FOR MISS JANE, THE guiding light that always shines

CHAPTER  **1.**

HE CLEARED THE THROAT THAT didn't need clearing, adjusted the tie that didn't need adjusting and reached for a joke.

"Ladies, gentlemen—and others," said Larry Felder. Guffaws welled up—from each of the three groups of reporters, he was pleased to see. Wasn't this how Al Gore softened up the press in 2000, before his personality and his fortunes did a 180? Wasn't this the kind of candidate it was always fun to cover?

"It is very strange to be on this side of the podium," Felder went on, his voice dropping a half-octave to signal that it was Serious Time. "Strange, yet very welcome.

"I am a candidate for Congress. I have put a tremendous amount of thought into this decision. I have abandoned a career that I dearly loved for a career that I would dearly love more. I believe I have the experience, the ideas and the knowledge. I ask for the support of the voters of the Eighth District."

Felder's swirl of rhetoric took place in a room that proved the oldest saw about suburban chain hotels. Whenever a grand ballroom is called grand, it is merely big.

It will be decorated in slightly peeling, cheap blue wallpaper. It will have track marks dug into its medium-brown carpet by many wheels of many buffet carts. It will never be a place where legions of Americans will come some day, for political inspiration, to mark the spot where a noteworthy career began. The grand ballroom of the Bethesda Hampton Inn was a soulless cave—a place for conventions of stamp collectors, expos of Tupperware and the occasional Bar Mitzvah.

Yet conventional political wisdom said you had to announce for Congress in a place that didn't "scream wealthy." Felder had briefly considered a busy street corner in Rockville, the largest and busiest suburb in the all-suburban district he hoped to represent in a little less than a year. But Charlie had deep-sixed the idea. Too noisy for TV crews. Too susceptible to a caterwauling catcall from a passing car full of teenagers.

"You want dignity at all times," she had told him, in that mildly preachy tone she loved to use. He had kissed her lightly and patronizingly on the bridge of the nose, wondered for the thousandth time how someone only 34 could have become such a shrew and, picking his battles, had relented.

Vic Printz waited until the TV roustabouts had repacked their gear and the radio kids had unclipped their microphone flags from the podium. Long known as the most sentimental reporter in the business—not a compliment in the saloons of 11th Street—Printz lumbered up to Larry and clapped him on the back.

"Masterful," he declared, in his well-worn whine. "As good as Ed Muskie in 1968, without the tears."

"Thank you, Vic," Larry replied. "But that's pretty faint praise, don't you think? Muskie didn't win. Or have you forgotten that?"

"Hardly. I believe you just evoked the wonderful emotion of his campaign, if not his unfortunate histrionics. Muskie could *compel* an audience, Larry. Today, you did, too."

Larry stripped off his gray herring-bone jacket and draped it over his right shoulder, Sinatra-style.

"Crapola," he said.

"I beg your pardon?"

"Crapsky, Vic. Total junk. Typical press exaggeration. Classic attempt to define me in terms that don't fit."

"Larry, I was trying to be your friend. . . ."

A big smile, and a counter-clap on Vic's shoulder. "And I was trying to jerk your chain, you moron. Now, before I insist on feeding you a chicken salad sandwich that has been sitting in the upstairs display case for three weeks, tell me: What's new downtown?"

Vic glared warily. He didn't take teasing well, because he was never sure when teasing was teasing. The only time he was sure was when someone teed off on his clothes. Right out of the Hecht Company catalog—for 1947—an intern had once bottom-lined. But gossip about the newsroom, that was where Vic shone.

"Cassidy is just back from some editors' conference in Puerto Rico, looking tan and fit. Ginny said that a little sex will do wonders for a man who carries so much stress. Mills said what makes you think it was a little? Parkinson was reassigned to sports. No loss. Never got it about Metro, anyway. New kid in Style looks excellent. Writing reminds me of Cusimano in the old days—brisk without being strident, you know what I mean?"

"And the campaign of the year?"

"Well, Larry, I'm here, aren't I?"

"You? You're going to be covering me? I don't believe it. Why aren't you in Iowa with all the other 60-something alkies? Why aren't you writing another Death Is Coming to the Democrats analysis? Don't tell me you asked to cover this epic Eighth District campaign?"

"1 did, Larry. I'm afraid I did."

Charlie pointed at her right wrist with her left index finger. The campaign was ten minutes old and it was already ten minutes late.

"Vic, you know Charlie. My better half—and we're not even married. Proof positive that a man always needs a woman to tell him what to do, even without benefit of a ring."

Charlie had the good grace to react as if she had never heard the line before. Vic wrote it down, "so I can use it later." Larry begged him not to. Vic, now feeling comfy, said he had been beseeched, bothered and bewildered by better candidates than Larry Felder. Larry said he had been covered by better journalists than Vic Printz. They mock-sparred. They beamed. They hugged.

"Charlie would never understand. She has no ink in her veins," Larry offered.

"I'll be fair to you from Day One to Day Last. Dead-solid down the middle," said Vic, who had retired the Paragon of Rectitude trophy a long time ago.

"Wouldn't expect more—or less."

A hotel porter was already removing the lectern. An electrician had already dismantled the bank of freebie Internet terminals. A banquet captain was stalking the space, detailed printout in hand. A 50th wedding anniversary was due in six hours. Another opening of another show. Hate to hurry you along, gentlemen, but. . . .

The elevator arrived. Vic shook Larry's hand, and held on a little too long. "Nineteen-seventy-seven," he said. "Still clear as a bell in my memory. Too much hair, too much attitude, but I knew on your first day at The Rag that somewhere inside Larry Felder was a star."

"Just spell it right," said Larry.

Vic boarded. Larry waved. Charlie yakked into a cell phone. The kid assigned to drive the campaign car—Felder One—stood off to one side, fidgeting nervously.

The ship had sailed.

Well, he might have offered me luck, or a prediction that I'll win, Larry thought.

But then again, Vic had to be objective about his old pal now. No cheering in the press box.

"Silver Spring senior citizen day care center up next," said Charlie, reading notes from a clipboard. Her platform heels clacked on the concrete as she made for the car. "Their big issue is government retirement and health care benefits. They don't want either of them cut. They want to hear that from you."

"They shall, Charlise. They shall."

A memory of Matthew Felder welled up and flashed past. Old man always hated journalism because it gave you a front-row seat, but never a role on stage. "Do, don't watch," the father had said. For 35 years, Larry had dodged that advice. Now he could embrace it.

★ ★ ★

Vermilion berry bushes lined the length of the driveway, on both sides. They were wonders of nature for two reasons: One, they were hardy perennials, always robust in color and always brimming with juice. Two, they were trimmed daily to munitions-factory tolerance levels by a squadron of groundskeepers. It was as if the 240 patients might get sicker if the bushes were allowed to get the slightest bit shaggy. In point of fact, none of the 240 would ever know, one way or the other.

"Devonshire Facility," said the discreet brown wooden sign at the point where the driveway becomes the entranceway. On Day One, Felder had recoiled at both words, the first because it had so obviously been chosen by a consulting firm for its non-offensiveness, the second because it was so maddeningly vague.

Facility? Was this a federal office where they drew up specs for grain farming? A great big rest room? The journalist in Felder wanted tip-your-hand transparency.

But 14 years later, he barely glanced at the sign any more and barely cared. Kat had been at Devonshire longer than all but three other patients. Signs didn't matter. Nothing did except loyalty. His.

Felder took the linoleum-covered stairs two at a time down to Level M. He rounded the bend into the intensive care wing. The rotund nurse from Grenada was on duty, the one who spoke slurred French and perpetually buried her head in a movie magazine.

Sometimes she didn't look up as Felder whipped past. Tonight, though, perhaps because an article about Russell Crowe had made her dreamy, she offered him a cheery, "Bon soir, monsieur."

"Ca va?" said Felder, exhausting his storehouse of eighth-grade French.

"Comme ci, comme ca," said the nurse. What she always said. But it was the whole drab truth and nothing but the truth.

Like the greeting and counter-greeting, the next exchange was a ritual. Felder reached into his inside-right jacket pocket for his checkbook. The woman from Grenada tapped on her keyboard. A printer began to whoosh. In 20 seconds, a bill had emerged.

The woman extended it toward Felder with her left hand. He wrote a check for $400 and placed it in her right hand. Bingo, bango, Kat had another month's care. Or rather, Felder had covered the five percent of her next month's care that the insurance didn't.

Charlie never believed it and never would, but being able to pass along 95 percent of the tab was the make-or-break detail, the one reason Felder would have stepped back from the starting gate and ducked the entire Congressional dream.

If the retirement package from The Rag had not included continuing coverage for dependents, Felder could not have afforded what Charlie called The Great Caper. He would have been consigned to a future like the past. Hacking—pun intended—would have been his lot, until some distant day—hard to visualize, but it was the denouement he hoped for and half-expected—when someone would have found him sprawled across the keyboard, beyond the reach of even the most generous long-term care policy.

His obit would be gushing and too long. The photo would be 20 years old, hastily grabbed from his personnel file. The list of survivors would be brief:

"His wife, Katharine, of Bethesda." And then, in classic newspaper style, a final sentence that raised more questions than it answered.

"A son, Bert, died in 1992."

Now, though, Felder had added at least six more inches to his final appearance in print, win or lose.

"Larry Felder, who renounced a successful career as a newspaper columnist to become a six-term member of Congress . . . ."

Well, if the polls had their way, they could set that baby in type right now. He was showing at a firm 56 percent. The closest of his three pursuers was at a flabby 18 percent. And yet Ed Muskie had been ahead by more than that.

"Larry Felder, who renounced a successful career as a newspaper columnist to run unsuccessfully for Congress. . . ."

Maybe the act of imagining this plot-line would keep it from coming true. Hell, he had imagined all sorts of stuff for Bert Felder--baseball games, graduations, science experiments in the basement, a fatherly clap on the son's shoulder before Bert's wedding. Bert had never come true, not unless you counted a fitful 16 hours attached to some machine that tried to breathe for him and couldn't manage it.

Meanwhile, down the hall, in intensive care, where Kat had been rolled at a speed that still astounded Larry all these years later, there had been a drama and an outcome that he had never spent a second imagining during the pregnancy.

On the door of room 208 was their wedding photo, browning and curling slightly now, inside a cheap, blue plastic frame. The social worker had suggested putting it there—for the benefit of which Felder, it wasn't clear. Larry-about-to-marry looked boyish and self-conscious. Kat looked upswept in a Bride's Magazine hairdo and downswept in her grandmother's ever-so-modest peau de soie dress.

She had told him that morning that she wanted to be pregnant by that evening.

Larry had tried to oblige, but their chemistry was cranky. Kat didn't place the fateful call until eight months later.

"I'm at the doctor's," she had said. "Say hello to the incubating Bert."

"And what if it's Alberta?"

"A woman knows," Kat had said. "Sorry to be an Old Wife. But their tales were mostly right, you know?"

Ultrasound confirmed it. Larry was so enthralled that he tempted fate—cigars for everyone on the copy desk, even though Kat's delivery date was still five months off.

Parsons The Cynic was always good for something tasteless at a time like this, and he didn't disappoint.

"At least one part of your body works, Felder," he said. "Your brain does only occasionally."

Matthews The Stickler had congratulated Parsons for inserting the modifier "only" after the verb "does," not before it.

Pillston The Veteran had offered his nightly beef about newfangled newspaper employees. "In the old days, someone would have said, 'Hot damn!,' and someone else would have uncorked a bottle," he said. "Now we get these God damned mama's-boy pedants who are such know-it-alls that they can't stop knowing it all, even when someone's having a baby."

Larry asked for silence. "May my son avoid the newspaper business so he can avoid the likes of all of you," he said.

"Lawyer, lawyer, pants on fire!" predicted Parsons, twisting the old saw in an uncharacteristically imaginative way. Larry giggled. Matthews grumped. Pillston coughed. And everyone went back to work on the first edition.

Felder didn't recreate that scene in his mind every time he strode into Room 208, but he did it often enough. It was a touchstone, a moment when all was well and gave every hope of staying well. Ever since the night when Kat had gone into the hospital, her cervix having dilated and her water having broken an hour earlier, good moments had been evanescent, and never entirely good.

"Hi, baby," said Larry. But it was for his own benefit. Kat couldn't hear him. Or smell-see-taste-touch.

She was hooked to a ventilator, as always. Her hair was streaked with blond—a monthly gift from her mother, who paid for the stylist religiously. But Kat's smile was a rictus, not a sliver of radiance. Her hair said she was dressed for the dance. Her limp posture said she had no horizon beyond her bed.

"It went pretty well, Babe," said Larry. "A good turnout from the pencil press, and wall-to-wall from the electronics. No bitchy questions. Nobody trying to make me squirm so he'd have a killer sound bite that would make the first block of the 6 and be repeated on the 11. Plus, Vic Printz is covering me for The Rag, and he said he'd treat me fairly throughout the campaign. How bad can that be, to be covered straight-up by a guy who's the patron saint of good political reporting?"

Kat's eyes were closed, as always. Her mouth hung slightly open at one corner.

The neurologist had coached Larry never to attach any significance to that, or to any other physical activity that Kat might produce.

"She might belch, she might google-eye you, she might do neither," the doctor had said. "You have to understand that her brain is essentially in Park. She can't shift to Drive or Reverse. She can't see you, and she will never know who you are. Please don't take it personally."

The way that Larry managed that was to orate at Kat without looking at her. He had not sat down. He never did. He paced the room as if he were a caricature of a Fortune 500 CEO, getting ready to exhort his troops gathered in the board room to a bigger and better fourth quarter.

"I wore the tie you bought me in New York that time," Larry said. "The one you always used to call Deep Purple. And my charcoal suit. Charlie was very helpful in helping me pick them out. She has a very good sense of fashion."

And so did you, Kat! That yellow sweater you bought me in Miami during the Super Bowl was a huge step forward for a guy who preferred down-the-middle and off-the-rack. But I went with it because I loved you, Kat. Loved you more than I thought I could love anyone. And now. . . . Now you're a duty. I am perpetually the Bar Mitzvah boy I was at 13. You are my mitzvah.

"The coverage should be pretty good tomorrow morning. I'd be surprised if it isn't. I mean, hell, Kat, who's going to rip me for being in favor of safe retirement for government employees and health care for every American? The voters know that I know what I'm doing. The scribes do, too."

Kat's blood pressure fluttered and flashed in green numerals across the digital monitor--120, then 118, then 124. Why would it fluctuate at all, Larry wondered, if she hadn't exerted herself, and never would again? But technology had a mind of its own. Voters do, too. Don't be cocky, Felder. This woman in this bed is reminder enough that the best-laid plans . . .

"Well, sweetheart, gotta go. Two fundraising coffees tonight in Potomac. Got a fresh shirt in the car. I fed the cat this morning. I'll go to Bert's grave over the weekend. And I'll call your mother. Promise."

Larry pecked Kat on the right cheek. It was clammy, as always.

Could she die? Would she please, please consider doing so, for heaven's sake? She (and he) deserved to be delivered, didn't they?

The doctors held out the option to him, every year, when he and they had their status meeting. The power of attorney gave him the right to pull the plug, no questions asked. But Felder balked at the prospect of blood on his hands, and blood in the water for his Congressional opponents to stir. Elect someone who preached the sanctity of life but didn't preserve the sanctity of his own wife's life? That was a one-way ticket to Obituary Version Two.

Felder rose to leave. The patterned wallpaper still galled him, as it always had. Little blue figurines—were they drummer boys?—created so as not to offend. Did their inventor come home from work one night and crow to his wife, "Guess what, baby? I just made a wallpaper pattern that will electrify every nursing home in America!" Probably a machine made it, coached by a computer program. A machine that couldn't imagine the passivity of the sick or the doldrums of the well.

"Oh, yes, forgot to mention one thing," Felder said. "The balloon payment from the insurance settlement came yesterday. Five million and change, just what we expected after the lawyers take their slice. That's it, Babe. That's all we get. The cookie jar is now officially out of cookies. But the campaign can be self-financed now, for the most part, if that's how I want to go. I'll still need help in the general. But the primary should be no sweat."

Could he say thank you to Kat without sounding like a fool? Thank you for choosing an anesthesiology resident who, according to his testimony, had been awake for two straight days and nights when he fumbled the dosage? Could Felder be that crass? Did it even matter any more?

It didn't. The campaign did. It was Kat's gift. And Bert's.

"Thank you, sweetheart," said Larry Felder. "Thank you for letting me take a shot at the career I dreamed about when I was a little boy."

★ ★ ★

February 1, 2006
To: Amanda Prosser
From: Charlise Carpentier
Re: Who Else?

Hi, Mandy. Hope you aren't burning to a crisp. I never did buy that business about the dry heat in the desert being easier to take than the drippy heat here in Washington. Or is it just that drips cause all the heat here in Washington?

I'm as funny as ever, obviously!

Mandy, I need to turn you into Ann Landers again. I'm stymied by Larry and how obtuse he always is. I want to ratchet this thing up to the next level, but he simply won't pay attention. Short of ripping off his clothes—or mine, or both sets—I just don't know what to do. I thought you might.

It's pretty simple, girl. The guy turns my motor, floats my boat and rocks my world. He is everything I've always wanted in a man—poised, witty, full of purpose, rich enough. Plus he has just the right kind of body—slim and slight, no paunch, no pecs. He doesn't look like a former college football player who would break 17 ribs the second he hugged you.

Larry reminds me of what we used to say back in high school—remember? When that first boy would get down to the brass tacks of actually Doing It, we'd say, "Be gentle." Larry would be gentle, I just know. He wouldn't need to be told.

But how do I get this man's attention, Mandy?

I'm with him, up close and personal, almost 16 hours a day. He relies on me totally—he tells me so. Maybe this is girlie fantasy stuff, but it's great to be needed. I can really imagine a life with him, long-term. As for the short-term, well, I've told you everything I need to tell you. Whenever I'm close to him, I just kind of start to, you know, HUM . . .

No woman should operate on hums, or trust them completely. But this here woman has a humdinger of a hum! I want this guy, and he's got to be a complete spaz not to know it.

So what's your bottom line, old friend?

Yes, the wife is still a vegetable. Yes, he's still married to her. Yes, I'd be willing to accept him as my squeeze even if he doesn't divorce her. It would be a stepping stone, I figure. If I make him mine now, he'll be mine then, whenever then turns out to be. Possession being nine-tenths of the law, and all that.

I know these are the rantings of an obsessed woman, but I confess. Larry Felder is my obsession. I want very much to see him win the election, and I think he will. But that only increases the pressure, Mandy.

I need to "seal the deal" now so he isn't looking over his shoulder all the time as a sitting Congressman. Yeah, I know, a lot of Congressmen have very creative personal lives—isn't that how you phrased it once? But we are dealing here with the Last Moral Man In The World, Mandy. I need him, I can't live without him and I'm worried that I'm going to make a big fat fool of myself pretty soon.

Advice?

Hope Bill and the kidlets are treating you well. Loved those photos of Christy's ballet recital! She is cuter by the day.

Write when you can, Arizona Girl. Hugs! Charlie.

February 2, 2006
To:Charlise Carpentier
From: Amanda Prosser
Re: Female She-Devil

Hey, Charlie Girl! The fam sends hugs back atcha! When ya coming down to the land of sunshine, illegal immigration and crazed conservatives? Don't ask if I'm ever coming back to D.C. Been there, done that, been undone by that. Enough!

And enough of your whining, girl! Where are your feminine wiles? Where is the Charlie I knew at Duke—the one who said she'd do whatever it takes this side of the cops to get what she wanted? The one who wasn't getting asked to the big dance by the big campus politico, so she asked him?

Dum-dum Felder isn't taking the hint(s), so you need to take direct action instead.

I think a frank talk while you're returning from a campaign appearance might do wonders. I think a letter left in his campaign briefing book might turn the tide. Perfume optional. And—this is serious—he might be one of those men who needs something even more direct. Like grabbing him and kissing him. Or grabbing him elsewhere, if you catch my meaning.

In one way, Charlie, I hate to give you advice like this. I believe in marriage. I believe in MY marriage. If I were ever in a nursing home for 14 years—or even if I weren't—I wouldn't take some other woman moving in on my man very kindly.

But this is a special situation. This is a guy who's worth it, and who needs a little Charlie Salesmanship.

You go, girl! Let me know how it goes. I can just imagine the expression on his face when you lay the word on him. "I never knew you cared, Charlie. . . ." Well, whether he ever knew, he'll know from that moment forward!

What is it that they say? "A woman without a man is like a cat without a bicycle?" Or is that some dumb T-shirt slogan I saw in Myrtle Beach 15 years ago? I'm telling you, Parker has been so cranky this week—and he's been costing me so much sleep—that I hardly know what I'm saying.

Just promise me that you and Felder-man will never have a one-year-old. It can fry your brains!

Yours in hopes and hollers, Mandy

....

February 2, 2006
To: Patricia Finkel
From: Charlise Carpentier
Re: Legal advice

Hi, Patsy. Hope this message won't reach you until tomorrow. You work far too many hours, young lady, and it's all for a bunch of profit-crazy white-shoe lawyers. At least when I do my 16 out of every 24, it's for a higher purpose: Felder for King. Or President. Or whatever the heck he's running for.

Patsy, I need some advice.

It's along the lines of what I was hinting at when we met for drinks a few days ago. I shouldn't put any of this in an e-mail, but here goes:

I am crazy-nutso-over the top in love with Larry Felder.

Check that. In lust with him.

Yes, I know he's "all wrong." He's almost 56. I'm 34. He's a public person. I'm a quiet, unassuming, get-it-done policy wonk. He has no hidden wild side. I have a major one. He's headed for a huge career in the House, and maybe even that bigger house at the other end of Pennsylvania Avenue. I'm headed for delinquency on my condo payments.

Seriously, Patsy, this is the man for me, and I want to make a major play for him.

I need your honest advice about. . . .

- Whether I'd be in any legal danger if I sleep with or live with a married man.

- Whether he'd be in any legal danger if he sleeps with a woman who isn't his wife, or moves in with her or both.

- Whether he'd be in any serious political danger if he "takes up with me." I know this is a judgment call, but judgment is what you advocates claim to have!

Answer as a lawyer, please. But please also answer as a single woman.

I'm not going to tell you that my biological clock is about to blow a gasket. I probably have ten years before the prospect of Little Charlies (or Little Larries!) is extinct. But my sanity is going to be extinct if I don't get my hands on this guy pretty soon.

Can I? Should I?

Thanks, lady! Next lunch on me. Cheers. Go Duke!

February 2, 2006
To: Charlise Carpentier
From: Patricia Finkel
Re: Legal advice

Charlie!

The easiest legal question I've faced all day!

Buy a new dress.

One with a scoop neckline!

Make sure he gets a good peek as you're getting into the campaign car. It will work, I promise you!

Keep me posted!

Patsy

February 2, 2006
To: Larry Felder
From: Charlise Carpentier
Re: Tomorrow

Hi, Larry. Glad it went well with the folks at Leisure World. Thank you for taking them seriously. They might give you all the votes you need, right there in that one gated community.

Larry, I need to talk to you privately tomorrow night, after the debate on Channel 9. Can we get a glass of wine or something? A milk shake if you're in training!

Thanks in advance, Charlie.

February 3, 2006
To: Charlise Carpentier
From: Larry Felder
Re: Tomorrow

Well, actually, tomorrow just became today.
YOU'RE NOT FIXING TO QUIT THE CAMPAIGN, ARE YOU?
Call me right away if that's what you want to discuss. If it isn't, sure, wine after Channel 9 sounds fine. Larry

February 3, 2006
To: Larry Felder
From: Charlise Carpentier
Re: Wine

I would never quit. On to victory in November! No, Larry, it's personal. Thanks for saying yes. Charlie.

Larry fed the cat and spent 15 minutes reading The Wall Street Journal. He turned out the lamp on the end table and fluffed up the four pillows. No more phones, no more photo ops. Pre-sleep was Larry's prime think-time.

"She's getting married," he told the cat. "Can't be anything else."

"Hey, baby?"

"MMMMMph."

"Very articulate, baby. One of your better qualities."

"MMMMMph again."

"Does that mean what I think it means, baby? Commit upon yourself an anatomically impossible act?"

The young woman stirred, stretched, swiveled and squealed. "I was actually thinking of the anatomically possible," she said. "Even if remembering my name is proving difficult for you." She bopped the alarm clock to death at precisely 7:11 a.m. and reached for him.

Ms. Whatshername had nearly killed him just six hours earlier with her energy and her effortless gymnastics. But when you're nearly 56, and a 26-year-old taste treat invites you to dance, what are you gonna say? Call me in a week? Let me sleep so I can handle my four client meetings today?

Not if you're Barry Mauskopf, Boy Wonder.

The young woman kneaded and stroked. He lay there and let her do it, without making so much as a feint of reciprocation. His mind flitted from the ridiculous (Federal Election Commission filings he had to take care of by the noon hour) to the sublime (she let me take her home and she never even ASKED about my dyed sideburns!).

Suntan lamps had turned his skin a little more crinkly than he might have liked. Wasn't this what the oldies in Miami Beach looked like—gorgeously tanned but hopelessly saggy? Weren't they the definition of pathetic? Was he?

But Barry could be whining about—and caving into—far worse physical problems at his age. Success in the career world was wonderful, and he had seen much of it. Cornell with high honors. Columbia Law. House in the Hamptons. Kids up and launched. Alimony readily covered by his senior partner's salary and annual profit sharing.

Very soon, Larry Felder would be extra-glad he had hired Mauskopf—had come home to Old Friends Ltd., as it were. The campaign contributions had flowed from the beginning. It was as if the fattest cats were afraid not to give— not because they were so sure that Felder would win, or that he'd treat them well once he did, but because they were afraid to anger Mauskopf.

This was power. This was influence. This was what lawyers like Clark Clifford and Bob Bennett had spent a lifetime chasing and getting. And now Mauskopf, too, could command serious cash from just about anyone he cared to chase, with just a short e-mail.

Yet when the One Great Scorer came to write against his name, notches in the proverbial rifle would be featured prominently. His high-school pals called him Mighty Mouse for a reason. Now, as he approached the back side of the mountain (his phrase), he still turned his laser focus on the three-hour mark. If he couldn't charm a young woman into his Lexus within that time—the younger she was, the better—Mouse would think he had lost a step. And if he couldn't rock around the clock, as he dated himself by putting it, he would need at least three martinis to blunt the funk.

"I may be a fabulous lobbyist. Few could argue," Mouse told Felder, the day before he agreed to serve as his official campaign treasurer and unofficial chief campaign rabbi. "But where I'm truly fabulous is in the rack, Larry. Truly Olympic caliber."

Felder had gone into skeptical-reporter mode right away. "And if I asked some of these young ladies about you?," he had asked.

"They'd tell me that they'd been with boys before, but the Man is the Mouse," said the Mouse.

"The only Olympic medal you'd ever win would be for Freestyle Bragging," Felder had said.

"Ain't bragging if you can back it up," Mouse retorted.

That night, he had called Larry at home—at 1 a.m.—and had asked him to hold on for a second.

"Hi, is this, like, Larry?" a soft female voice had asked. If she was over 23, she hid it well.

"Yes, this is Larry Felder," he said, a little officiously, a little carefully. Never knew who had a notebook or a tape recorder these days.

"Barry wanted me to tell you that he's a great lover," the young lady said. "Well, he certainly is. He CERTAINLY is. He. . . . Barry, you stop that!"

Felder hung up before he began to wonder if it was all a set-up. Maybe some actress Mouse had hired for a fast 20 to place the call.

The next morning, at their regular status meeting, he saw the deep circles under Mouse's eyes. He knew The Accounting was on the way. Mouse didn't disappoint.

"Four times," he said. "She's 5-feet-ll and a natural blonde and she has moves like a broad jumper. Hey, come to think of it, I guess I'm the broad jumper!" Without shame, Barry giggled at his own lame, inadvertent pun.

Felder said it wasn't this way in the Bronx, when they were kids.

That's why I wanted out of the Bronx, The Mouse said.

Women there thought that sex was what you traded for health insurance and a charge plate from Alexander's. In Washington, Barry had discovered women—many, many women—who believe that copulation with near-strangers is one of the seven basic food groups. Especially if the man is powerful. Especially if he is forever on the front of the Lifestyle section. Especially if he dresses in basic power-blue Brooks Brothers and doesn't go for the open-collar, gold-chains, 39-and-holding look of pure desperation.

Barry Mauskopf would never abandon nubiles in their moments of need.

* * *

Graystone Manor Drive had its name half right. The homes weren't gray and weren't stone. They were well-weathered, cream-colored stucco, trimmed with brown beams. But the homes were manors, for sure--most of them six-bedroom, six-bath extravaganzas, most sitting on rolling 2.5-acre lots. It was the kind of street where for-sale signs always said, "By Appointment Only." Cruise-by, Sunday-afternoon, open-house riffraff wouldn't do.

Locusts and poplars dotted the deep-turfed back yards, as if to say: "We trees have been here for 100 years and we expect to be here for the next 100. Same with the people who own the house. And same with their fortunes. This is rich that doesn't wither and doesn't worry."

Except that, in the conference room at the rear of the first floor of 9718 Graystone Manor, Lorraine Bartlesby had just smashed a coffee cup against the wall.

"I'm frustrated and I'm ticked," she had said, unnecessarily.

Her campaign brain trust sat there glumly, as they had recently learned to do.

Lorraine had looked good—damned good—three months earlier. She was self-financing most of her campaign—always an advantage. She was polling very well among all sectors—even, a bit surprisingly, among Hispanics who don't speak English at home. She was the kind of Democrat who looked great in TV ads—her hair just a little bit gray, her eyes just a little bit crinkly with concern. And her personal life was bulletproof—two photogenic kids who had never crashed a car while drunk, an outstanding career as the head of the largest family foundation in the county, service on innumerable non-profit boards, a husband whose grandfather had named a downtown law firm and whose enormous gold wedding band squashed all rumors and all hopes.

"I learned in tennis that you always change a losing game," she said. "And kiddos, we are losing. Big."

The final PowerPoint chart still sat on the screen. It showed Bartlesby nose-diving, from 60 percent in early summer to 18 percent now. This despite plenty of advertising and plenty of visibility at plenty of public events. This despite early editorial support from the one county daily. This despite traffic on local political blogs that any candidate would die for—the young, the old, the white, the black, all calling her the obvious choice and the inevitable winner.

"Felder," she scowled. "Felder is all I hear. Felder the nicest guy in the world. Felder who learned the county cold as a reporter. Felder with the wife on life support. Felder with the dead son. How could he come up so far so fast?"

No one offered an answer. None was needed. Larry Felder had been a public figure in a way that Lorraine Bartlesby hadn't.

The bylines, the TV appearances, the bookings to speak, the radio pops. Lorraine had done much more to make the county solid via direct infusions of bucks, time, shoe leather and concern, not necessarily in that order. But politics was about who got visible and stayed visible, who seemed cast for the role and who seemed likely to be able to handle it. A woman whose heart had always been in the right place wasn't necessarily Congressional material. A man whose words and face had been out there for a quarter of a century.... He seemed to be a form fit.

Lorraine started to go around the table for brainstorms, but immediately thought better of it. She knew where she wanted to begin.

"Follow the money," she said. "John, Jim, I want a full report from the federal elections people about who has given Felder how much. We'll have to chase every dollar and hope he has made a mistake. Otherwise, I don't see how we can make up so much ground."

Bill Bigelow, the courtly consultant who had brought home eight previous winners in the county, urged Lorraine to hang tough, stand firm and cool off.

"Nobody votes for anything for three months," he pointed out. "You can go up and he can go down. John Kerry did the first and Howard Dean did the second."

Lorraine double-clutched for only a second. Then she fixed her face in a scowl of determination.

"Nope, Bill," she said. "No time to waste. If we stay underwater the way we're underwater now, there's no way we revive. No, I want to tar him with the one piece of junk that will work: a dirty campaign."

John Mallinger, the campaign treasurer, had the kind of voice that always undermined what he was trying to say. It was equal parts squeaky and squawky. He was 26 and sounded 12.

"Lorraine, you can bet the ranch on Felder's people," he said. "They won't have made a mistake about their fundraising, in part because Felder knows where to look for trouble from his career as a reporter. This is a strategy that can only backfire." His voice cracked on "back."

Jim Phillips, the uber-communications czar, pointed out risks on the publicity side.

"Let's say this idea works, Lorraine," he said. "What do we do with the information? We'll have to leak it to The Rag. But don't you think that could come back to haunt us? It very well might, because it will make us look like The Sour Grapes Campaign, even if Felder isn't kosher."

Lorraine was cooling off now. She began to gather up the shards of the smashed cup. She grunted slightly as she bent from the waist to fetch the now-detached handle.

"Change a losing game," she said. "I want to hear from Bill and Jim in 48 hours."

★ ★ ★

Calloway Cassidy III had a name that only a mother could bestow and a desk that any mother would abhor. It contained every scrap of paper that the editor of a major metropolitan daily newspaper would need to do his job. The trouble was that the paper looked as if it had been arranged by a Category Five hurricane.

There were stacks, but they represented no rhyme or reason. There were piles on the floor, but one pile would often begin to encroach on another, rendering neither distinct and both useless. Meanwhile, on the office couch, there sat a tuxedo (never hung up in the closet after last night's reception), a pillow (hand-made by his Mama—it said BOSS across the front), a briefcase (whose contents were as disorderly as the office's) and a framed photo of baseball iron man Cal Ripken's record-breaking day at work years earlier (the photo showed the scoreboard—it displayed just one word: CAL—Cassidy had been known by that nickname since Ripken was knee-high to a batting cage).

Cassidy had been editor of The Washington Record (known far and wide as The Rag) for 15 years. During his tenure, the staff had won ten Pulitzer Prizes

(Felder had accounted for six). Cassidy still burst off the elevator every morning as if the next ten seconds might hold a story greater than Watergate. As his hair thinned, his enthusiasm soared. He told his closest associates that he was better at his job than ever and more eager to perform it than ever.

"Kind of like sex," he would say, regardless of who was listening, regardless of whether a lawsuit might lurk behind his salty frankness. "The more you do it, the more you fear not doing it, so the more you enjoy it."

His palace guard would always chuckle, even though they had heard the line many, many times. Cassidy's rear end still needed kissing. He wouldn't be in the big chair forever, and he who had puckered most often would probably be in position for an endorsement.

Cal Cassidy was 60, which gave him the ability—if not necessarily the right—to wax gooey about the good old days.

He knew that the Web was about to redefine the business he loved—hell, that had probably happened already, irretrievably. That's how fast the earth was moving under everyone's ink-stained butts. But Cassidy could not give up career lessons so well learned.

He still wore a suit, a tie and a starched white shirt to work every morning. "What if they send you to cover the White House?" he still said, to every one of his 375 reporters, forgetting that he'd be the one doing the sending, not the one doing the going.

He still insisted on a personal briefing, by phone, from every reporter whose stories were going on Page One the next day. "Delegating is for sissies," he once told his assembled pucker-uppers. "No offense to any of you, but did Patton delegate?"

The silence was deafening.

And he still called his secretary Millie, the art director and the personnel person "honey." None of the three women had sued, or even objected very seriously, perhaps because of an annual bonus that Cal personally slipped to each, perhaps because a woman knows when "honey" means benign respect and when it means that a boor is at the wheel.

The TV in Cassidy's office flickered, as it always did. Newsroom wags had made book on how long it had been pumping out electrons without a rest. The prevailing guess was 1968.

Few picture tubes could have withstood such a marathon. But the sound could probably have withstood anything, because Cassidy almost always kept it on "Mute." He would allow sound only when the world was trying to come to an end or when some TV reporter was in the process of scooping The Rag. The first had happened far more often than the second.

In the tallest stack, at the right side of his desk, paper-weighted down by the diamond cufflinks Cassidy had worn the night before, sat a sheet of paper. It showed the latest inductees into The Rag's 30-Year Club—and also the names of all the previous ones.

Cassidy's eye fell on Larry Felder's name. He began to muse.

Their goodbye had been awkward. Neither man knew who was supposed to initiate the hug. Cassidy finally broke the ice, with a wrap of his arms all the way around Felder and a squeeze so serious that it might have saved the younger, smaller man from choking on a piece of steak.

"You sure?" the editor had asked.

"I'm sure," Felder had said.

"You're an effing bastard, you know that?" the editor had observed.

"You're not so wonderful yourself," Felder had said.

And so, on a wave of macho posing, the men had severed ties. Felder had made it a point to tell Cassidy that he didn't expect favorable treatment—and he wouldn't dream of asking him to wire an endorsement by the editorial page, since that wasn't part of Cassidy's domain. Cassidy had replied that he wanted to make one thing crystal clear: He couldn't root either for or against Felder, but he wished him all the luck in the world just the same.

"Just don't ask my mother for money," Cassidy had wisecracked. "I'm hoping to cash in on every cent the rotten old lady has."

Felder had to say it, so he did.

"Cal, no reporter has had the kind of run I've had. I owe you everything. I'd have done this job happily, forever, if the road to the Eighth District seat weren't so wide open."

"Just keep this in mind, buddy boy," said Cassidy. "If this fantasy of yours doesn't work out, you'd be welcome back in a heartbeat."

"Thanks, Cal."

A moment of awkward silence.

"Yeah, we can always use a floor sweeper, I'm told."

Just like Cassidy. Could never stay completely serious for more than five seconds.

Each man squeezed the right shoulder of the other. Felder waved and walked out.

Cassidy breathed deeply, once, and exhaled as if he were expelling all the carbon monoxide the world had ever produced.

Then he sat down and picked up his Dictaphone (E-mail was beyond and beneath him).

"Millie, honey, please circulate a memo right away to the Maryland desk and everyone who covers campaign finance. Felder may have been ours, but he isn't protected by that. I want vigorous, continuous coverage of him for the rest of the campaign. No home team stuff. No pulled punches. The guy will get the white-hot lens of The Rag.

"And if any of you ever use a phrase like that in print, I'll have your ass. "Signed, Cal."

2.

BEFORE RAUCOUS FANS SCREAMED incessantly on radio talk shows, before blogs routinely drew blood, before ESPN spewed high-action highlights 25 hours a day, there was Dick Young.

He owned New York City in the time of Mickey Mantle and Yogi Berra. He covered the big fights, the big horse races and the burgeoning interest in the National Football League. But mostly, he lived to bust bullshit. That's what a marquee sports columnist did in the 1950s. That and win hearts, including the one that belonged to Lawrence Alan Felder.

If you looked up Grand Concourse on a map, that's what you called it. If you lived there, you called it "THE Grand Concourse."

The name was a triumph of intentions. Grandeur would have been possible if the street were a wider-than-usual road that wound through the East Side of Manhattan, rather than through the central and east Bronx. But The Grand Concourse was not Park Avenue. Right after World War Two, it quickly became a long-running strip of sociology—people leaning out of grimy apartment windows to yak with pedestrians below, pushcart vendors selling vegetables that were anything but grand, trucks spewing fumes and causing the pavement to tremble at all hours.

It was Eastern Europe come to America—a totally urban, totally tumultuous environment. It was the only home young Larry Felder ever knew.

He used to find copies of the Daily News in trash barrels. Dick Young always ran on the back page. Young had the rare ability to write as if we were lecturing a drunk on the next bar stool—and as if he liked the poor sap at the same time.

Young was no effete statistician, no philosopher seeking Deep Meaning in games.

He wrote about how it *felt* to watch DiMaggio canter after a sinking line drive, how it *smelled* when Archie Moore took the ring. Young knew his readers were subway-and-a-shot people, not I-used-to-live-in-Brooklyn-but-I-moved-to-Long-Island. He assumed that athletes would always try their best, especially if they were getting paid. His prose would routinely savage them if they didn't.

Larry Felder devoured Dick Young throughout his childhood. He shared in Young's enduring outrage after the Dodgers and Giants moved to California. He knew that "Scooter" was Phil Rizzuto's nickname, so he got it when the columnist never bothered to explain what Scooter's given names were. Larry would read Young's interviews with "railbirds" and "clockers" at some mythic place called Belmont Park, and a big stakes horse race would come alive for him.

In fourth grade, students in Miss Moriarty's class were asked to write an essay about what they'd like to be when they grew up. As in the rest of the world, this was an exercise for posterity—to be found in a trunkful of memories 40 years later, to be chuckled over at a large, overfed family Thanksgiving.

Larry Felder wrote a very short essay. It said: "I want to be a sports columnist because Dick Young is the greatest man in America. I want to be as great as he is." Miss Moriarty gave him an "Excellent," and this comment: "Keep working hard, Larry, and I'm sure this dream of yours will come true."

It almost didn't. When John Lindsay became mayor of New York in 1964, Felder reclaimed his heart from Dick Young, dusted it off and presented it to Lindsay instead. The urbane, wavy-haired mayor was everything Felder doubted that he'd ever be—stylish, avuncular, snappily dressed, unflappable, effortlessly Gentile. Perhaps believing that some Lindsay stardust might rub off on his scrawny, straight-haired self, Felder leafleted "The Concourse" on Lindsay's behalf. It was a violation of the prevailing Jewish ethic of the day. Republicans like Lindsay were not only born with silver spoons in their mouths, according to lean-out-the-window wisdom along The Concourse, but they couldn't see past those spoons, to the problems (and attributes) of groups like Jews.

If Dick Young had been a city-streets columnist, he would have found a ready and willing subject in Matthew Felder, who sold shoes by day and who dreamed of an ascendant Zionism by night. Larry Felder, on the other hand, saw a path to a less doctrinaire, less limited future. He would go to City College, major in government or history and then plunge into politics. Some day the silver spoons would give way to silver tongues. Larry Felder, Orator, would some fine day become Larry Felder, Candidate.

Not for the first time, a woman changed a dreamer's plans. At the first meeting of the student government in 1968, Felder met Marnie Moskowitz. Like him, she was looking for deliverance via politics. Like him, she was eager to end the war in Vietnam—by talking it to death, if she could. Like him, she was a child of The Concourse—her parents Polish Jews, her politics loud and vehement. And like him, she was a virgin. They decided to take each other out of their mutual misery one night in early 1969, at a seedy hotel in Harlem whose cost they carefully and righteously split.

Marnie insisted on playing a Rolling Stones LP as a backdrop. Afterward, Felder felt more woozy than emancipated. But at least he could now compare notes with his chum from the Bronx, Barry Mauskopf, who had been bragging about his conquests—yes, plural—since the age of 15.

Larry and Marnie. . . . the couple was inseparably a couple. Class together, movies together, furtive smooching together. Actual sex was rare, because opportunity was, too. But Marnie and Larry would cinch their pea jackets against the cold and agree that being soulmates was better, anyway.

She was the first to declare for president of the student government. Larry had planned to run for months, but they had never discussed a possible conflict. He had assumed that she would support him. She had assumed that student government president would be far below his "level of hope," as she put it.

He asked her to withdraw. She shot back that women didn't automatically do what little puppy-dog, hurt-feelings men wanted them to do—not in the new world of 1969.

Stung, Larry decided to teach her a lesson. He would beat her, big.

He raised funds in front of the student union. He spent them on campaign handouts and a tape deck that endlessly repeated a recording of Felder's platform. He electioneered in person at dances and anti-war rallies.

Polls hadn't made their way into student political races yet, so Larry couldn't gauge where he stood. But the spill-back was all good. The smiles on the faces were genuine. He was almost sure he was in.

Almost.

When she beat him by 130 votes, out of 806 cast, Marnie could not resist being smug.

"Fairly close," she allowed.

Larry had become a political columnist for the student newspaper by dusk.

It suited him from the start. He liked awarding gold stars or demerits in print. He liked advancing ideas that no one else had thought of (or so he hoped). He especially liked the fact that he would write again on Friday regardless of how his Tuesday effort had been received.

Columnizing was better than straight reporting because it allowed you to reach for the Tabasco sauce. And it was better than politicking because you didn't have to shake a million hands or solemnly swear to spend someone's $2.50 wisely.

Young in The Daily News gave way rather quickly to Anthony Lewis in The New York Times. Felder's father made one last try. Wouldn't his only son and only child consider a career as an academic? He could use his summers to work for the liberation of the Jewish people.

Sorry, said Larry, but summers would be for internships on newspapers. The Jewish people would do just fine without him, Dad.

The old man broke into tears before he broke into shouts. Larry always liked to think that perhaps this was a form of blessing.

Having touched the workaday world of political organizing, Larry was reluctant to adopt the political chastity of journalism. He and his fellow student news-niks would debate endlessly whether a political reporter could and should vote, whether he could or should cover someone whose views he shared, whether he could or should go out of his way to cover someone whose views he abhorred. The debates led to jumbo cardboard boxes full of grease stains and pizza crusts, and zero consensus. It wasn't until Cayenne became editor that Larry went all the way over to pad-and-pencil lore and ethics.

Cayenne was large, sweaty, Jamaican and furious, not necessarily in that order.

He never used his last name. He may not have had one. He was "maybe in my sixth year here, maybe my seventh. I've lost track." No one ever tried to pin him down about this because they might have gotten pinned down in return—literally. Cayenne had been named after the pepper by his mother, he endlessly revealed. She hoped that he'd be as exciting as the spice. She hadn't been disappointed.

Cayenne might have seemed like an unlikely candidate to argue for journalistic propriety and detachment, but he always did.

"Larry, my guy, you can't be a little bit pregnant and you can't be a little bit objective," Cayenne would say, as he fiddled with his Afro-pick comb. "You've got real talent, Larry, my guy. But you will never be able to show it—never be able to work for a real newspaper downtown—if you don't understand that you are an observer only."

Cayenne picked up two pizza crusts. He ate one in a single bite and threw the other at Larry's head. It missed only because Larry snapped his head out of the way at the last instant.

"No more rhetoric in your copy! No more describing Republicans as 'arch!' You want journalism, you'll have to make journalism want you! And that means believing in shoe leather and fairness deep in your soul," Cayenne thundered.

Larry, who by now was never missing a Tony Lewis column, was already on board. Thanks to Lewis, he knew that a columnist is a reporter first, but an advocate for the good guys, too. Columnizing was not an excuse to hang your views around the necks of readers, or to indulge yourself by floating far-out trial balloons. It was a way to persuade, to coax, to implore, to root for outcomes. Conventional politics was a way to spend hours making deals—most of which would come unstuck at the last minute, anyway.

Felder traded his work shirts for buttoned-down, off-the-rack broadcloth and began to hound the Manhattan borough president. His scoop about a no-bid contract that had been awarded to the president's nephew for the repaving of the college's front walk won Larry an interview at the *White Plains Journal-News*.

The editor didn't much like Larry's three-day growth of beard, and he liked Larry's columns about the paving scandal far less than he liked Larry's straight-up news stories. But he decided "to give you a shot, young man." Larry agreed to report in six weeks, right before Memorial Day.

In journalism, the race goes to the dogged and the careful. But luck never hurts. Larry Felder was thrashing away at his first beat—the White Plains Police Department—when an administrative assistant he had just met decided to lob a question at him.

"I have a neighbor who does contracting work," Gloria Gonsalves told Felder. "He has been working at the chief's house for months, always at night. Maybe it's private. Maybe it's just a moonlighting kind of deal. The chief has always been a pretty straight shooter from what I can tell. But who does major contracting work at night? Maybe it smells."

Felder had no wife, no children, no outside interests. He could devote every evening to the stakeout he undertook. After two weeks of parking across the street and observing, it was obvious that the chief's house was undergoing a total makeover.

But why? It sat on a street of beautifully kept, modern homes. It looked to be in excellent shape. This was no rehab job after a hurricane or a fire. Was the chief adding marble bathtubs and granite counter tops just because he wanted or just because he could? Or could this be a case of public money going improperly to a private place?

Felder walked down the obvious trail—to the on-site workers (who said money was money and they didn't know the source), to the city permits office (which said that all the paperwork was current and proper), to neighbors (who said the chief and his wife were the salts of the earth, and what was wrong with home improvements, anyway, mister?).

Then. . . . the luck.

Deep inside the city's budget was a line item called "Routine Police Department Maintenance." It listed $550,000 for the current fiscal year. But there were separate, additional budgets for patrol cars, station houses and storage sheds. So where was that unspecified money going? And why?

Like Woodward and Bernstein, Felder knocked on the doors of top police officials after dark, rather than relying on the telephone. He came up empty.

But when he tried the door of Malcolm Morgan, whose MM Contracting Company was doing the work at the chief's home, Marjean Morgan said she was glad to see him.

"My husband has been very weird about what he's doing for the chief," she said. "He usually tells me everything that's going on with the business. But this job has been going on for months, and my husband just says it's going fine. Won't say more. Very unlike him."

Felder asked if he could see MM's books. Marjean said funny you should ask, I'm the chief accountant and I was just looking them over myself.

She produced the current year's ledger. Not a jot about the work at the police chief's house.

Did Mrs. Morgan have any ideas about what might really be going on?

"I think my husband is stashing a lot of money somewhere, and the chief knows about it," she replied.

Then. . . . more luck.

A routine bust of a teenaged methamphetamine dealer produced a remarkable courtroom scene. At his arraignment, Charles Thomas, age 22, began shouting that he was just a small fish, but he knew much bigger ones. A bailiff whom Larry Felder had befriended told him about the outburst later the same day.

More digging. Turned out Thomas had a rap sheet longer than a proverbial arm. Always drug busts. But, unusually, he had been remanded to a community service organization after his second arrest (at age 18), rather than to a family member.

Larry Felder soon discovered that Malcolm Morgan served on the board of that community organization. Hmmm. He also discovered that the police chief had been taking more unscheduled leave over the past two years than he had ever taken before. Hmmm again.

Journalism doesn't pay off to hunches, but imagining never hurt a flea. In the shower, at the coffee place on the corner, in bed at night, Felder tried to link two and two and come out with four. He finally came up with a working scenario—Charles Thomas, Malcolm Morgan and the police chief were somehow tied to meth.

Felder thought he saw how to break the story free from maybe. He asked if he could visit another meth dealer who was well known to the White Plains Police and who was doing time in the Westchester County Jail. After a short delay, permission was granted.

Bruce Carman was excited about talking to "a real live reporter. You like one of those guys on TV?" Larry Felder, in brown oxfords, brown socks, a dark brown suit, a cobalt blue tie and a shapeless haircut, could not have made it onto TV without a search warrant. Even his driver's license proclaimed his ordinariness—brown, brown, 5-10, 160. He was a recycled 1950s package surrounding a 1970s body. But he won Carman's trust by promising to do "what I can" to shorten your sentence in return for Carman's cooperation.

Of course, "what I can" was really "nothing much." Reporters do not have subpoena power. They are askers and persuaders, not muscle. Sometimes they mislead or overpromise, as Felder did with Carman. But if they win the confidence of a source, it's as if they were the Attorney General.

So it went with Bruce Carman. He knew all about Charles Thomas—since Thomas was a rival dealer. He also knew that Thomas liked to brag about how much money he was raking in. And the clincher. . . . Malcolm Morgan, Charles Thomas and the police chief were all related.

How did he know? "Because my grandmother is the unofficial historian of White Plains," said Carman. "She tells me all this stuff."

Next stop, Charles Thomas. When Felder interviewed him, in the visitors' room at the county jail, Thomas was agitated and uncooperative. Felder left. But when he tried again two days later, Thomas melted in Felder's hand.

Thomas laid it all out—how he had approached the police chief at a family meal about bankrolling some meth deals when both were well lubricated, about how the chief had arranged to slide maintenance money out of its public account, about how the chief had been vacationing regularly in Aruba and Curacao on the proceeds, about how the contractor had found out and had blackmailed the chief, about how the chief then decided to pay for the contractor's silence with a great deal of illicit high-end home improvement work.

Larry Felder did not win a Pulitzer Prize for his series about the White Plains meth ring. Pulitzers are supremely political, and the best lobbyists are the biggest papers. The White Plains paper had never won a Pulitzer, so it had no track record or traction with the selection committee. But Felder did win every investigative prize in New York State, and most of the big ones in the middle Atlantic states. He was booked on "Good Morning Westchester" and various radio shows. He got calls from agents. He also got a regular weekly column—"Larry Felder At Large."

At only 24, he had won his spurs.

★ ★ ★

Maryland's Eighth District had been an odd duck ever since World War Two. Once full of staunchly religious Republican farmers and burghers who lived their lives peacefully and uneventfully just northwest of Washington, D.C., the Eighth had flipped almost completely during post-war suburbanization. As it tripled in population, it veered suddenly and sharply Democratic. Along the shaded streets of Rockville and Silver Spring, families dug roots—and wanted little to do with Joe McCarthy, the partisan view of the Cold War or the traditions of border-state racism. These were educated, caring, engaged people. They wanted big government. They believed in peace and pudding and puppy dog's tails. They voted for any candidate who smiled a lot and promised to do the right thing.

Politics may make strange bedfellows, but the real problems arrive when there are too many bedfellows. So it went for Democrats in Maryland's Eighth during the Kennedy and Johnson eras. More than a dozen candidates filed for the congressional primary every two years. They killed off each other's bank accounts, stamina and prospects. In the general election of 1960, and those through 1988, a station wagon-driving, God-fearing, deficit-disdaining Republican named Everette Wheatley tiptoed into office, defeating a better-funded and more telegenic Democratic opponent each time.

Wheatley never won by more than 2,000 votes. He did so each time in the face of increasing Democratic registration, by stressing common sense and constituent service. Time Magazine called him "The Wheatley who defied political gravity."

Wheatley made sure that the government employees in his district—more than 90,000 strong—always got their calls returned. He never offered a single piece of landmark legislation. He never took a junket to 11 exotic countries. He was a workaday fellow in a snap-brim hat. And he exemplified a lesson that it took Democrats nearly 40 years to learn—that Maryland's Eighth wanted quiet strength more than gaudy partisanship.

Everette Wheatley retired after 14 terms. At a party in his honor at the Germantown Lions Club, he trotted out a rare joke. "If anyone ever names a park or a school in my honor," he said, "I'll come back from the dead and run again." With that, he loaded his wife, his dog and some old campaign posters into his ancient station wagon and moved to Florida, forever.

By 1988, Maryland's Eighth was undergoing vast changes yet again. Immigrants from Central America and Southeast Asia had become a large, visible and vocal minority. McMansions had begun to replace two-bedroom "kit" houses in Bethesda and Potomac. The Eighth's huge, widespread wealth might have been expected to signal a Republican resurgence. Close-in Connecticut, exurban Chicago and the suburbs of the Southwest had seen precisely that trend. But the Eighth's discomfort with party orthodoxy remained. Widely smiling Democratic candidates came and went—and all came up short on election day. Wheatley's former chief of staff, Martin Morrison, who was once an accountant and who looked it, coasted to victory for nine terms.

But Morrison couldn't avoid the political quicksand around the war in Iraq. He attracted a Republican primary opponent for the first time—an Iraq veteran who had been reconstructed at Walter Reed Army Medical Center and who had stayed. Corrie Corporan came within a whisker of winning the 2004 primary. Morrison smelled the future. Only six months into his tenth term, he announced that he would retire in 2006.

The story of his decision ran on page three of The Rag—beside a dull-as-dishwasher takeout about environmental legislation and below a yawner day story about the Pentagon budget. Page three was not quite the equivalent of newspaper purgatory. That would have been page 90. But it was not exactly screamy prominent, either.

As Vic Printz loved to say—and say, and say—there's only one page in each morning's Rag: the one that's right out front. Every other page and every other story is a bow to duty or a half-hearted feint toward being the newspaper of record. For sexiness and curb appeal, page three might as well be the gutter.

Larry Felder had been a little late to work that morning. He had been meeting with the sales staff of The Rag's syndicate. They wanted him to do a tour over the winter—of some wavering dailies that now subscribed but might drop. In the lurching, desperate, can't-feel-the-bottom-of-the-lake world of print journalism, where profits and old assumptions were tumbling by the minute, syndicated columns offered up from Washington were becoming highly expendable. Still, Felder had star power. Perhaps a smile and a cup of coffee with local editors would entice renewals in Omaha and Topeka.

When Felder walked onto the newsroom floor and toward his flyspeck of an office, it was 11 a.m. Yet only half the chairs were occupied. As usual, the place looked like a combination of college dorm and warehouse—jackets draped across desks, mounds of files stacked under (and sometimes on) chairs, clumps of people giggling and gossiping, great balls of gray dust collected around electric plugs and file cabinets.

The Rag's wags had long dreaded a rumored visit from some time-and-motion genius, who would take one look at the sprawling cavalcade of filthy rugs and two-day-old cups of coffee and pronounce the entire place in need of condemnation.

Besides that, no one seemed to be working.

Little would that expert understand that what seemed like passivity was really a great gearing up. To read that morning's product—and perhaps two other papers—was the journalistic equivalent of calisthenics among the great unwashed. Got to see what's shaking the world, and what the competition is doing. Once it was time for the staff to chase the day's stories, phones were lifted, notebooks were opened and the pace went from stop to red line instantly. The big, boxy room was once again on track to produce the proverbial Daily Miracle—via a mixture of disorganization and rigor, intuition and shoe leather, cynicism and idealism, flair and burrowing straight ahead. The formula had somehow stood the test of decades.

Felder's assistant, Lindsay Baron, had already clipped the story about Maryland's Eighth and had laid it on Felder's keyboard. Trim, intense, unmarried, canny, pushing 40, she had worked for Felder for more than 15 years—long enough to see him rise from fledgling political voice to Mr. Authority.

"Lindsay knows what I'm thinking before I'm thinking it," Felder had said, at her tenth anniversary luncheon. "Keeps the bills paid," she had replied. The slightly odd couple hugged often. They flirted or fornicated never.

Lindsay slid the clipping under Felder's nose as he was folding himself into his work pod. He glanced at it, and whistled.

"Inter-r-r-resting," she declared, in her best South Philadelphia-ese.

"You can say that again," said Felder.

So she did.

He giggled.

She smiled.

It was that office ESP that so many seek, and so few find.

"Instructions, chief?"

"Don't call me chief."

"Are we going to have that debate about Jimmy Olsen and Perry White again?"

Felder turned mushy. "I could never debate someone as wonderful and as gorgeous as you, Linz," he warbled.

"Careful, I'll bring you up on charges of skirtchasing," she said.

Felder moved his left hand right under her nose. "That wedding ring gold enough for ya?" he asked, pointing to his fourth finger.

It always was.

Lindsay Baron had often drifted briefly into Felder Fantasyland, but she had never landed there. The guy was just too loyal to his lady, too Boy Scout, much too unimaginative and unromantic. The kind of man who, if propositioned, would reply that he'd take the offer under advisement. Then he would whip out a yellow pad and draw up a pros-and-cons spreadsheet to analyze what he ought to do about it. No Errol Flynn, no sweet nothings murmured, no blood pressure surges. He stood 5-feet-10, right down the middle. He weighed 160 pounds, right down the middle. Brown eyes, brown hair, type A blood, glasses for reading only—his driver's license vitals were a study in average.

If they ever made love, Lindsay decided, it would give new meaning to the words plodding and clinical. And he would probably wear his watch throughout.

Lindsay was often asked by friends and family what it was like to work for a legend. She replied that no columnist is a hero to his valet.

Evidence: "When he gets all wound up and he's deep into writing, he'll sit there, staring at his screen, mumbling 'Purpose!'," she'd reveal. Maiden aunts who were hoping for more sauciness would change the subject.

Larry read the clip from page three. She stood beside him as he did so. Halfway through, he ran his hands through his hair and blurted, "Inter-r-r-resting!" As he finished and tossed the clip onto a two-foot-high mountain of paper beside his bookcase, he blurted:

"Clear path for a Democrat, I'd bet."

"You," said Lindsay.

"Me?" said Larry Felder.

"Benjie's," said Lindsay.

Down the street from The Rag was a coffee joint that had been a shot-and-a-beer joint until reporters went straight in about 1975. Now, lattes went for $3.50. Then, Heurich lager had gone for 25 cents. Felder wasn't particularly a fan of either, but he would often spring for a frosted concoction for Lindsay and bemoan the passing of time. Benjie's was still Benjie's among the Raggers and Ragettes, although the sign above the door now said Starbucks.

"What was ever wrong with a hole in the wall that was home to half its customers?" he'd grumble. "Who needed fresh paint and baristas in mauve aprons? Now you've got a chain that wouldn't know a customer's name if their lives depended on it."

"They know *my* name, Larry."

"Small wonder. You put the bucks in Starbucks."

"Beautifully put."

"You always did appreciate my originality."

A swallow of frostedness, then:

"Larry, I've been your Girl Friday for a whole lot of years. I know what you're thinking before you're thinking it. And when I saw this story this morning. . . . (she had brought along the clipping, which she now again shoved his way). . . . I saw one door opening and another closing."

"Clichés are illegal."

"But going for the gold isn't. This is you, Larry."

"What? Me? What do you mean?"

"You should run for this seat. You should show yourself and half a million people in the Eighth District that you don't just report and write well, but that you can serve well."

She stood up, in mock-military posture. "Purpose!" she called out.

"Sssssh! People will hear you!"

"As long as they hear me in the Eighth District, I'm good with that," said Lindsay. She gazed hard into Felder's light gray eyes. "Here's the campaign slogan that will launch a thousand ships—'You've Read Him, Now Elect Him.' "

"Needs big work."

"But your heart doesn't, Larry. You can do this. You should do this. And I've got to say, I can imagine you wanting to do this. Larry Felder has been pounding a keyboard for a very long time. He's almost 56 years old. Windows are closing—windows that you didn't even know could open. You're never going to take three years off and sail around the world, Larry. But a seat in Congress—this could be Felder II."

Larry promised to think about it. That was usually the kiss of death, Lindsay knew. But a door nudged open might fly open...

They walked back to the office. The DON'T WALK light was on at the corner of 11th and K. No cross-traffic was coming. But Larry Felder refused to cross just the same.

"You are virtue itself," Lindsay called out, over her shoulder, as she scampered across the street. "And virtue wins elections!" she added, once she had reached the other side in one piece.

"Shhhh!" Felder stage-whispered, with an index finger held up to his lips. "People will hear you!"

★ ★ ★

Kalman Radin declined the champagne and waved off the canapés. He had work to do. Lots of work.

Once upon a sainted epoch, flying business class between Europe and Washington was a straight shot at "found time"—eight beautiful hours to tuck into reports, analyses, tons of stuff that the regular workday never let Radin begin, much less finish.

But now, all these airlines were run by marketing MBAs, not by aviators and certainly not by businesspeople. Which was why Smiling Sarah and Grinning Gertrude had already interrupted his concentration six times to offer him things he didn't want—and they were only two hours out of Paris, for God's sake.

Radin briefly considered writing out a sign, in longhand, that would read: "NO, NO, A THOUSAND TIMES NO," and hanging it from the edge of his seat. He thought better of the idea only because the phrase was unoriginal.

Grumpiness was not Kal Radin's usual state, however. He had many reasons to grin. The most successful businessman in Maryland's Eighth District, and perhaps in the entire state, he was that 21st Century rarity. His company made beverages. But they were not sugary and not named Coke or Dr. Pepper. They were low calorie, very refreshing and very environmentally sensitive.

The line of drinks was called AaaaaaH. As in what you said after you took a long pull on a guava goodie (their best seller), or a pineapple smash, or a blueberry boffo.

No marketing MBA had thought up these names. Radin's then-preschool-aged daughter had. She still starred in the company's ads, even though she was now in college.

"Hi, folks, I'm Sarah," she had been become famous for saying, all over television, for 15 years now, "and if you want a great drink that won't make you fat, won't leave you thirsty and won't pollute the planet, there's only one smart choice."

Then a big swig.

Then a big "AaaaaaH."

The kids at Duke would walk past her on campus, recognize her and say, "AaaaaaH." But Sarah was used to it. Her father was equally used to consistent, smashing profits. AaaaaaH had routinely added 20 percent each year to its sales. It was fending off takeover bids and buyout offers every month. Kal Radin was pretty much on top of the world.

Expect he didn't feel as if he was.

The best businessman is the one who is always testing the floorboards for looseness. Radin had not gone all the way over to paranoia—that would have been unseemly when he was worth at least $400 million in AaaaaaH stock. But he knew that, without help from somewhere, his fixed costs to buy the fruit he needed could cause big trouble not very far down the road.

In his hands was a report from his brand-new business development and corporate strategy manager. It recommended increasing the share of fruits AaaaaaH bought abroad from 40 percent to 80 percent. "Wages and wage expectations are much lower in Europe and the Third World," the report read. "AaaaaaH could save millions."

Radin ran his fingers through what was left of his hair. Gosh, getting to be like the old man, and I'm just 50, he thought. But, as he well knew, he was his father's son, in the big ways as well as the small. He expected to get his way. But he had worked for that privilege, and he expected to keep on working for it.

AaaaaaH could run its operations from anywhere. It could have done what the Toyotas and the Boeings did and run away from unions, to southern states where there were few or none. But Kal Radin's old man had run a small grocery chain in suburban Maryland, and he had not dodged the United Grocery Clerks of America. So Kal wouldn't move or duck, either. He would keep the company in northern Montgomery County, Maryland, on an 800-acre site just off Interstate 270, until hell froze over. Or, as his daughter liked to joke, "until 270 runs at more than 30 miles an hour." Home was home.

As for the recommendation to import more fruit, Radin made a note to have a word with this stars-in-his-eyes kid down the hall. Didn't he realize that tariffs on imports would crush most of the possible savings?

Then again, maybe there was a way to win both coming and going.

He began jotting some notes. . . .

CHAPTER 3.

EVEN IN WASHINGTON, where gray hair is ubiquitous and wrinkles are a badge of honor, it's sometimes hard to peg the actual age of a near-oldster. Channel 9 helped out with that in a very reliable way.

The station's official name was WUSA-TV. It was the CBS affiliate in a town that Walter Cronkite and Dan Rather once owned. Its local news shows at 6 and 11 had been kings of the market for more than half a century. The station billed more than twice as much as any of the competition. It operated out of a glass-and-steel palace near one of the city's highest points, Mount St. Alban.

But the joke around The Rag—retold often by Larry Felder and Lindsay Baron, among others—was that WUSA was really a piece of litmus paper.

People older than 50 always called it Channel 9, because that's where they had set the dial when they were young. Anyone younger called the station by its longtime branding nickname, The Big U.

By virtue of its market dominance, and to cement it, WUSA hosted every election-year debate for every major local political race. In 2006, it chose a Tuesday evening for the first face-off between the leading Democratic candidates for Congress from Maryland's Eighth District, Larry Felder and Lorraine Bartlesby.

The Big U swaddled itself in civic sanctimony whenever it did a Montgomery County public affairs broadcast. "Underscoring and aiding the democratic process," said a WUSA press release, as bombs burst in air.

The truth was in the pocketbook. Maryland's Eighth was a "dream demo"—home to thousands who regularly bought expensive cars, took expensive vacations, called their brokers every day and thought nothing of remodeling their kitchens to the tune of $40,000. The more they kept it on Channel 9—or whatever the right place was on their fancy cable systems—the happier WUSA's advertisers would be. Especially since this year's Montgomery debate was bumping one of the top-rated cop shows.

The anchor of "The Big U at 6," Granville Cameron, welcomed everyone in his usual dulcet baritone. He flicked on his usual wide smile. Then he explained the ground rules. Opening statements, five minutes each. Then rotating questions from a panel of three reporters. One candidate answers each, then the other comments. Answers two minutes each, rebuttals one minute each. Then each candidate gets a three-minute closing statement. "And then voters will be prepared to exercise their all-important civic responsibility," Cameron intoned grandly, no doubt inspired by rockets' red glare.

Everything that happened over the next half hour was entirely predictable. Bartlesby, far down in the polls, attacked Felder for being an inexperienced newbie who couldn't possibly grasp the concerns of a place as complicated as the Eighth. Felder played not to lose. He stressed his listening skills, his experience in Washington and his dedication to little-guy, lunch-pail, streetcorner issues. He withheld all specifics.

As the credits rolled, the candidates shook hands half-heartedly. No love had been lost between them ever since Felder announced for the seat five months earlier.

"Lots of luck, Lorraine," he said.

"How very sincere, Larry," replied Bartlesby.

They shared a glare. Then Charlie came out of the shadows and grabbed Larry by the arm.

"Nicely done, good sir," she said. She added her own glare, straight at Bartlesby's heavily made up eyes. Bartlesby nodded, coldly.

"I don't imagine that you're going to be on her Christmas card list," Charlie cracked. As Larry nodded, an intern rushed up with a clipboard full of Items That Couldn't Wait.

A prospective major donor wanted a private coffee—sure, set it up.

A reporter from the New York Times who said he was on a crushing deadline—absolutely, book him.

A condo association in Gaithersburg wanted Larry to speak to their monthly meeting—lots of potential votes there, but better check with Charlie.

The intern scrawled a couple of notes and skittered away. Charlie had just finished a 14-hour day, but the major agenda item of the day—at least in her mind—still lay ahead. She had just ducked into the ladies' room to freshen her lipstick. She used it to smile broadly and wetly as she said:

"How about that drink you promised?"

"Oh, yes, sure," said Larry, who had obviously forgotten. Not a great sign for Ms. Carpentier. His head was still on Primary Day, not on her. Or maybe it was in the clouds, where it spent far too much time. But the next few minutes might be about to change that.

They hopped into Felder One—the burnt bronze Dodge station wagon that used to ferry Felder to grocery stores and Kat's bedside, but was now crammed to the gills with table tents and posters on sticks. Charlie drove the three and a half blocks to The Grotto.

Maybe not the greatest choice, she worried, especially since Tuesday nights at "The Grot" are half-price pizza nights. The joint was jumping with libidinous and three-quarters-bombed American University undergrads who didn't know the meaning of sssssh. But Felder had never been a monk or a librarian, she reminded herself. He had done plenty of time in Grotto-ish places while covering hundreds of campaigns. Tonight would begin the Charlie Campaign. She felt preternaturally confident.

For about one second.

Larry Felder, the detail-driven reporter, wanted to be the detail-driven congressional contender. Still in campaign mode, he ran through a top-of-the-head list of I's to dot and T's to cross. Charlie jotted them all down in her laptop. "Ever the faithful servant," she heard herself say.

Drinks arrived—a chardonnay for her, a scotch and water for him. The AU kids were deep into Buds. No one was sitting in either of the neighboring booths. Time for Charlie to trot out the mousetrap.

"Larry, there's something I've been meaning to talk to you about. . . ."

He crinkled into a smile. "If it's about a raise. . . ."

"No, Larry. I'm not in this for the money. It's about you and me."

"I thought you told me you aren't quitting."

"I'm not. Don't give it a second thought. I'm in this to the bitter end. Although I don't think the end is going to be bitter."

He took a slight pull of scotch and crinkled again. "Attagirl," he said, somehow managing not to make it patronizing.

"Larry, you know how you always believed in total honesty when you were in journalism? You know how you'd always work a source by saying it was in his interest to come completely clean, because half of the truth would only muddy the waters?"

Larry nodded.

"Well, it's my turn to lay it all out, Larry."

Another pull of scotch. "Did someone die?"

"Good grief, no, Larry. It's something . . . personal."

He stared, his mouth slightly ajar. That was Felder-ese for "Please go on."

"Larry," said Charlise, with a slightly sharp intake of breath to steady herself, "I want to discuss the possibility of becoming a couple."

He picked up his tumbler of scotch, swished the scotch around the ice cubes and then placed it back on the table. "Could you explain what you mean by that, Charlie?" he said, mildly.

"Oh, Larry, you're doing your reporter thing on me, trying to draw me out so I'll spill my guts. OK, I'll spill my guts. I just spilled a major portion of them, but let me finish the job. I'm attracted to you. Very attracted to you. I want you. I want to be your, uh, lady, I guess you could say. I want a relationship with you."

Felder had made a cottage industry of never saying the right thing at moments like this.

When Marnie Moskowitz had offered herself to him in 1968, quite graphically and quite passionately, his first words had been, "Are you sure?"

When a fellow reporter in White Plains had sent him a letter—special delivery, no less—requesting his presence at her apartment that Saturday night, "and make no plans for Sunday," Larry had called her and said, "Should I bring a jacket and tie?"

When he and Kat were just lifting off the runway, all those years ago, she had told him that he launched "a thousand fires in her belly." Ever the gentleman, he had offered her a Tums.

It was no surprise that he was known at The Rag as The Geek For All Seasons.

To keep his streak alive, Larry Felder looked into Charlise Carpentier's eyes—full of brightness, full of eagerness—and declared: "My marriage vows have always meant a great deal to me, Charlie."

"I knew you would say something like that, Larry. And I don't want you to get the wrong idea. I am not a homewrecker. I'm a home *builder*. I'm not proposing some sordid quickie. I'm trying to lay out for you my deep—very, very deep—feelings. I'm trying to say that I want a life with you, as far as the eye can see, whether you win this campaign or not."

"Charlie," said Larry. Then three more times, a little more pityingly each time. "Charlie, Charlie, Charlie." He looked as if he was about to scold a nine-year-old who had defaced the mirrors in the boys' bathroom.

"Charlie, I've been in the public eye for a long time, and I'm trying to redouble that. I can't be running for Congress and having an affair. That would be sudden death."

Charlie was ready to tumble down that rabbit hole.

"Larry," she said, taking her first—and, as it would turn out, only—sip of the chardonnay, "I'm not talking about some kind of deal where one of us sneaks up the rear staircase. I want to build on what we already obviously have. I want couplehood. I want babies. I want two names on the mailbox. Larry Felder (pause two beats for emphasis). . . . I want you."

"Thank you for being so honest," said Felder, deliberately. "Thank you for being so open. I just . . . I mean. . . . I don't know what to say."

"How about a simple yes?"

"What would I be yessing to? Would you move into my house tomorrow morning? Would I divorce Kat the next afternoon? This is an awful lot to try to digest, Charlie. Especially with only a few weeks left in the primary campaign."

"Larry, all your life you've made everything look easy. They want you to do TV shows in addition to five columns a week? No sweat. They want a quickie book about the 1988 campaign while you're taking a week in Puerto Rico? Done. Are you seriously saying that there's no room for me in your life just because you're spending great hunks of it speaking to women's clubs at Leisure World?"

Another pull of scotch, a bit longer this time. An AU kid screamed for another pitcher. A waitress told a drunken regular to wait his damn turn. A far-off jukebox rumbled to life with some Springsteen.

"Charlie, may I please sleep on it?"

"Of course you can sleep on it, Larry."

More scotch. "I haven't said no yet, Charlie. Not bar-the-door, not-ever no."

"You sleep on it, Larry. I'll keep my fingers crossed."

Her cell phone buzzed—was it at the wrong or the right moment? She looked at the read-out of who was calling, sighed, said "Damn!" once very forcefully and then said sharply into the machine: "Trouble?"

Larry couldn't make out the voice on the other end. Must be a campaign operative. Funny how they always smelled trouble where there usually wasn't any. Then again, as Vic Printz used to make a career of saying, just because you're paranoid doesn't mean they aren't out to get you.

"Uh, huh...uh, huh...." Charlie's eyes were not giving anything away. "OK, thanks, I'll let him know right away." She clicked off.

"That was Chesiree, Larry. She just checked The Rag's web site. Really favorable story about your performance in the debate. Seven mentions of stuff you said and only three for Lorraine."

"You know that journalism doesn't play favorites that way, Charlie."

"Here's what I know, Larry. We are going to win this thing. And once we do, I am hoping to win the longest, toughest battle of all. I just explained what that was."

Larry Felder patted her on the head, as if she were a wayward terrier.

One month later, Charlie would summon that moment of humiliation and turn it into ammunition.

CHAPTER

"BY STERLING SIDNEY SADLER

"Special to *The New York Times*

"ROCKVILLE, MD, March 15—Larry Felder had won every possible prize in daily journalism. He had written six books and won six Pulitzer Prizes. He had his own highly-rated TV show for more than a decade. He routinely commanded $20,000 fees for 20-minute lectures. He could have stayed on the same influential, lucrative glide path for the rest of his career.

" 'But this opportunity to run for Congress looked irresistible,' said Felder, the well-known political reporter and analyst for The Washington Record.

" 'So I decided not to resist it.'

"If that sounds like bravado or overconfidence, Felder is quick to dismiss any such notion. His principal opponent in the race for the Democratic Congressional nomination in Maryland's Eighth District, Lorraine Bartlesby, has vast sums of personal money to spend on the race, and she has assembled a team of battle-hardened campaign experts.

"She announced first. She had a commanding lead in early local polls. Felder has never viewed himself as 'anything like a shoo-in,' he says.

"But Larry Felder has begun to pull ahead in the contest, according to more recent independent samplings. If he prevails in the May primary, he would be a strong favorite to capture the seat in Maryland's Eighth. Voter registration there runs more than 3-to-2 Democratic.

"Even so, Republicans have held the seat for more than 40 years. Felder says that, because of the 'natural cycles of politics,' it's time for a change.'

" 'I got to know the Eighth District as a reporter, and it's a snapshot of America,' said Felder, a slightly balding, slightly stooped 55-year-old whose speech still reflects his Grand Concourse boyhood. 'I believe that my second act will be to represent that snapshot in the People's House.'

"The Eighth District is a wealthy bedroom for Washington's power elite—but also, in recent years, the new home for thousands of immigrants. Average annual household income is $110,000, one of the highest such rates in the world. But 40 percent of students in the district's public schools are poor enough to qualify for free lunches, and gang activity has become a major law enforcement problem in the eastern third of the county.

" 'I don't want to represent paradise,' said Felder, 'and I won't. I want to represent an Eighth District that works hard and cares. Sort of like me.' "

"Felder is married to the former Katharine Goodman. She suffered severe brain damage during childbirth and has been institutionalized for 14 years. Their son, Bert, died shortly after he was born."

Barry Mauskopf had been prancing around his office as he read the Times story aloud. Now he slammed shut the front section and declared:

"Not bad, boychick! Not bad at all!"

"Well, that settles it, I guess," said Larry. "I now have the blessing of Barry Mauskopf. What more would any poor struggling politico need?"

Mauskopf rang an intercom. More coffee appeared. He paced up to and then back away from what he had always called the "wonderfuls" on his ego wall—college with high honors, law review while in law school, grip-and-grins with half the Supreme Court, a cover of Washingtonian Magazine whose streamer screamed "Washington's Best Lawyers." Mauskopf had been chosen for this honor 11 times.

He was down to his shirtsleeves, his monogrammed white cuffs rolled back, his gray pinstriped jacket hung loosely over the back of his ergonomically excellent office chair. Barry Mauskopf loved to orate, and he was about to loose a major oration on his boyhood buddy.

"Here's how I see it, Fel," he began, as he rubbed his hands through his brown Brillo mop. "You are looking mighty, mighty strong. Know how I know? The Republicans aren't saying a word about you yet. How easy it would be for them to make snide cracks about how you have a typewriter ribbon for a brain, or you don't know how to manage because you've never managed anything tougher than an expense account. But they know you can't be touched. And they'll know it again in the general. They won't come close to you in fundraising."

Larry had been coming to see Mauskopf about once a week ever since his announcement. It was just a couple of old pals—off the record and never to be repeated. Supplicant comes to see rabbi.

Felder had a staff of nine that knew politics cold, and knew how to get him in front of the right voters. But Barry Mauskopf had been advising Congressional candidates—and members—for three decades, especially about the intricacies of federal election law. He didn't get to be The $700-An-Hour Man without knowing what he was talking about.

Their meetings had the slightly condescending air of big-brother-advises-little-brother. Larry Felder was making all the key strategic decisions for his campaign—where to advertise, where to hand out bumper stickers, when to stand at which Metro stations on which weekday mornings, which editorial writers to stroke. But Felder needed a disinterested savant. It didn't hurt that Mauskopf made him chuckle. Felder seldom did much of that.

Mouse paced, Felder sat. Mouse offered up "mousedrops of truth" in his I'm-never-wrong, orotund style. Felder shifted his feet, occasionally took some notes, seldom interrupted.

"Let's play some Twenty Questions," Mauskopf said. "Has Larry Felder studied up on federal hiring and promotions?" A nod from the red leather armchair to Mauskopf's left.

"Has Larry Felder memorized how many federal jobs reside in the Eighth District, and how many more could easily be added once he's elected?" A double thumbs-up.

"How about the bigger national stuff? You've thought through what you'd say if somebody divebombs you at a community meeting about gay marriage or defense spending or immigration reform?"

"I'm for it and I'm for it and I'm for it," said Felder, with a slow smile.

"Not good enough!" thundered Mouse. "Everybody's for it! I need to hear a legislative strategy! I need to hear practicality, not just the vision thing!"

As Mouse surely knew, he had just lobbed a 60-mile-an-hour fastball into Felder's strike zone. The Big Geek smacked it into the upper deck. Gay marriage and not just civil unions. Freedom, but also vigilance via new weapons systems and better training of recruits. More liberal immigration policies, but also vigorous border security.

"Not an ideology, Mouse," he said. "Just a practical agenda that the country wants and needs."

Mouse strode about the room—five steps east, the same five west. More hands through Brillo. More tugs on cuffs. A few chews on the end of a $500 fountain pen.

Then:

"Fel, you are heading so firmly into the wind that I can't offer so much as a peep of criticism. Keep working hard. Keep being honest. Remember that you're playing a part here—Larry Felder The Aw-Shucks Guy Who Used To Type Columns. Keep the aw-shucks, whatever else you do. Chicks will love you!" Finished off with the classic, earthy Mouse guffaw.

Felder got up to go. Fifteen minutes late already and it was only 9:30 in the morning. He placed his cup and saucer on Mauskopf's Queen Anne end table, which had been oiled to within an inch of its life.

"May I ask a question, Mouse?" he blurted.

"Yes, Mr. Famous Former Reporter."

"Are you still bedding everything that walks?"

"They aren't walking when I bed them, Larry."

"I figured you might have figured out a way to accomplish that. Maybe pulleys or something."

"Very funny. Then again, did I ever tell you about the time in the Bahamas when. . . ."

"Save it, Mouse. I don't want to eat up any of your legendary masculine energy. You're going to need it."

"Thanks, old chum." They hugged. They patted each other's shoulders. And then, from out of the blue:

"Larry, how long since you've been with a woman?"

"Mouse, you know the answer to that. We've been over that a million times. It's fourteen years. A little more than that, actually."

"You mean that with all that travelling you've done, and all the notoriety you have, there hasn't been *one single time* that you've chased a skirt? Or been chased by one?"

"Not one single time."

Mauskopf shook his head. "I can't figure you, man. If I went 14 years without a woman, I'd be like a seething volcano." He mock-punched Larry in the gut. "I guess you're pouring all that intensity into the campaign, eh?"

"Guess so."

"Well, your old pal, the Mighty Mouse, can hook you up anytime you say. My Rolodexes have Rolodexes, Larry! Tall, short, thin, thick, whatever floats that Felder boat, I can do ya."

"Mouse," said Felder, suddenly and unexpectedly melancholy, "if I ever did this—if I ever called you and said I'm ready to come off the slag heap—it wouldn't be about lust. It would be about love."

"Good God, man! You sound like some women's magazine! May I please offer you yet one more mousedrop, for your delectation and edification? Lust comes first. Love comes second. If it comes at all."

Larry nodded. To have argued would have been like trying to roll a boulder up Mount Mouse. But Felder knew his core, and he knew his history. Kat was his rock, even now. The I-do girl. There couldn't be a second, or a substitute, as long as she lay, drawing shallow breaths at Devonshire.

★ ★ ★

Bert. . . . Bert. . . . Over there, Bert. . . . Take a bunch of those campaign-posters-on-sticks and jam them into the grass, please. . . . That's right, Bert. . . . Over there. . . . Be careful when you cross the street. . . . Look both ways. . . . That's my guy. . . . Thank you, hon. . . . Now put them about 15 feet apart so people can read each one. . . . Good, very good. . . . You're being such a huge help. . . . Can't wait to tell Mom all about it. . . .

For the first two years after the disaster, Felder had fantasized every day about The Stages of Bert That Would Never Be. At four, tearing around the back yard on a bright yellow plastic three-wheeler. At eight, moving up to two wheels. At 12, pimples and requests for help with homework. At 16, could I please have the car tonight? Then, at 18, college and probable paternal irrelevance.

Larry knew he was beating himself up unnecessarily and unmercifully with all the what-ifs and might-have-beens. But he couldn't prevent himself from sliding off into recrimination and regret. It was almost a touchstone—a way to remember the pain, and therefore the tiny person who didn't make it for even a full day.

Bert reveries would hit at the least opportune times—while interviewing governors, while checking yellowed clippings in The Rag's library, while washing his hands beside a flag-rank editor in The Rag's one and only fifth-floor men's room. Bert chased Larry's tail. Bert, in a macabre way, kept Larry rooted in the past. Bert made it impossible for Larry to move on, even though time had moved on.

Bedtime at 9807 Greentree Road, Bethesda.... Tossing, turning.... Up to get a snack, then more toss, more turn.... Sit on the edge of the bed.... Gather wits.... Say it aloud, for the thousandth time: "Larry, you have got to get a grip and get some sleep. Bert is dead. D-E-A-D. You didn't kill him. You can't help it. You must, must, must live in the moment and in the future, or you'll be dead, too. Emotionally dead."

But hadn't Larry been close to dead emotionally even before that horrible day?

His colleagues would mock him—"That Felder, heart of stone, never even reached for a hanky when he covered a plane crash." His neighbors steered clear—"Don't know what to say to such a silent, moody, into-himself guy, especially after what happened to Kat and the boy."

If there had been a brother or a sister, past might not have continued to be present. But he was an only. Kat was, too. No cousins, no uncles, no aunts. Just Kat's aging mother, who had never liked him and wasn't the sort who would lend a shoulder.

Felder was used to riding the waves by himself.

Self-preservation being what it is, Larry had made one move toward normal over the past 14 years. For the first two, he had kept an eight-by-eight poem in a gold frame beside his desk at The Rag. He had written it one sleepless night.

A boy named Bert
Was the apple of a man's eye
The apple didn't fall far from the tree
The tree has been pitted and dented
But it is determined to stand

One Friday, he had run over to the Justice Department to pick up some press releases. As he rounded the bend, into the corridor that led to his office, already scanning the press releases, he overheard two colleagues clucking about him:

"Poor Larry...."

"Just can't let it go, can he?"

"Two years already...."

"Can't be helping to have that poem right in front of him every day...."

Felder tucked the poem into his desk drawer that same day and never removed it. The last thing he wanted was to be an object of newsroom pity, or possibly scorn.

He rediscovered the poem on his last day at The Rag. He held it over his trusty gray rubber trash can for a long moment. Damned thing wasn't going to threaten Walt Whitman or Emily Dickinson, was it?

But then he crammed it into his briefcase and took it home to 9807 Greentree. Purpose was Larry Felder's gasoline. Sentimentality was his siren song. To have chucked the poem would have been to nullify all the drive he had somehow summoned to get out of bed all these mornings.

It had sat ever since on his bathroom shelf. Must reading while shaving.

Well past 2 a.m. . . . up to snack on celery and grapes . . . can't hurt to grab a look at tomorrow's campaign agenda. . . . Click, click, yup, yup, National Association of Retired Federal Employees. . . . Then Chamber of Commerce in Germantown . . . Then coffee at the Silver Spring Starbucks with that guy who knows federal contracting . . . the one that Charlie insisted he see. . . . Probably will turn out to be a mid-sized donor. . . . Must remember not to commit to any staff positions for his nephew or anyone else. . . . More grapes. . . . More clicks. . . . Then a sudden, sharp veer. . . . How would Kat have been as a candidate's wife?. . . .

They had never done much Dream Baking (Kat's phrase). Her college sorority sisters had recommended it, and perfected it. Make cookies for Mr. Promising, pack them into a picnic, spread out under a tree, start munching and start imagining. The house with blue shutters. The 2.2 children. The occasional trip to Spain. Kat had ducked down that fantasy alleyway just before they took the final plunge. Larry—two feet always nailed firmly to the floor—had brushed it off.

"Kat," he had said, as they shared yet another order of meat dumplings at yet another nondescript Chinese restaurant, "I want to marry you because I love you and respect you, not because of some Disney fantasy."

"Larry," she had said, as she declined the same hot red sauce that she always declined, "I want to marry you because I love you and respect you. But how are we going to keep each other smiling?"

"I hadn't thought about that," Larry said.

"I have," Kat said. "Larry, I may not like the hot red sauce here very much, but there has to be spice between us. There has to be something beyond making the mortgage payments on time. Can we agree on. . . . gosh, I don't know . . . maybe a madcap date once a month? You know, hanging out at a biker bar, something like that? Or are you perpetually beige?"

Larry fiddled with the bright red paper sheath that always surrounds chopsticks. "I don't do madcap very much or very well, Kat," he said.

She married him anyway, because he was solid, stolid, sure. Her sorority sisters were on board. Good catch, Kat. . . . You don't marry for giggles, Kat. . . . He seems like an oak tree. . . . Never bends. . . . He'll be as strong in 30 years as he is today. . . . Your kids will be stars. . . . You can be the woman we all want to be. . .

Her mother worried about the newspaper life. Would he ever be home for dinner? Would his salary ever achieve liftoff? Was he married to his career more than he'd ever be married to her?

"Mom," said Kat, "he's the one." That's a hard slammed door to open, or re-open. Mrs. Goodman relented. She smiled her blessing. Her deep burgundy silk dress was the talk of the wedding.

Young in Washington can mean in each other's way in Washington. Kat had been climbing the rungs in public relations—a first job with an ambitious young liberal Congressman, then a mid-level position at the local office of a national firm, now a partnership with three refugees from the previous White House press operation. She was 33 and strapped in for success.

But after she and Larry has returned from Costa Rica, he raised it for the first time: Was there the seed of a conflict of interest here?

She looked up the phrase in the dictionary-- the ten-pounder that had seen her through college—and triumphantly announced that there was nothing to worry about. He occupied one orbit, she another. They could simply agree not to write about or flack about anything that might connect to or conflict with the other.

Larry did his signature up-and-back, up-and-back—ten steps to one end of the kitchen, the same ten back, his head down, the proverbial black cloud forming over his head.

"I don't know how to say this," he announced, "so I'll just say it. One of us is going to have to have a different profession. And I don't think it should be me."

Coffee curdled in both cups. Smiles morphed into grimaces. Neither gave ground. They did what every marriage manual says that newlyweds (and old-ly-weds) should never do. They went to bed angry.

She arose first. She sat in the den of their apartment—too small for just Larry, now hopeless for Larry plus Kat—and made a list. The calico cat prowled as she scrawled.

PROS OF QUITTING MY JOB: Adventure, flexibility, can always get another, wifely thing to do, would probably do it soon anyway if/when we have a kid.

CONS: Good salary, partnership stake, good colleagues, great future. AND IT'S MINE!

"Beat me to the bathroom, I see," said Larry, forcing a smile, as he shambled up to her and pecked her once on the cheek, sportingly but not lovingly.

Her return smile was just as tense. "I've been making lists," she declared. He nodded. The pros-and-cons sheet was right in front of her. She nudged it toward him. He studied it, studied it again.

She said, "Well?"

He said, "You can stay with Capital Solutions. But this is revisitable whenever either of us says it should be."

With that, a handshake and a mutual tickle with the two pinkies—their secret way of agreeing. She felt vaguely uneasy, as if they had settled this huge issue without truly understanding the attitudes of the other.

But her Larry was no male chauvinist dinosaur. He neither joked about barefoot-and-pregnant nor sought it. Kat would call all tunes, they had agreed—where to live, how to live, when to reproduce, whether to reproduce. Larry told her that marriage would help stabilize him. Her uneasiness was all about whether that stability would simply make him a better reporter, and therefore a more distant partner. Did he care—or even notice—what staying at Capital Solutions would mean to her and her alone? Was she just a caboose now clipped to the rear of The Larry Felder Limited?

They had met in the most innocent fashion imaginable. Larry was blasting down the stairs of his apartment building, uncharacteristically late for an interview. Kat was blasting up—toward a wine and cheese get-together of some college pals who happened to be Larry's neighbors. Blasting Down couldn't stop in time and smashed right into Blasting Up. As the best man, Mouse, put it during his wedding toast: "They didn't kiss on the first date. They didn't have sex on the first date. But they had serious body contact on the first date."

Larry was all apologies and chivalry. Kat was all get-this-unwelcome-encounter-over-with. He helped her up and insisted on walking her to her friend's apartment, to be sure she was all right. Thus was formed a bread crumb trail. Larry followed it a week later, with a knock on 4B.

"Hi, I'm Larry Felder from 6A," he announced to the very blond, very apprehensive Stacy Stein of 4B. "I bumped into a girl on the stairs last week. Friend of yours, I think. I just want to be sure she's doing OK."

Stacy, a child of North Jersey and sitcoms, was quick on the draw: "That's none of your business, pal."

Larry had been put off far more elegantly in his newspaper life. He volleyed: "I'd like to make it my business. I wonder if you could tell me how to contact her, please."

A year later, Stacy would recount the story at the bridal shower and declare: "I never knew I had destiny in the palm of my hands."

"Let me tell you how Larry feels in the palm of MY hands," said the bride-to-be. Just bawdy enough—that was our Kat.

Dates had often been working dates. Few movies or wine bars for this purposeful pair. They'd sit in coffee bars and sift through papers—notes and congressional reports for him, client meeting records for her. "Editing each other made us love each other," Larry would often pronounce, if someone at The Rag asked how lightning had struck. Jokesters would usually reply that Kat had nothing to worry about on that score, since editing at The Rag was so rare.

He was 38 and she was 29—a gap wide enough to separate them but not divide them. He remembered the Beatles' legendary appearance on The Ed Sullivan Show (she didn't). She thought Bruce Springsteen had invented danceable music (he knew it had been Bill Haley and The Comets). He tried not to patronize her. She tried not to worry about his early-onset stodginess. They kept moving toward a decision, even when they sometimes didn't want it, seek it or recognize it.

The ring had been on display for ages at a small crafts shop near his apartment. Gold, with inlaid amethysts. Larry gulped at the price, but decided that he could handle amortizing it across . . . what, maybe 40 years?

"In the category of things you do only once," he said to himself, aloud. Three hundred large. He paid in cash.

"I'm not much for soupy scenes," he began, as they sat down at the local Tex-Mex place and opened the menus whose contents they already knew by heart.

She thought he was about to break up with her. She began to sniffle. He grabbed both of her hands in both of his and patted. She let him, warily.

Then he reached into the pocket of his light brown corduroy sports coat—wooden buttons, dark brown felt elbow patches, frozen in the 1970s—and produced the ring. Kat glowed the way women do in ads. He smiled a little, more self-conscious than elated. He had rehearsed seven times the speech he now gave.

"Kat, I want a life with you. I want a life together. I want you to marry me. Will you, please?"

She would later tell her sorority pals that Larry sounded as if he was buying a stock, not arranging a lifelong romance. But unalloyed bliss was clearly not Mr. Felder's game. He was so serious, so straight ahead. She already knew that he would call a source more than ten times if that's what it took to get past no. Was she just another project? It was more than a little possible. Her eyes were open.

Newspaper people are always clannish, as if only they can understand the joy of making journalism sausage every day. But the clannishness redoubles when PR people appear. Much of it is jealousy—newspaper salaries simply can't compare. But a lot of it, too, is the discomfort newsies feel when they look into their future and see PR as their likely landing pad. They will have sold out once that day arrives, so they fire up disdain and arms-length-ness to keep their professional adolescence alive just a little longer.

Kat was not welcomed into Rag-Land. It wasn't even halfway subtle.

Larry brought her to The Dump (a newsie bar on the corner) a couple of times. She was tolerated but shunned, either interrupted or ignored.

One night, a very well-lubricated Pillston The Veteran asked her how it felt to represent crackpots, criminals and Third World regimes that don't let women out of the house. Kat never went back. Larry never pressed it.

They fought about current events (she believed in national leaders, he said the jury was always out), about religion (she was interested, he wasn't in the slightest), about issues (she thought children should be allowed to vote at age 14, he scoffed), about sex (she could go from zero to 60 in a blink, he wanted kissing and lots of hugs). But they never fought about money. Mostly because they never spent much.

"Larry," said Kat one winter day, "I am totally sick of being around that ratty winter coat of yours. We're replacing it." She grabbed the car keys from the wicker tray in the front hall, grabbed him and started for the door.

"Only if you let me keep the old one," said Larry.

"And why would you want to do that?"

"In case I don't like the new one."

"Then we'll return it and get another."

"No, we'll return it and I'll get another couple of years (he still pronounced it 'yee-uhs') out of the old one."

"There is a difference, Mr. Felder, between thrifty and pack rat."

"Not to me."

She stared at him, as if at an extraterrestrial. He shrugged. So their arguments would end, with a whimper, never a bang.

Felder was having an especially productive year at work. He had won the two top Middle Atlantic Press Association prizes for explanatory journalism, and Cal had nominated him for his first Pulitzer. "Gave that baby a special goodbye kiss," Cal had declared, as he told Larry about the bulging package of tear sheets he had just had mailed to the committee the day before. Then Cal added, very sotto voce, that he had just slipped Felder a five percent raise—his third in five years.

"Knowing you, that'll be better than sex," Cal boomed. Felder protested. But Cal knew his man. Achievement, accomplishment, recognition—those would animate Larry Felder far more and far longer than the random tumble.

Kat was businesslike when the moment of reckoning came. They were having brunch in Annapolis, at a nautically themed bar near the Naval Academy. It was a spring Sunday. Larry was going on (and on) about his latest struggles with the chief of staff to a ranking Republican congressman when Kat tapped the table with her knuckles. Like the pinky tickle, this was their private signal: Attention, please.

"Yes, Miss Goodman?"

"I have a question."

"Yes, Miss Goodman?"

"Are you ever going to ask me to marry you?"

"I'm considering it."

"Is that some kind of joke?"

"I wouldn't joke about something like that. Give me a little space, OK?"

Two days later, at the local Tex-Mex place where they knew the menus by heart, Larry began: "Kat, I want a life with you. . . . "

Had she pushed him into it? Did Larry need pushing into everything except his latest three-part series? The Tex-Mex Declaration (she named it as if it were an anti-ballistic missile treaty negotiated between the U.S. and the Soviet Union) was hardly the romantic play-out that little girls dream about. Especially the utter humorlessness of it.

Kat needed the occasional antic burst of laughter. "I'm brunette," she liked to say, "but I'm as dizzy as a blonde." She was given to great guffaws over TV shows, and discombobulated blather after two glasses of wine. Larry would be her anchor, for life. But would he also be her millstone?

The wedding was small and spare—elegant but not showy. They rented an old mansion on N Street in Georgetown. The slats across the front facing had been painted over so many times, over so many centuries, that paint drools had collected in the corners. Yet that passed for charm—Georgetown always kept a stiff, historic upper lip.

The oak-paneled parlor where the ceremony took place was creaky and cranky. Floors gave slightly when you stepped in the wrong places. Ancient radiators hissed when the federal judge asked if anyone had any reason why this couple should not be forever joined. . . .

The assembled newsies applauded after the vows—and headed straight for the bar. Kat's sorority sisters posed for photos and clucked about corsages. Kat's mother kept smoothing the train of her daughter's dress. She had her doubts, but she swallowed them.

The toasts were brief: "Kat agreed to marry me because I wore her down," said Larry. "I have found a genuinely good man," said Kat. More applause. More trips to the bar. At last, the cake, atop which a scale-model groom was holding a microphone and doing a stand-up, as if he were a TV star, and the scale-model bride was out-to-here pregnant.

"Is this a promise or a threat?" asked Larry.

"You have a face made for radio," said Pillston The Veteran.

" I meant the pregnant part."

"Some things you just have to figure out on your own," said Mouse, who was escorting his gumdrop du jour, a young thing who was no more than 24, and might have been a lot less.

That night, at the Capital Hilton Hotel—like Larry, low on allure and high on practicality—the new groom had hung out the Do Not Disturb sign, adjusted the temperature in the room to 64, checked the 11 o'clock news to be sure that the world hadn't ended while they were getting hitched and gargled and peignoired. Then he gathered up Kat in his thin arms and told her that he was the happiest man in the world.

CHAPTER  **5.**

PENNY ROMANOFF STIRRED her tea, stirred it again, removed the tea bag, squeezed it dry by wrapping it around her spoon—all without looking up. The she delivered the line that is always a blade to the chest of any candidate.

"Let me think about it, Lorraine," she said.

Lorraine Bartlesby was making her first stop of a 12-stop day, so she was vastly overdressed for the in-the-kitchen-on-two-bar-stools conference she had just had. Her suit was salmon, her shoes soft mocha, her stockings a muted gray, her blouse pearl. Stop Six would be a women's club lunch at a country club in Rockville. An excellent opportunity to collect some volunteers, some dollars and some votes. So. . . . best foot forward into the closet, and best dress onto the back. Pants suits were for 20-somethings. Lorraine Bartlesby was running for Congress from behind, so she needed every possible "click" she could get.

Penny should have been a hefty one.

They had met 15 years earlier, when both had daughters in the same day care center. As they loaded the girls into their respective Volvos on that first day, they parried as new friends will—my husband and I *really* wanted a station wagon, but we're trying to save money. . . . I read all the safety reports, and a Volvo handles a crash better than any American car. . . . It's nice to see you loading Amanda into her car seat in the back seat. . . . Much safer there. . . .

A play date was booked. And another. A month later, a dinner for four, featuring a cavalcade of toilet training war stories and tips. Then mutual baby showers when each couple had a second child. Followed by unending committee work for the day care. Long, consoling phone calls between the women when parents died. And veiled complaints about husbands, duly dissected.

Through it all, loyalty was assumed. Not only were secrets routinely kept—Amanda's bed wetting was never revealed to anyone, even though Lorraine had known about it for years—but projects were routinely and cheerfully undertaken.

A gala for autistic kids? Lorraine was right there, with the backing of her family foundation. A donation to the all-girls prep school in Connecticut that Lorraine had attended? Penny had never even set foot on campus, but she routinely made a gift to the annual fund, in Lorraine's honor.

And now, Lorraine's campaign ship was taking water. Money wouldn't solve every problem, she knew—and had repeated often in Penny's kitchen. "But I have to get out ahead of Felder with young women, Pen, and you know how busy they are. It's going to mean tons of radio and TV advertising. Only way to reach them. And that means raising the money to pay for it."

Penny had done campaign work for many local candidates before she settled into life as a Chevy Chase housewife. Her questions were as pungent and as pointed as her central Maryland accent:

- Why didn't Lorraine self-fund the commercials? She surely could. "Because I need to show the national Democratic campaign donors that I can raise money among influentials in my own district. Raised money leads to more raised money."

- Why didn't Lorraine aim her campaign more sharply at older voters, who vote in greater proportions, and with stronger loyalty, than younger voters? "Because the Eighth District is changing, Pen. Lots of move-ins. Lots of new, young families. Lots of Asian and Hispanic money. It isn't just church ladies and horse farm ladies any more. I believe young women will vote for the female candidate in the race, if I can reach them."

- Why had Lorraine lost so much of her early lead? "Felder has been very effective with his aw-shucks stuff. He has made his total inexperience look like an asset. But I have the real record of accomplishment. All I have to do is help the voters realize this—or help him self-destruct."

- Self-destruct? How? "Any campaign has made mistakes. I'm working night and day to find a few of his."

- And if you find them? "I will have the delicious pleasure of leaking every detail to The Rag. Where someone who has no doubt been jealous of Felder for years will have the delicious pleasure of laying it all out for one million readers on Page One."

- Are swing voters really going to care about campaign flubs? "They will if the goods are good enough."

- What about the old money in the Eighth, Lorraine? Where is it going? "To me early. Then I started getting some slippage. Some people even started avoiding me, and fibbing about it. I started hearing from some of the biggest traditional donors that I must be wrong to be soliciting them, they weren't Democrats any more, despite what the county registrar's lists said, so they couldn't vote in the primary. Isn't that great? If they don't want to give me a donation, then don't. But don't make stuff up. Computer registration lists don't lie."

- How about celebrity endorsements? "Nobody really major has committed yet. But this is an area that worries me. All the big state politicians say they're weighing their options. That means they're checking the polls, which means very bad news, Pen. But I'm working on two former governors. If I get them, that has to help, right?"

Penny stared at her, caught somewhere between wanting to say, "No, not really," and saying nothing. She fiddled with her shirt collar, cursed the bar stools in the kitchen for being too flimsy, vowed to ask Mark whether they could afford to replace them, ignored a ringing phone, checked her BlackBerry, checked it again.

"Pen?"

"Yes, Lorraine."

"Pen, I could really use a significant donation from you."

Out came the blade.

"Let me think about it, Lorraine."

"OK, thanks, please do think about it. And when you do, please don't forget how well you know me. You know I'm a fighter, Pen. You know I'm going to do every last single thing I can do to re-aim the needle in this race. You know I'll be the best candidate and the best member of Congress."

"I'm rooting for you, Lorraine," said Penny. They air-kissed. They patted shoulders. Lorraine didn't realize how mad she was until she had fired up her dark blue Toyota Camry—the new I'm-not-rich campaign car of choice that her advisers had recommended.

She pounded the steering wheel hard enough to bruise the heel of her hand. She barely avoided a tumble into tears—only the fear of drowning her eye makeup prevented it. Self-pity washed over her.

To do so much, so right, for so long, and now to be caught in this downdraft.... And if you can't count on your oldest friends....

"I need some luck," said the candidate.

As the Toyota hummed in neutral, she recalled the favorite saying of her girlhood tennis teacher, who had repeated it every morning, right before the oldie about changing a losing game.

"You make your own luck, Lorraine," he had said.

She had never quite been able to do that, and had surrendered her tennis career eventually to a lack of strength and agility. But that didn't make the saying untrue, in tennis, love, war or politics.

Out came her BlackBerry. Into the notes field, she typed: "Develop Felder dirt—somehow."

✸ ✸ ✸

Charlie's mother had been bitterly critical, more than once, but Charlie didn't care. When you had gotten to be 34 years old, and you knew how to feed and clothe yourself and make a living, what difference could it possibly make if you parked your bike in the living room?

To Muriel Carpentier, the bike was a rebuke with 20 gears, a living reminder of why Charlie did not have a husband.

"Who in the world will want you if he has to compete with.... that?," Muriel had said, every time she visited from central Pennsylvania, gesturing at the sleek, cherry-red $3,000 British racing machine as if it were a dead hamster?

"Mother, you want to pay for a place for me to store it? I live in a big city, Mother. Space isn't free, Mother. I have to cut some corners sometimes."

Muriel shook her head sadly and silently. Her long-departed husband had often done the same—over bad stock market news, over yet another failure of his beloved Phillies, over his only daughter's choice of careers. Perhaps the old saw needed revisions. Perhaps long-marrieds not only finished each other's sentences, but adopted each other's negative gestures.

Charlie knew that the bike was just the beginning. Here came the worries, followed by the offer of financial help.

"Charlise, I'm not getting any younger, you know," said Muriel, who was 59 and who wasn't ancient by any definition. But that didn't stop The Speech:

"When you get to be my age, you want two things. Safety and security for your daughter, and grandchildren. That means a man, honey. That means a husband," she said.

"Mother, don't you think I've thought about that? I'd love to have a guy and a baby. But you can't just go to the store and buy either one of them, Mother."

"Charlise, I know the world is different for you than it was for me when I was your age. But it's so, so hard to be on your own. I've learned that ever since your father died. No companionship. No security. No . . .well, you know."

"Sex is anywhere, Mother. Sex is everywhere."

"Yes, I suppose it is. But that's not what I really care about. What I really care about is knowing, on my deathbed, that my Charlise is on the right course."

Charlie's phone began to beep, squawk and rumble. She punched three buttons, muttered "Damn," and pushed a speed-dial button.

"Get him there right now!," she barked, as if the person on the other end was a dimwit. Perhaps he was.

"Trouble, dear?"

"Nothing that I can't solve and didn't just solve. Some kid who's responsible for getting Larry to his campaign stops. Just hired him last week. Probably shouldn't have. So wet behind the ears that his ears are drowning. He just texted me to say that he was lost in Poolesville. How can you get lost in Poolesville? There are only two main roads in the whole place. But these interns in politics these days. . . ."

"Charlise, I know you take this campaign very seriously. But have you considered what's going to happen to you if Larry loses?"

"Larry won't lose."

"Al Gore couldn't lose and he lost."

"Larry won't lose."

"I'm just looking out for your best interests, dear."

Charlie had forded this generation gulf before. She hitched up her designer slacks and made ready to do so again.

"Mother, I know this is hard for you to understand, but when you say that I should have a husband, and that I should spend all my time and energy looking for a husband, that's a way of demeaning my career and casting aspersions on how well I do it."

"Charlise, I never. . . ."

"You always. I can see right through you. You think that running a congressional campaign is like going to summer camp—a nice diversion. Mother, this . . . is . . . what . . . I . . . do! This is the career I've had for years, and that I may have forever. If a husband happens, great. But even after he happens, he's going to have to understand that I'm a serious person, in a serious job."

"Honey, maybe if you changed your hair. . . ."

"Mother!"

"OK, OK, it's not that simple. And by the way, I like your latest haircut a lot! I really do!"

"I'll tell Federico you said so."

Muriel got up from the graduate-student-era couch with the skinny arms, sidestepped the bike, approached the triple-track bay window that looked down on rainswept R Street and stared.

"Looks like more rain," she announced.

"You hungry, Mother?"

"No. No, thank you. I'm trying hard to reduce. Do you notice anything?"

"You always look trim, Mother."

"So do you, dear. Even with the schedule you're keeping."

Charlie picked up that morning's Rag from the granite-top kitchen counter and scanned the local front. Nothing about Larry, Lorraine or the Eighth. She flipped to the obituary page. No one prominent from the Eighth had departed overnight. Then to Page One. Nothing seemed to have happened on Capitol Hill that would change the course of rivers. So Larry's talking points would not need to be recast, as they so often had been over the last two months because of Iraq, climate change or proposals to adjust the federal employee cost of living increase.

"Mother," said Charlie.

"Yes, dear?"

"Mother, I have a problem."

Muriel reassumed her seat and leaned forward, her hands clasped as if in prayer. This was body language for "I want to help in the way that only a mother can."

"Does she ever respond to me sincerely?" Charlie asked herself, for the umpty-umpth time. "It's as if I have a mother who has been made from a box of Bisquick. Just add water and it'll always come out the same. Totally predictable."

But you go to war with the mother you have. Charlie poured herself another cup of orange pekoe tea. She cleared the throat that didn't need clearing, a la Felder. And she lobbed this rocket:

"Mother, I'm in love with a man."

Muriel wanted to smile, but she knew that it might be misunderstood. Into the Bisquick box she reached and out came . . .a furrowed brow and a cliché.

"That's wonderful, dear! I'm so glad you told me! Who is he?"

"Mother, I can't tell you that right now."

"Oh, my, gosh, Charlise, is he married?"

"Sort of."

"What do you mean, 'Sort of?' "

"He hasn't gotten a divorce. He hasn't even said he wants one, to be honest with you. But that hasn't stopped me. I know he's the right one for me."

"Charlise, dear, this is a blind alley. This is nothing but trouble. This isn't what I want for you. Another woman's husband? Nothing but trouble."

"Mother, what I want from you is a promise."

"Yes, dear?"

"I want you to give me your emotional support no matter how this turns out, OK?"

"You know you have that, dear."

"Good. Because I'm going to need it, I have a feeling."

"Dear, does this man know about the feelings you have for him?"

"Not at all."

"Are you going to tell him?"

"Not right away. But soon."

"What if he says he isn't interested in you?"

"I've been there before, Mother, heaven knows. Remember that guy Bruce, in college? Remember Riley right after I came to D.C.?"

"Yes, of course I do."

"Then trust me to get the timing right, OK?" (God, I sound like a pouty four-year-old).

"I trust you, dear. I trust you totally." (But maybe I shouldn't—that Bruce was awful to her, and that Riley only wanted sex).

"Mother, I know you want to know more about him (and maybe I should spill all the beans. . . .)."

"Only if you want to tell me, dear (Oh, my, is there something wrong with him? Besides being married, I mean? Is he handicapped? Is he destitute?)."

"I'd love to tell you, Mother. But I just can't right now (because you'd toss me right out the window if you knew)."

"Charlise, have you, uh, I mean, um. . . ."

"No, Mother, I haven't. We haven't. It hasn't gotten to that point."

"I'm so relieved! The last thing you need is some lawsuit from some mistreated wife."

"Mother, this will never be about some quickie affair, I promise you. This man is a total keeper. A rock. I hope he'll be my rock. But I realize it might not work out."

"Charlise, there's always some element of mystery to all this, even when it does work out. Why, when your father and I. . . ."

"Mother, I've heard this approximately a thousand times!"

"All right, dear, all right." She was squelched—again. Charlie knew how to find and push that button.

"But, Mother, I do want you to know that I'm getting a little impatient with this man. I see him regularly—let me put it that way. But he never seems to be aware that I exist. Well, let me take that back. He never sees me as a possible mate. Just as someone who flows into and back out of his day. A piece of female wallpaper in sensible shoes. Not good enough for me, Mother."

"Dear, you know what they say about feminine wiles. Some new stockings? A new dress?"

"Won't work on THIS guy."

"How do you know?"

"I've tried! I've tried other tricks, too. He's beyond tricks."

"Maybe he loves his wife."

"He does. He surely does."

Then, a burst outside the box marked "Careful."

"Charlise, I did NOT raise you to be a homewrecker! I will NOT allow you to break up a happy home!"

"I won't allow that, either, Mother." Measured. Cool. Refuse to be drawn into a fight. "My strategy is to bait hooks, set traps. Let HIM make the key move."

"I like that a lot better, dear. There's no shame in marrying a divorced man. Why, when Edwina did it. . . ."

"Please don't start looking for mother-of-the-bride dresses quite yet, Mother."

Muriel got up, strode surely across the room and planted a light kiss on Charlie's right cheek.

"No harm in thinking about it, though, dear, is there?"

Charlie pecked her back, and thought for the thousandth time that she never changes. Then again, Larry Felder doesn't, either.

★ ★ ★

Kal Radin got to the Golden Goose first, at 7:50 a.m. It was a typical Radin tactic.

Early was his equivalent of on time. On time was his equivalent of late. To win in business, you needed any edge. Seeing to it that Larry Felder arrived second was Radin's time-honored way of getting the drop, as movie cowboys always tried to do with unsuspecting bad guys.

Radin slid into the red leatherette booth and pointed once at his coffee mug. A waiter noticed from 50 feet away and was right there with the orange-collared Pyrex pot. No interrogation about decaf or regular was offered, and none was necessary. At the Goose, the self-proclaimed "Bethesda's finest," they knew that, for Radin, it was always decaf after 8 a.m., always regular before.

Felder arrived at precisely 8, his smile firmly in place, his blue suit freshly pressed. Radin did not get up. He extended his hand, shook once and said it was nice to meet a man he'd heard so much about.

"So nice to meet you, too, Mr. Radin."

"Please, please, make it Kal."

"OK, Kal."

"And may I call you Larry?"

"All my best friends do."

"Well, then, we've got that taken care of."

Up curled Radin's left eyebrow. That brought the waiter at a near-trot. For Larry: A veggie omelet and whole wheat toast, hold the butter, please. For Kal: Finely chopped pineapple, oatmeal with 2 percent milk and a side of Canadian bacon.

Then the right eyebrow, with his face at an angle that only the waiter could see. That was code for: The check is mine.

"They don't have Canadian bacon on the menu," Radin reported, "but I've been coming here since the day they opened. And when they needed a loan to expand, I was right there for them. So, for me. . . ."

Felder nodded. These power players were the same the world over. Always looking for leverage, and bragging once they've found it.

For a fleeting second, he wished he were wearing the worn-thin gray sport coat of an investigative reporter, not the perfecto blue uniform of the wannabe public servant. If this were six months earlier, Felder would already have had his notebook out, and he'd be making a note about Canadian bacon. But now, and perhaps for good, he was trying to make his breakfast date feel comfortable, not fry him on the griddle.

"So, you wanted to discuss my campaign," said Felder, a touch impatiently.

"Yes, I did. How's it going?"

"Very nicely so far. I've gotten endorsements from all over the Eighth District, and I'm expecting endorsements from all the major county papers. My polls are excellent. They say anything over 55 percent is a landslide in a contested primary. I'm at 69 percent in the latest newspaper polls. My own polls are even higher."

Radin plucked a packet of Splenda from the bowl beside the napkin dispenser and rolled it nervously into a cylinder.

"If you're that far ahead this early, you must be a lock, then, right?"

"Wrong, Kal. Or at least I have to guard carefully against that possibility. The worst thing I can do is to be complacent. So I'm out on the trail every day, for 12 hours. And I'm raising money vigorously. I can't be sure of winning unless I neutralize Bartlesby and all her personal money."

Radin unspooled the cylinder and replaced the packet in the bowl. He picked up the plastic jug of ketchup and studied it.

"Never did understand who could want ketchup with eggs," he mused.

"Guess it's people who want to go their own way with breakfast, Kal."

Kal looked hard at Larry and wiped the half-smile off his face.

"I think that describes me pretty well, Larry. I like to go my own way, for sure. That's what I've done with AaaaaaH and what I'll always do. I like to win. And I like to get the right help when the right help is what I need."

"Can I give you some of that help?"

"Maybe you can, Larry. Maybe you can. I'm having some trouble with my business that my local Congressman might be able to help me clear away."

"What kind of trouble?"

"Import tariffs. They're high and going higher. Tariffs on basic materials that keep my business afloat—pun intended. Do you know anything about any of that?"

"Zero. But I'm sure I could learn."

"Would you be willing to do that? After all, I'm one of the larger employers in your district. . . ."

"Whoa, Kal. It's not my district yet."

"But I'm pretty sure it will be. And I'm prepared to help that happen. You know what I mean. A donation. But I need to know what that money would buy."

"Kal, I can't promise you that a donation will buy anything definite. That would be illegal. But I can promise you that I'll try to help you with the right people."

"And who would that be?"

"Whoever the party places in leadership in the Commerce Committee, which handles import tariffs, or the Ways and Means Committee, which sets taxes."

"Why wouldn't you be on those committees?"

"Because I'd be a freshman, Kal, with no power and no seniority and I'd have to take committee assignments that I might not want. Probably lesser stuff. Probably out-of-the-limelight kind of stuff, like Government Operations, since I'd have so many federal employees in my district. Possibly Energy, since I won one of my Pulitzers by reporting on oil pipelines."

The food arrived. Kal attacked his by sawing at it vigorously with both his knife and fork, as if he were dismembering a flapping bird. Larry picked at his with fork only.

"Look, Larry, I tend to speak very directly. That's always been my habit and my style. I won't apologize for it. It has served me very well."

Larry nodded.

"I want to support you. But I will definitely need your help in return. Can I expect that?"

"Yes, Kal, you can. I will support you the way I would support any influential resident of my district."

Kal shook too much salt onto his food, followed by too much pepper.

"I've got to say, Larry, that I don't like being compared to other influential residents of the district. I'm a key guy with a particular problem. In business, that means we have the potential for a deal, you see what I'm saying?"

"Tell me more, Kal."

"I am prepared to give you the largest donation I can give you by law, Larry. But I'm also prepared to give you much more."

"I'm not going to accept a gift that exceeds the federal limits, Kal."

"What if I said the gift wouldn't be from me? What if I arranged for lots of gifts to land on your desk, from each one of my senior employees? No single gift would break the federal limit. But put them together, and you know, they might wrap around the world about 45 times!" He chuckled at his own metaphor.

When Larry was at Kat's bedside the previous evening, talking at her instead of to her as always, he had promised her that he'd never court legal trouble in his campaign. "Why would I do that, Kat?," he had ruminated. "That would make me just as big a skunk as the guys I always wrote about. To paraphrase Richard Nixon, I am not a skunk."

And now he was staring dead-on at skunkdom. Yet even skunks need the renowned lubricating power of dough.

He took a sip of coffee. He looked down at his fingernails. He picked a sautéed hunk of green pepper out of his omelet. And he said:

"I'd be grateful for your support in any way, Kal. I'd have to be sure this is legal. But I'm sure it is. And once I assure myself that we'd be OK with this approach, I'd be all in."

"I WISH THEY ALL COULD

be California gir-r-r-rls...."

The five-part harmony of The Beach Boys was Larry Felder's unwavering shaving music. Whiskers had been disappearing to this group's signature tune, and no other, for nearly 40 years. Kat had tried to wean him onto Bonnie Raitt or Willie Nelson, but he had refused to stray. Just as he wore the same blue pinstripe shirt for decades, the same shoes until the soles started flapping, the same black socks that he had bought 20 years earlier, so he stuck with his musical tastes of puberty. It was yet another form of Felder geek-dom. For him, familiarity never bred contempt.

"Keep their boy friends warm at ni-i-i-i-ght...."

Felder was up at 6, as usual, not having been warmed by any girl friends, as usual. In and out of the shower by 6:06, running the hot water for his shave 10 seconds later, lathering up his chin 30 seconds after that. And planning. Always, always planning.

If he had learned nothing else from trailing political campaigns around the country for decades, he had grasped what happens to candidates who float, or try to "feel" where they're going. They end up practicing law back in Sheboygan—again—or spending the next five years living with their mothers-in-law so they can pay off their campaign debts. Larry Felder, armed with a silver Samsung pocket dictation machine that sat beside his mug of shaving soap, wouldn't fall into that well-worn pit.

CLICK...."Thoughts about the campaign for Charlie for Tuesday morning.... Charlie, I really need some research about whether and when the Army Corps of Engineers dumped live residue from chemical weapons experiments in the district.... I hear it happened right after World War Two... A plan to remediate this could be an excellent wedge to attract young enviros...."

CLICK. Shave the right side of his sallow face. Pay special attention to that troublesome ridge along the jaw bone. CLICK. "I'll need some remarks prepared for the American Legion of Gaithersburg appearance on Wednesday... Please check to be sure which wars these guys fought... I'm sure it'll be everything from World War Two to Vietnam, but I'll want to know the population breaks for each era...."

CLICK. Carefully rake razor across Adam's apple. Cuts wouldn't do. "Charlie, I haven't been happy for quite some time with that radio commentator... You know, Abrabanel from WQST... Real flamethrower... Would be damned dangerous if he ever knew what he was talking about.... Maybe we should have a private sit-down with him, to try to woo him?... I'll kill this idea in a flash if you think it's too dangerous or too unlikely to produce results... But the guy does have big numbers among older independents, if I recall right...."

CLICK. Wipe face with towel. Check for patches he might have missed. Notice new areas of baldness on top of noggin. Sigh. Curse ancestors. Muse.

"Well, East Coast girls are hip.... I really dig the clothes they wear-r-r-r...."

The first thing he had noticed about Charlie had been her culottes. Hardly the badge of usual for an ambitious female Washington career political operative. That species tended toward black sheaths (if Democratic) or cranberry blazers (if Republican). Not since Marnie Moskowitz had he seen this old-but-now-new-again fashion—and Charlie's culottes were deep purple, of all things.

He never commented on personal appearance—not wise, not professional. Could only be misunderstood. But the culottes had pulled him out of his shopworn shell.

"I really like those pants you're wearing," he had said, casting caution to the winds. He and Charlie had just met at a Capitol Hill press conference. It was thrown by a once-bright Illinois star who was starting to tumble in the polls and who was facing a primary challenge for the first time. Charlie was there representing her boss, an Ohio Democrat who was worried about a primary challenge himself and wanted some politico-intelligence. Larry was there to troll for column material.

"Maybe my candidate needs to wear purple culottes. He'd be huge with the transgender vote," Charlie replied. They chuckled together. But no sparks. No deep glances into the pools of the other's eyes. No tendrils of let's-meet-later. Wit leavened the business of politics, which needed all the leavening it could get. But wit often operated for its own sake.

Mental note/Larry to Larry: This girl has a nice freshness to her, a genuine sauciness that she didn't just learn from some late-night TV comic. Not a simpleton, not a babe on the make. Seems smart. Seems connected. Might be a good source on some story some day.

Mental note/Charlie to Charlie: This Felder has a kind of wounded innocence about him. Self-absorbed, but all the biggest journos are. Distracted, but wasn't Bob Woodward distracted? Maybe I should offer to help him with a story some day. Maybe, inshallah, he isn't married? Or at least he's a Democrat?

She called him to book coffee. He broke three dates in a row—"sorry, I'm on deadline." The fourth date took place, successfully, at a Cosi on K Street. Black, no cream, no sugar for him. A salad with dressing prudently on the side for her.

They talked first about the Hill, second about his career, third about hers. Then they gazed at a fantasy future.

"Have you ever considered another career?"

"Why would I? Journalism has been everything I've always wanted, and more."

"Because lots of journalists get tired of sitting in the third row. They'd rather be on the playing field."

"If I ever had that kind of itch to scratch, I did it years ago by going into TV and radio. They always said I had a face and a voice made for newspapers, but I proved them wrong!"

Lame, but she laughed in an agreeable fashion nevertheless. She was enjoying this guy, despite his reserve, his lack of flair. He wasn't so famous that he repelled efforts to get closer. He put her into a comfort zone that congressional aides rarely approach, much less achieve, with media heavyweights. Their age difference would usually have been a huge hurdle. Their status difference would been another. But with Larry and Charlie, hurdles never even seemed to surface.

"Larry, I think you could be a heck of a public servant."

He didn't understand her at first. "Do you mean working for the government?," he had asked. The cringe in his voice had been hard to miss.

"No, silly. I mean running for office."

He was genuinely surprised.

"Me? What? Are you serious?"

"Totally."

"Which office? Dogcatcher?"

"Larry, you could run for any office you wanted. You're so well known. You're so good with issues. You're just the right age and just the right combination of experience and idealism. I seriously think you could run for Congress and win."

Larry ran through all the obvious objections. No campaign organization. No independent funds. No experience. No party affiliation, because of The Rag's conflict of interest rules. He would look like a hypocrite, a changeling or the victim of a midlife crisis after writing so searchingly about the flaws of other politicians for so long.

Yes, he had name recognition, but so would Willie Sutton. A political columnist is not necessarily a politician, he half-lectured her, as if to slam shut the door.

It creaked open for: "Oh, yes, one more thing. I don't have the right lieutenant. Someone who has been through the wars, and is willing to go through them one more time. Someone who can happily play Number Two. Someone who is super-organized and super-committed. I don't have that person, Charlie."

"Yes, you do, Larry."

Big bats of her eyes. Look of surprise on his face, followed by a slow welling look of comprehension.

"Really?"

"Really."

"But. . . ."

"Before you do the buts, Larry, promise me that you'll at least consider it. Give it two mornings while you're shaving. For you, that'll be enough for a yes or a no. I wouldn't be in it for the salary, so don't fret about that. I'd be in it to help you win."

The Beach Boys had no opinion about this wackola idea. They were too busy extolling the pleasures of "girls, girls, girls, I dig the girls, girls, girls." As they air-hugged and parted, Larry had indeed promised Charlie that yes, he would at least consider it.

Yet he wasn't going to get shoved into anything rash. That was not the Felder way. If he was even half-serious, or could ever get to that point, he would first have to run the idea past several colleagues who were actual adults and not boiler room culottes-wearers. Also past several party moguls and several potential funders. Then Mauskopf. Then possibly Cassidy.

And he might still not do it.

But if he ever did, he knew from the very first who his campaign manager was going to be.

Charlie had promised not to breathe a word of this conversation. But who would ever know how quickly she leaped into Google that night for every Felder morsel? Uh, huh, uh, huh.... Grand Concourse, White Plains, Rag. Uh, huh.... Six Pulitzers in fewer than 20 years, the best such batting average in newspaper history. Yup, yup... the TV, the radio, the procession of collegiate columnists who imitated his style even more often than they imitated David Brooks. And way down deep in the bios, a brief mention of the wife, and the son who was no longer with us.

That night, the kind of humid, hanging evening that gives Washington summers their dismal reputation, Charlie had dragged her bike down the stairs and gone for a 10-miler through Rock Creek Park.

She listed the positives—he could win, he could last for many years, he cared about the right things, he would never become a Capitol Hill phony who lived only for the bright lights.

And the negatives—he wasn't the kind to say exactly what any and every audience wanted to hear, he wasn't glib, he wasn't photogenic, he might have written something over the course of his career that would come back to bite him.

Amanda Prosser, one of her gal pals at Duke, had fallen for a man who had all the panache of the Roto Rooter man. Not distinctive. Not distinguished. Not especially aware, either of her or of the world. Prematurely tubby. Already losing his hair when they met. Liked to play Dungeons and Dragons, and hearts for the pulse-pounding sum of a tenth of a cent a point.

Yet she was enthralled from the first second. They now had three kids, and were still giddy 10 years later.

Amanda had explained her choice by trotting out an old 78 RPM recording of "Bill," the showstopper song from "Showboat." The money lyric said it all:

"I used to dream I would discover
"The perfect lover some day
"... I always thought that I would find
"One of those special kind of men
"With a giant brain and a noble head

"Like the heroes found in the books I've read

"So I can't explain

"It's clearly not his brain

"That makes me thrill

"I love him because he's. . . .

"I don't know. . . .

"Because he's just my Bill."

Yes, Amanda's guy was named Bill. He lacked anything close to a noble head, and he tended to discuss (endlessly) science fiction and sitcoms, which would make him the dullest dinner partner in history. But if he was right for Amanda Prosser, why couldn't Charlie settle down with her favorite balding-but-budding national leader?

He was no life of the party, either. And he dressed terribly. And he probably hated quickie vacations to the Caribbean. And biking. And Duke. And he probably made love with his socks on.

But even if it took a million long days on the campaign trail before he thought of her in THAT way, well, that would be a price worth paying.

★ ★ ★

"Mr. Felder, it's SUCH a pleasure to meet you!". . . . "Mr. Felder, I've been reading you for years, but I've never heard you speak before!". . . . "Hey, Larry, I grew up on the Grand Concourse, too. You ever have an egg cream at Harry's, man? No? Must have been before your time.". . . . "Mr. Felder, it would be an HONOR to vote for you and an HONOR to have you represent me. You're not like all the rest of them."

Rule One of Electoral Politics: It isn't just what you say from the stump, or how you say it. It's how—and how well—you schmooze right afterward with the audience.

In the 21st Century, it's tempting to think that a political campaign can be conducted wholesale. By the batch. Remotely. Aiming at thousands, or at least hundreds. Technology made that thinking seductive. But the truth was walking up to Larry Felder right after he had finished his standard speech to the current events club of Calvary United Methodist Church in Rockville.

Sixteen people had lined up to (choose at least one) ask him a question, bask in his glow, thank him for coming or ask if he knew their cousin Charlotte. Sixteen votes could be locked at this moment, or permanently lost.

Larry was eternally even, placid and polite. He asked for names, and repeated them back, accurately and disarmingly, when he addressed his questioners. He never rose to the bait of a contentious comment. He never made promises, or anything that could be construed as one. It was all vanilla ice cream. Go down smooth. Don't leave a bitter aftertaste. Project that you're caring, you're one of them, you're a winner. Make them feel good about you, the process and the future, not necessarily in that order.

Charlie stood to one side of the after-speech pack, copying down as many names as she could manage from all the HI MY NAME IS slap-on badges the crowd was wearing. Billy the intern was asking those who had finished their one-on-one time with Larry to fill out index cards—What do you think the most important issue is in this campaign? . . . Would you be willing to volunteer? . . . Would you be willing to make a donation? . . . Are you a likely voter or a maybe voter?

The primary was a month away. Newton's Third Law of Politics—a candidate leading then would almost certainly win--was in full effect. Reporters were calling Charlie to see if they could interview the candidate for pieces about his "inevitability." The wonkiest of the scribes was even trying on a different kind of glass slipper—would Larry get a spot on the coveted Democratic Congressional Campaign Committee, which would place other Democrats in his debt and might make him a contender for higher national office?

But neither the roar of the greasepaint nor the whiff of success could stay Larry Felder from total, habitual reliance on caution. It was how he approached everything.

If he was shopping for batteries for his dictation machine, he would compare brands, prices, model numbers and special deals as if he had never done so before. In fact, he did so every time he shopped for the same batteries.

Caution and conservatism were not identical. Felder could be quite bold in his policy positions—Pell grants for every would-be college student, a dedicated federal fund for reconstruction of the Interstate highway system, expedited federal cancer research funds. But rushing to judgment was for the hot-tempered, and for those who truly pined to be talking heads on CNN. Larry Felder was determined to be a deliberate legislator. He liked to joke with Charlie and the staff that he would be the only member of the House who would actually read every bill on which he voted. Except that it wasn't a joke.

The Eighth District was notorious for early-to-bed-early-to-rise, so it was no surprise that the current events club meeting had wrapped up by 8:45 p.m., or that The Felder Express had nothing on its schedule afterward. Charlie proposed a beer in Silver Spring. Larry grimaced revealingly, but said OK.

The Conchapreague had been selling overpriced seafood and underpriced draft beer for 45 years. When they arrived, the place was full of tradesmen with their first names woven above their left breasts and women who averaged 50 unneeded pounds each. Many were smoking, even though the law and the Surgeon General said they shouldn't.

Charlie and Larry slid into a corner booth, both of whose burgundy linoleum-covered seats had split open from age. They each ordered a National Bohemian.

"Charlie, I'm feeling good."

"Larry, you really must be. You never say any such thing."

"Charlie, I'm feeling so good that I want to look ahead."

"So look."

Larry stacked and restacked a pile of campaign documents, as if to gather his thoughts, or maybe his strength.

"Charlie," he said, "I'm thinking of you as my chief of staff."

Charlie allowed a smile to build. "Congressman," she said, "I'd be honored."

Then the geek reappeared.

"I think we can work out the right salary and the right staff for you," said Larry. "I don't think we'd get any spillback from Bartlesby, or anybody who'd run against us in the future. You don't have any skeletons in that closet of yours, do you?"

Charlie said the only issue with her closet was why Larry Felder's clothes weren't hanging in it.

"You keep returning to that," Larry said.

"And I will keep returning to that," Charlie said.

"Haven't I made myself clear?"

"You have. But things sometimes have a way of changing."

"Not this thing."

Charlie drained her Natty Boh. "Larry, I promise you that I will always keep my professional life with you separate from any other kind of life I can imagine with you. But it is damned hard. And it is getting damned harder."

Larry was half a glass behind her. He took a studied sip.

"Which Charlie am I seeing here?" he asked. "The dedicated, talented Capitol Hill operative? Or the victim of hormones?"

Charlie scowled. "I'm not a victim of anything, Larry. I'm a woman who's being honest. I've always been honest. And I'll lay it out for you again. I want a relationship with you. For more than just a minute or an hour. I want a life with you. And I'm not talking just about our career paths intersecting. I'm talking about . . . well, you know."

Larry shook his head three times—In surprise? Dismay? Scorn? Hard to tell. Felder the reporter had learned through thousands of interviews and encounters not to tip his hand.

But his soliloquy left little doubt.

"Not going to happen, Charlie. Can't happen. First of all, it would be too close for comfort. I couldn't work with you every day and shack up with you every night. I need some space, some alone time. Second of all, it would lead to lots of gossip and probably lots of negative publicity. Can't you just see us in all those web sites about how the rich and famous live? Who needs that? Third of all, I am married, Charlie! How can I suddenly give that up after all these years? Can't. Can't possibly."

Charlie had not planned it. She had not hoped for it. In fact, she had planned for Larry to fold that very evening. She had even carefully brought along two types of birth control—a condom and a diaphragm—in case lust started flooding, and they wanted options. Plus a clean pair of underpants for the morning after.

But now Charlie was out of options. She stood up, smoothed out her basic-black skirt and announced that she was quitting the campaign, as of that instant.

"I wish you the best, Larry," she said. "But you won't have me to kick around any more." She was halfway to the front door by the time Larry had collected himself and called out to her. She never turned back.

★ ★ ★

By Vic Printz
Staff Writer
The Washington Record

"In a staff shift that could have major consequences in Maryland's Eighth Congressional District, the campaign chief for Democratic candidate Larry Felder resigned yesterday.

"Charlise Carpentier, who had worked for Felder since he announced for the open seat five months earlier, announced that she was leaving immediately.

"She offered no additional details except to say: 'I'm not going to be spending more time with my family because I don't have a family.'

"Felder, a longtime political reporter and columnist for The Rag until he became a congressional candidate, said he would miss Carpentier and would not try to replace her immediately, or perhaps ever.

" 'With fewer than three weeks until the primary, I couldn't hope to duplicate the work she did,' Felder said. 'We'll just continue down the path she planned. The greatest praise I could give her would be to win the primary, based on her strategies.'

"Lorraine Bartlesby, Felder's chief opponent in the primary, said in a prepared statement:

" 'Now we'll see if Larry Felder really has the skill and the DNA to represent our district. It was common knowledge that he simply did whatever Charlie Carpentier told him to do. On the contrary, our campaign is run by me, and only by me. The voters will soon see—and sense—who's the better candidate.'

"The most recent Washington Record poll shows Felder far in front of Bartlesby—by an average margin of 65 to 20 percent, with a three percent margin of error. Felder has more than tripled Bartlesby's reported fundraising results. Much of Bartlesby's campaign has been financed by her family's foundation."

Cal Cassidy read the story twice. Then he marched out into the slum that was The Rag's newsroom and bellowed for Printz.

Cal ushered him into his office with an over-grand sweep of his hand. This usually meant that an idea was percolating in what was left of Cal's brain.

Printz sat down stiffly on the couch right below an oversized mock Rag front page. Its headline read:

WASHINGTON FOUND TO POSSESS HUMAN BEINGS AFTER ALL.

"Printz, what's really going on in this campaign?"

"What I wrote, Cal. The girl left his staff. Larry said he'd keep calm and carry on, kind of like what the Brits did during World War Two. Not much there."

"Your nose must be stopped up, you old bastard. Here's what I smell: A much better story. No one quits a campaign that's about to win by 18 lengths. There's more there. I know it. Go find it."

Printz nodded and shuffled immediately off to a desk that had recently been placed near his. Lindsay Baron had relocated there after Larry left. Her job was now to provide editing and guidance to Rag bureau chiefs, on request. In fact, they needed little, wanted less and requested never. She spent her days reading opposition newspapers, finishing crosswords and pining for the old days.

"Linz, the old man wants more on Charlie Carpentier and the decision.

Whaddaya got for me?"

"Nothing that I would give a lecherous old nobody for nothing."

"I love you, too, sweetie. But come on, this is business. I need a push in the right direction."

"The only place I'd push you, Printz, is off a cliff."

"Such sweetness. Such camaraderie. Makes me miss my third-grade teacher. The one who corrected my spelling mistakes with a paddle to the rump."

"It obviously didn't keep you from becoming an ass."

"Please. And here I thought you were a lady."

Lindsay tossed an eraser at him. It missed. She grinned. The preliminaries were now over.

"Here's where I think your story is, Vic," she said. "Larry has been running an immaculate campaign. No seedy donor deals. No back-channel attempts to influence him. No need to sell out to the national party to get their support. He's the Larry he always was when he was here—the geek of higher purpose."

"Yeah?"

"I'd see if Bartlesby or her people can flesh something out. I don't mean that reflexively negative quote that was in today's. Typical attack-dog junk, written by some think tank refugee. No, I mean a story with real people in it, not just talking points. Try her strategy person. Bill Bigelow, I think his name is. But for God's sake, don't tie it back to me."

Printz had him on the phone 90 seconds later. Bigelow said he'd be only too happy to meet for lunch. Would the Golden Goose be OK? Tomorrow at 12:30?

CHAPTER 7.

"DEAR MARJORIE: I HAVE recently broken up with the guy of my dreams. I had such high hopes for us, but now that I have a little perspective, I see that he was never as serious about us as I was.

"I know I should heal my wounds and move on. But there's a big piece of me that wants to get even, so he'll feel the pain and know how much of it he caused me.

"Is it wrong to feel this way? I'm not talking about tearing out his eyeballs—just placing a few unexploded mines in his path. Or should I simply try to forget him as best I can?

"(SIGNED) CAUGHT IN A CONUNDRUM

"DEAR CAUGHT: It's only natural to want to lash out. But the person you will harm longest and most is you.

"Remember that you have to live with yourself every day for the rest of your life. If you try to get even with this man, how will you feel each morning when you look at yourself in the mirror? Crummy, I'd venture.

"So. . . . You might consider a biting letter. Or that scrapbook you made after your trip to Mexico with him—you might leave it on his doorstep. No poison-pen note necessary. But anything heavier or deeper would only make you feel worse, not better.

"Time heals all wounds. Vengeance keeps them open."

Marjorie Townsend had been the advice columnist for The Rag for more than 30 years, and it showed. Her prescriptions were platitudes. Her writing was shopworn. Her judgment was locked somewhere between the Girl Scout handbook and The Little House On The Prairie.

Yet Charlie never missed a day of Marjorie. It was one of her guilty pleasures. Also a way to reassure herself. If actual people are writing actual letters about actual problems to an advice columnist, how bad can mine be?

Bad.

Very bad.

Charlie had barely been out of bed for three days. She hadn't ridden her bike in four. She was ignoring a bad cough and a sudden outbreak of split ends. She kept saying "Dammit" a lot. She was subsisting on crackers and Diet Dr. Pepper. She re-read Marjorie's advice to "CAUGHT" and said to herself: "No way I'm going to be quite so reasonable."

The Felder campaign had never had a formal headquarters. Part of the reason was frugality—Larry's. Why spend $20,000 a month for a storefront office on Wisconsin Avenue that would look as if a good gust of wind could carry it away? The only records that needed to be handled carefully and securely were the donations. Charlie had volunteered to play Human Safe Deposit Box for those, until Billy the Intern could find time to enter them into the master campaign data base. But he never had—damned interns are worthless, always. So the records sat in a cardboard accordion file—the best that Staples sold for $4.99—organized from front to back, on 8-by-11 sheets, according to amount.

On a Tuesday morning, as yet another couple ranted live and in color about their awful sex life, Charlie began to comb through the file.

She would know bloody fingerprints when she saw them.

The early money that flowed into the campaign had been easy and expected. Doctors. Lawyers. People who lived in the Eighth and had business agendas that only Capitol Hill could fix.

All of them were scrupulous about the rules because they had more to lose by violating them than they had to gain by contributing. And as Larry had so often said, this kind of money gave to both sides of the river, pre-emptively. "Probably Lorraine has cashed checks of exactly the same size, written on exactly the same days," he had said. The interns had nodded as if this was wisdom they could have acquired nowhere else.

But the early money was speculative. Six months ago, no one could have foreseen Larry's surge in the polls. Since then, slowly but steadily, he had proven the old saw: Money begets money.

When the well-off residents of the Eighth and the superintendents of national PAC money licked their index fingers and held them up to the wind, they felt the gusts of success. Larry's fundraising had been average-plus in the first month, average-minus in the second and third, stupendous ever since.

His average donation was nearly $500—better than almost every other candidate for Congress, incumbent or insurgent. He was even beginning to get sniffed by the biggest conservative money—insurance, American Medical Association, defense contracting—because word had it that he might somehow get a seat on the Appropriations Committee. This was a friend that serious lobbyists needed to make, early.

Some of these donations might have been based on a misapprehension—that Larry in Congress could still cut ice with the influentials at The Rag. If anything, the opposite would be true. But Agenda Washington often didn't understand that. It assumed that newspapers worked the way every other industry in town does—on the basis of whispers, handshakes, old friendships and connections. They never believed it when reporters and editors crowed about their ethics. They were wrong, regularly—but their money was still green, and Larry Felder wasn't too proud to accept it.

All day, accompanied by a package of pita bread and an eight-ounce tub of hummus, Charlie flip-flip-flipped and chowed-chowed-chowed. But she found no smoking guns in the file. Not even any smoke.

Here was $100 from an old lady who lived on Democracy Boulevard. The address sounded like a condo, not an office tower. No whiffs of the untoward here.

Flip-flip-flip. . . . $600 from the Montgomery County Chamber of Commerce—no surprise.

Flip-flip-flip. . . . $1,000 (the legal limit) from Alphonse Arcola, a well-known dentist and social gadabout in the county. Probably looking to get invited to parties when Beyoncé was booked to entertain, so he could impress his kids.

Then another $1,000, from the Rockville Cement and Contracting Association. . . . hedging their bets on illegal immigration, no doubt. A mid-campaign $500 gift from the Montgomery County Committee for Better Schools. . . . they're hoping to have their phone calls returned. A $250 gift from a kid named Benjamin Berger, of Derwood, with a note that said it was half his bar mitzvah money and he had always been fascinated by politics, so here goes. Not the slightest stench.

Charlie was about to devote the rest of the afternoon to some excellent white zinfandel when she came upon nine $1,000 gifts, all received on the same day. Each was drawn on a personal checking account. Each was made out by hand. But what made Charlie stop was the handwriting. Same on each.

She checked the swirls of the L's and the whorls of the W's. No question. Any penmanship teacher would have sniffed it out in a second. One hand had written all nine.

Google demystified the discovery in a few clicks. All nine benefactors worked at the same place. They seemed to be the senior brain trust of AaaaaaH Beverages.

Otherwise, they had nothing obvious in common. They were black and white, 35 and 55, Presbyterian and Baptist, smiling and scowling, singles and grandpas. But they all lived in Maryland's Eighth District, and they had all made their donations without a cover letter.

This was a bit unusual, Charlie decided, especially in the polarizing politics that were now built into the American woodwork. If money was passion—and wasn't it, since it seemed to excite many people more than sex?—then giving money was the equivalent of giving lifeblood. To support a congressional candidate was to say, in effect: "I'm trusting you to point my personal ship—not just the public ship—in the right direction."

Charlie was not the kind to unearth one strand of evidence and start leaping to conclusions. She wasn't even sure it was evidence. Couldn't an AaaaaaH secretary have written out all nine checks as a favor to the executive team? Couldn't one of the nine wives have done it at a Sunday football-watch party, while she was bored? Couldn't an accountant have done it as a favor to nine clients whose tax returns he prepared each April?

"Slowly, girl," said Charlie, to her west living room wall. But slowly didn't mean leave it all alone.

Out came the master bank statement for the Larry Felder campaign. Charlie studied the date just after the nine checks had been received. Yup, there they were, among the 110 deposits for that day—all nine as line items, all nine having sailed right through. So there was very little chance of fraud on the front end. The money wasn't misappropriated, the checks weren't rubber, and they hadn't been flagged by some bank algorithm because they smelled as if they might have been laundered.

This was $9,000 of legitimate.

So were the nine AaaaaaH checks received on the same day, written in the same hand, just a coincidence? Charlie's nose didn't think so. She left the bank statement sitting in the middle of the floor and took a walk around the block to think more clearly.

Hypothesis One, as she lumbered past the new Whole Foods: Felder had arranged all nine gifts at one campaign event. Possible, but unlikely. Even if AaaaaaH's executives had been at the same coffee on the same day, they might not have coughed up donations right then and there. And each of them might not have coughed the exact same amount.

Hypothesis Two, as she loped past the Studio Theater on 14th Street: AaaaaaH's boss was a Felder fan, and he had strongly suggested a donation from the senior staff. That usually translates as: Pony up or I'll break something in your lower body that you were planning to use. Hard to prove this one, even if true, without some inside information, Charlie decided. And to sniff for such inside info would be to cause trap doors to snap shut.

Hypothesis Three: It was all an illusion. So nine guys had one somebody write checks for all of them? So what? It would never stand up in a court of law without more juice underneath it.

Juice. Who could find it if there were any? A private detective? Too expensive and too leak-prone. A congressional investigator? He'd be fired if he took on a task like this. A Felder enemy? Charlie wasn't sure the man had any.

Wait a minute.

Did that brain of mine just say the word, "Leak?"

Bingo.

You're brilliant, Charlie Carpentier, you know that?

★ ★ ★

"Hello?"

"Hi, Chuck, it's me."

"Hi, me."

"Chuck, please don't choose this moment to be a wise guy! I need some advice and I need it now."

Lorraine Bartlesby had a public image that was as carefully pruned as the rhododendrons in front of her $2 million home. But she no longer shared that home with Chuck because of her private, rarely pruned self. By turns, she could be imperious, selfish, peremptory and furious. Sometimes all four. Often all four at once.

It had been more than Chuck Bartlesby could take. They had been "good at first," he told Lorraine, the night they convened in the sun room to discuss their future. Chuck had asked for the conversation. It was the first time they had been in the same place together, and actually listening to one another, in a month and a half.

Lorraine armed herself with a Johnnie Walker Black over three cubes. Chuck sipped V-8 juice. He began.

"Lorraine, it's time to end this. I'm done. I'm packing up in the morning and moving in with my sister."

Lorraine did not try to stir the embers of their relationship. Embers had become ashes long before. Not all at once. It seldom happens that way. But irresistibly, through the many repetitive arguments about the personal costs of Lorraine's political ambitions, through Chuck's lectures about her drinking, through her return-lectures about his spectacularly poor run in the dot.com stock market.

They were not mortal enemies. They had just run out of mutual respect and pucker power.

"Chuck, I'm sorry," Lorraine said.

"What are you sorry for?"

"I'm sorry it's ending like this. I'm sorry it's ending. I never wanted to hear this coming from your mouth. I would rather have seen it end because of some bimbo."

"You know I don't do bimbos."

"Yes, Chuck, I know." She left unsaid that he hadn't done her much, either. Not since their second child had been born. Only a few months later, Lorraine's political ambitions had taken shape. He always felt it was a way to distance herself from him, even more than two children already had.

"Lorraine, I know this is very awkward, as far as timing goes. I know this isn't going to help your campaign. I'm sorry about that, too. I just hope you don't lose by two votes—old ladies who didn't vote for you because they thought you might have held onto me by cooking more pot roasts for me."

"All the pot roasts in the world couldn't have saved us, Chuck," she said. Deliberately not looking at him, she crossed to the polished oak bar cart and poured herself a fresh one. "I think I might have saved us. But to do that, I would have had to have been some other person, existing in some other universe. Nope. Not this girl."

Chuck was wearing head-to-toe Lorraine. She had bought his khakis (J. Press, online), his black loafers (Church's) and his permanent press plaid shirt

(Jos. A. Bank). He had never objected, so he had been stunned one night five years earlier when she ripped him for being unmanly.

What kind of Alpha male lets his wife shop for him, she had taunted?

"I never thought I was an Alpha male, " Chuck responded.

"I only wish you were," Lorraine said, half aloud.

When Lorraine said she was thinking about running for Congress, Chuck had put his foot deeply into it by suggesting the school board instead. This led to an epic, two-hour fight about why her ambitions couldn't be as big and broad as any man's.

Ever the prudent, careful, financial planner, Chuck had suggested starting small. "I'm not pushing Congress away," he had said. "I'm only pushing it back to its place in line." Lorraine had countered that Hillary Clinton and exactly 11 female members of the current Congress had never run first for lesser office.

"You're not Hillary Clinton," Chuck had said.

"And you sure as hell aren't her husband," Lorraine had retorted.

They slept in separate beds that night. In the morning, Chuck arrived at her bedside, looking for a makeup cuddle, or perhaps more. She rebuffed him with a swat. They had sex only four times more over the next four years— on each anniversary, Lorraine urging him to hurry up so she could get to sleep, Chuck trying not to focus too hard on how electric it had been at the beginning.

When Lorraine announced her candidacy—to the tune of a splashy press event complete with PR staff handing out color-coded campaign kits, red for the print press, blue for all others—Chuck was on hand as "the captive spouse," as he later put it to his boyhood pals, over a mass consolation cocktail spree at the Hyatt Regency bar right after they separated.

"I couldn't NOT be there that day," he had said. "But it was awkward. Lorraine was running because there was something in our lives that was lacking. Not even running the family foundation was enough for her. Her ambition eventually buried me, and buried us."

But the children glued them. Children always do. Graduations, ball games, recitals—both parents dutifully showed up almost every time. Lorraine did so even when she had to cancel or reschedule campaign events. Chuck used that fact to wonder aloud whether she was really serious about winning. She replied that she was doing just fine without his wise counsel, thank you very much. It didn't seem to matter to either of them that their children were hugely embarrassed by such sniping. They both told their parents, separately and together, that it would be better if they didn't show up at all if they were going to behave like six-year-olds.

So Chuck and Lorraine took their sniping private. He insisted on managing their common funds for as long as the kids were still at home. She had a lawyer call him and threaten him with a suit for misappropriation. More sniping. More threats. Finally, they agreed to marriage counseling for the sake of the kids.

But it soon became clear—to Chuck at least—that the counseling sessions were a prop. Lorraine needed to show herself as a concerned wife and mother if the truth ever leaked. Yes, even Congressional candidates face personal strains. But Contender Bartlesby could say that she was determined not to let anything nudge her away from her top priority—Chuck and the babies. She could say that she was seeking a life raft via counseling.

It was a sure-thing strategy that would appeal to the typical married voter in Maryland's Eighth. To have declared war against Chuck during the campaign, and to have waged it, would have been what her campaign manager called "a damned difficult swallow."

The appear-to-be-normal strategy worked for about two months. But The Rag blew it up.

A young reporter named Agatha Stern was on the make approximately 25 hours a day. She was assigned to the "glamour people" beat. It was up to her to define that. As Cal had told her, she had a dream assignment--as long as she boated big fish. She chased nothing but.

Stern didn't quite place Lorraine Bartlesby in the same class as Elizabeth Dole or Laura Bush, but Bartlesby had a modicum of glow—big money, big reputation, big house, big smile, big ambition. Aggie decided to check out the soccer game between the Olney Firebirds and the Rockville Demons to see if a Bartlesby story might lurk. The left forward for the Demons was 17-year-old Amanda Bartlesby.

As the game dragged on, parents rooted too hard and too much, even though they knew they shouldn't. They shouted instructions incessantly, even when they knew nothing about soccer or about a particular tactical situation. They wore T-shirts that read DEMON POWER or YOU GO, GIRLS.

Aggie Stern was waiting until the end of the game to interview both adult Bartlesbys. But she noticed throughout the game that they didn't stand together.

This was hardly a red-letter observation. Many soccer parents roamed during games, swept up in nervous energy. But to Aggie, it was downright strange—

especially in a tense scoreless tie—that neither Bartlesby roamed to within 30 yards of the other, and that neither spoke to the other once.

One soccer Mom was obviously the mother hen of the Demons. At the end of the game, which the Demons pulled out on a penalty kick with 30 seconds left, Aggie approached Pat Monaco and asked to speak to her.

Monaco, who had never thought an ugly thought in her life, and might not have thought a complicated one, either, replied:

"Sure thing, babycakes. I've always wanted to be in The Rag."

She soon was.

Asked by Stern whether there was any trouble brewing between the Bartlesbys, Monaco replied that the reporter would have to ask the Bartlesbys.

"I will," Stern said. "But I noticed that they didn't stand together during the game, and didn't say a word to each other."

"Well, honey," said Monaco, whose South Carolina effusiveness had never left her, "they never do."

It was a low-megatonnage line. But when Lorraine's press secretary was asked for comment the next day about a rumor that the Bartlesbys had split, or were about to split, and an explanation for their cold shoulders at the soccer game, the campaign had a full-blown mushroom cloud hanging over it.

"Who is this Stern?" raged Lorraine, to her senior staff.

"Some kid," said Rick McGee, her junior press person, his brow full of wrinkles, his red patterned tie askew.

Lorraine threw a handful of papers across the room and reminded everyone that they were far, far behind in the polls. "This kind of thing just can't happen!," she shouted. "Cannot! You're all being paid to prevent it. You can't just dismiss this, Rick! If I see a headline about Chuck and me in tomorrow's Rag, you're all on the street!"

"I'm on this," said McGee.

But the next day, Aggie Stern's story led the local front. It contained zero hard facts and a lot of squishy, unjustified speculation. But if you believe that a negative headline can sink a thousand ships—and most political pros did—the four words atop Stern's story were a mouthful and a handful.

BARTLESBYS KAPUT, OR KAPUTTING?, the headline read.

Chuck saw it at his office at 8 that morning. He immediately called Lorraine to commiserate. She accused him of planting the story to spite her, and hung up in a fury.

This was a truly horrid day for such a bomb to drop. Chuck had scheduled three conference calls with top New York brokerage firms. He needed the information these calls would provide to steer the investments of his best clients. But he needed peace with Lorraine even more.

He called her again.

"Lo, I think we need to talk," he began.

"I'm listening."

"Lo, I want to get back with you. This isn't the right answer for us. We need to give it one more try. Two more if we need two. Eighty more if we need 80."

"Chuck, as you surely know, I have much more on my plate and my mind right now than your syrupy romantic nonsense."

"It's our lives, Lorraine, not syrup."

She flatly refused to reconcile. She said her lawyer would be in touch.

But before she rang off, Chuck told her that he would always love her and would always want to mend their fences. "I would do anything to reset our clock," he told her. "Anything." But he was talking to a dial tone.

That night, Chuck confided in his sister, whose spare bedroom now housed him, his laptop and three jam-packed suitcases. "There has to be a way to make this go again. We've spent 20 years together," Chuck blurted.

"Maybe if you somehow helped her beat Felder, she'd repay you for it," said Bianca Bartlesby, who was a 45-year-old yoga teacher and looked congenitally on the bright side.

"I'll consider that, B," he told his sister. "You might have something there."

But he didn't really believe it. Only a bolt from the blue could bring his wife back, and his life back.

And now she was on the phone, seeking advice. He listened to the thrashings of an already beaten candidate.

"Chuck," she said, "do you think I should just quit? I mean, you always said that the first time you run for Congress, you shouldn't really expect to win. You're just introducing yourself to the voters. Should I just chalk this up to experience and try to knock off Larry two years from now?"

"And I also always said that politics can turn on a dime. You never know what can happen, Lo. It sometimes doesn't take long. What if Felder is caught carousing with a roomful of little boys? What if one of his staff members does something illegal? That would put you right back in the ballgame."

"A pretty thin reed," said Lorraine Bartlesby. "And I'm worried that if I don't beat him now, I never will. But thanks, Chuck. It's always good to hear optimism. And that's what you're always good for."

Was that faint praise? Chuck didn't ask, and Lorraine didn't elaborate. But at least they had stayed civil for three telephone minutes. That was a major improvement over their usual, and for him, a sliver of hope.

★ ★ ★

Charlie could never be replaced, but someone had to make the trains run on time. So Larry Felder took a well-worn and easy way out. He hired Blake Sonner, a 67-year-old former chief of staff to a Texas Congressman, for the three weeks left in the campaign. Lots of competence and experience. Sufficient loyalty. No drama.

And no promises of future employment. Sonner didn't want any. "This will be a temporary interruption of my poor putting and poor gardening, nothing more," he had told Larry.

"Can you give me all you've got?" Larry had asked.

"I may look old and useless, but for three weeks, I can run with the bulls," Sonner had said.

They negotiated a salary in 25 seconds. He began 30 seconds after that, just time enough to feed the meter out front. Ever since, Sonner's judgment had been bulletproof.

But now Larry Felder was sitting in an over-fluorescent auditorium at Richard Montgomery High School in Rockville and wishing he were anywhere else.

The occasion was a press conference organized by high school newspaper editors from all over the north county. Felder had strenuously objected to spending two hours of his life with them.

"Are there any votes there?," he had asked Sonner, testy with the veteran hand for the first time. "Or will I just get a bunch of kids who have written out 15 softball questions each and can't wait to learn my views about pre-marital gum chewing?"

Sonner had tried to soothe him. "Their parents vote, Larry," he had said. "And the shelf life of student newspapers is surprisingly long. Besides, aren't you the guy who worked for a newspaper forever and ever, amen?"

"I'm doing this only because I'm ahead," he told Sonner. "If I were behind, no way."

For this crowd, Felder chose crisply pleated gray slacks, a blue blazer and an open-necked striped blue dress shirt. A tie would have shouted, "I'm the fuddy-duddy you were expecting."

But he didn't go all the way over to business casual, whatever that had come to mean in 2006. There would always be a dignity and a reserve about Larry Felder. He always dressed at least two notches up from barely presentable.

The press conference had been advertised for two weeks, but as soon as Felder entered the main auditorium, it was obvious that few students other than the editors cared. The place was one-fourth full at best. Felder scanned the crowd for familiar faces. There was only one: Agatha Stern of The Rag. He nodded to her, once, barely perceptibly. She blew him a mock kiss.

"Good afternoon, everyone," said the moderator, who wore thick black glasses and seemed to think he was auditioning for "Meet The Press." "We are gathered together to ask Mr. Larry Felder a range of questions in an effort to determine if he is qualified to be our next member of Congress."

Felder's face gave nothing away. But he couldn't help cringe at the length of the kid's sentence. Had commas and periods lost their traction with today's student journalists? He could only hope that the questions would be sharper than the preamble.

He wasn't disappointed. The first one out of the box came from a beefy boy in a work shirt who looked as if he'd have been right at home in the 1960s.

"Do you believe in peace, Mr. Felder, or do you believe in perpetual war?"

The room rustled with discomfort—or was it anticipation? The question had been borderline disrespectful—or was it penetrating? Maybe this Very Important Adult was about to lose his cool or lay an egg. The kids leaned in to listen. This was sure better than second-period chemistry.

"I believe in peace, always," said Felder. "I will dedicate every day I'm in Congress—if I get there—to keeping the United States free, but also free of war. I do not believe you can win friends or settle scores with soldiers. I believe you can do that only through diplomacy, and by example. You know, there's a reason people from all over the world want to live in the United States. It's not because we have the best generals and the best tanks, although we do. It's because we believe in peace and freedom, and we're dedicated to achieving both. So am I."

Work Shirt was ready with a follow-up.

"Do you believe we spend too much money on the military and not enough on domestic problems?"

"In one way, yes, I do. I'm very worried about unemployment, job training, infrastructure, public transportation and public health. I can't imagine serving in Congress and not caring about those domestic issues every day, plus many others. But we simply have to have the best military in the world, to protect ourselves. Freedom has to be protected. Our open society is very vulnerable to anyone who wants to use our freedom against us. We saw that, sadly, on September 11. We might see it again on some awful day in the future. So don't make this a false choice. We can spend enough money on both the military and on domestic concerns."

Next, a smiling girl in black braids and a red sweater set.

"Mr. Felder, my parents are both government employees. They tell me all the time that they are disrespected and underpaid. What can you do about this?"

A rustle of nervous laughter spread around the room. Did kids always have to personalize everything, even at 16? Evidently so.

Felder brooded for a second. Then:

"As a journalist, I have had contact with hundreds of government employees. They have almost always been honest, helpful and knowledgeable. Government employees will never fail to get my attention, my help and my respect if I am elected. They are easy targets for people who are frustrated over the lack of easy, quick answers in our society. But our problems are very complicated, and they aren't going to be solved in 15 seconds by calling some 800 number and getting Big Daddy Government's magic answer. The problem is our lack of patience, not our lack of dedicated, skilled public sector employees."

Next, a shortish boy who looked like a math nerd. Nope, he turned out to be a policy nerd.

"Mr. Felder, we spend about 35 cents of every dollar on health care in this country. But our results are nowhere near as good as they are in other countries, all of which spend far less. How can you fix this?"

Felder had been honing his answer to this question for months. He needed to simplify it slightly because this audience wouldn't appreciate a barrage of figures and citations.

"We cannot afford a health system that's second to anyone else's. Health care is a basic right, and so is health insurance. We can do much better on both scores. I'd much prefer it if the private sector got us there, but if it can't or won't, I'm prepared to help lead a charge for change via government. And in case any of you think I don't care about the problems of doctors, I am prepared to advocate for a change in our malpractice laws. I want to cap the amount that any patient can seek or collect from any doctor. I know that's a platform that has been advocated by Republicans for ages. But they're right about this. And I'm willing to say that they're right about this. If and when

I'm elected, you won't get ideology from me. You'll get common sense and solutions."

On it went.... questions about Iraq, about why the Beltway was so congested in the morning, about why electric cars weren't everywhere, about why there couldn't be a massive federal effort to protect the wild gophers of central Maryland.

Felder was good-humored throughout. He carefully avoided sounding scripted. Meet kids halfway and head on, Sonner had reminded him. They are used to adult shillyshallying. They can smell it before it arrives. Be the adult who tells the truth.

"We want to thank Mr. Larry Felder for taking the time to meet with us this morning," said Mr. Moderator, who was reading from note cards. "We are lucky to live in a democracy that allows events such as this one. Please use our free press wisely, and please vote on May 19."

"None of them can," Larry thought. But he grinned nevertheless and shook about 25 hands. Six kids wanted autographs. Three wanted him to pose for pictures with them. One wanted to know how he could volunteer to help the campaign. One teacher came scurrying up to him—she had waited for last—and said breathlessly: "Mr. Felder, you are a rock star!"

"You're very kind," said Larry Felder. Always be the most modest guy in the room, Charlie had reminded him, until she was blue in the face. God, how he missed her tartness, her cleverness, her competence.

When the room was nearly empty, Aggie Stern approached. Her notebook was open to a blank page and her pen was uncapped.

"Nice piece this morning," Felder said. "I bet Lorraine's people were really delighted with it."

"Working on a follow-up for tomorrow," Stern said. "Coupla questions."

"Shoot."

"Any comments on reports of the split between the Bartlesbys?"

"No comment."

"Any comment on how that split might help your campaign?"

"No comment."

"Do you think the fact that you are still married 14 years after your wife's incapacitation helps you in the campaign?"

"I have no idea, Aggie. I'd rather the voters judge me on the basis of what I say and do in the campaign, rather than my marital situation."

"Do you ever wish you were back at The Rag, pounding a keyboard?"

"Only when I miss the huge salaries."

That brought a slight smile. "You made a lot more there than most people do, Larry," she said.

"And for the last few months, I've been driving all around the Eighth District, spending money but not making any. I should probably have my head examined," Felder said.

"One last question, Larry. Is there any way you can lose this election?"

"Of course there is. There's always a chance that the polls are wrong. There's always the chance that I'll shoot myself in the foot."

"Are the odds of that larger now that Carpentier has quit?"

"I'd like to think not. But Charlie was a very solid performer, and she got my campaign to where it is today. If I win, it'll be largely because of her."

"Thanks, Larry," said Stern. She flipped her notebook shut and recapped her pen. "Good luck."

"Thanks for coming out, Aggie. Best to everyone downtown."

Stern acknowledged the request with a slight nod. As she headed for the parking lot, she mused that she had never been around a political candidate who was such a lock to win.

CHAPTER **8.**

DESPITE ALL HER RESOURCEFULNESS, her tactical talent, her seeming sophistication, Charlie Carpentier had never dealt well with reporters.

It wasn't just the usual suspicion among political professionals that reporters wanted to spread manure everywhere they went, and would therefore treat her boss(es) unfairly. It was a true lack of common ground.

She viewed politics as having two poles and two poles only—elected representatives at one end, the people they represented at the other. The fourth estate was needed as a conduit between the two—that much she could get behind. But who gave some seedy reporter the right to shift the public agenda via what he wrote? To take up cudgels for one candidate by aiming his talking points at another, and cloaking those questions in holy-rolling objectivity? To claim that the reporter had the right to see secret documents and learn about secret conversations just because of some moldy old paragraph called the First Amendment?

Who the hell had ever elected reporters the saviors of the world, anyway?

But Larry Felder had been different—very different.

For one thing, he had done his work as a journalist tirelessly, honorably and relentlessly. He never sought a shortcut and never caved to laziness. Before Charlie went to work for him, she asked around about him. Even the staffs of far-out right wingers had praised Felder for his ethics and his fairness.

"Best thing I can say about him is that I could read 100 of his stories and never detect a whiff of partisanship," said the press secretary to a notoriously Neanderthal senator from Texas.

You need to respect a man before you can lust after him, Charlie had chuckled to herself, a few months later, when the campaign was in third gear and the hots had begun to creep into her every Felder thought. But it had definitely proceeded in that order. Felder was as close to a choir boy as the dirty business of journalism—and the dirtier business of politics--got.

And yet, in order to be elected in Maryland's Eighth, he needed to brand himself a Democrat, because that party had the registration edge and therefore had the votes.

Once upon a time, this mantle would have carried few deeper meanings. To be a Democrat was to be a man of the people—what could be wrong with that?

But now the word had been repositioned by many Republicans (and many editorial writers) to mean endlessly doling money to the underdeserving, endlessly opposing business and endlessly standing in the way of flag-waving presidents who wanted to start wars wherever they chose.

The D-word hung comfortably on Larry Felder. But if he won the party primary, he would surely be called out in the general election by an opponent who wasn't going to let him hide behind the political neutrality that journalism demands.

"If you're suddenly a Democrat, you must be yet another big spender and fuzzy thinker"—Larry (and Charlie) could almost hear his eventual opponent aiming such small arms fire at him.

They had never brainstormed a response that didn't sound mealy-mouthed or hypocritical. But now that item on the to-do list fell to Larry and Larry alone. Charlie wanted to cause him maximum harm, she kept reminding herself. She was not quite the woman scorned, but she was a time bomb in search of a fuse.

Tuesday morning on R Street. Coffee Number Three in her hand, sugar, no cream. The Rag spread out on the rug before her.

Charlie looked around her one-bedroom, still furnished in Graduate Student Modern after all this time, and felt a pang—maybe of jealousy, maybe of regret. If she had married that bozo right out of college—the one with the irritating mother, the one who had promised her all that Macon, Georgia, had to offer—she would have expensive curtains and a late-model mini-van by now. Instead, her bookcases were still unvarnished planks supported and separated by bricks.

Her bedspread was a beach towel with Dudley Do-Right's face all over it. Was this the future as well as the present?

Right there, beside her left foot, on the front page of The Rag, was a story about the Congressional mid-terms, by Vic Printz. He quoted many party professionals as expecting a Democratic surge in the House in November. One pro said that the swing toward Dems would be especially pronounced in districts that had been represented for ages by Republicans, but now had shifted demographically.

Charlie placed a mental check mark beside Maryland's Eighth. The Felder Juggernaut would hardly notice the resignation of one lowly campaign grunt.

Should she leak to Printz? Charlie immediately weighed the negatives. He was well-known to be an old pal of Larry's. He would never rush into print without checking deeply and more deeply, thus delaying a story about AaaaaaH campaign gifts past the point where the story might make a difference.

And what if Printz decided that there wasn't enough there there?

There might not be, by the way, Charlie reminded herself. All she had was smoke. Fire would be something really smelly—Larry posing for AaaaaaH ads in return for campaign gifts, or running off with Kal Radin's wife. The Soul Of Political Caution wasn't about to do anything close to that.

What if she approached Cal Cassidy himself? He'd treat her very respectfully and very enthusiastically, Charlie was sure. But she couldn't control which reporter he'd assign to check out her story. It might be some back-bencher who had no clout around The Rag and who might report, after three perfunctory phone calls, that it was all just a blip, just a rumor.

How about that old war horse, Billy Marx? Once had a big reputation on Capitol Hill. Had covered lots of presidents and lots of races for The Rag. Good with nuts-and-bolts political stories, especially those that touched on money. But Marx was in his 70s and was about to retire, rumor had it.

He and Felder had once had a fierce rivalry. That could be a plus. However, Marx wasn't a front-liner any more. Tight political contests were now assigned to much younger, more ambitious scribes. If Marx were a judge, he'd be on senior status, not on the bench every day. Besides, his skirmishes with Larry had been plowed under more than 20 years before, so it would be hard to expect any personal blood lust for the story.

Charlie got up to pour Coffee Four. She exhumed the local section from her stack of Rag. Her eye fell on a story below the fold—a piece about the new wave of women in politics and how they were rewriting dress-code propriety via fishnet stockings.

She cursed once, sharply.

She said to the cheap pine bedside table, "Right in front of my nose."

She picked up her mobile phone and dialed 202-223-5500. When a tinny female voice answered, she asked to speak to Miss Agatha Stern, please.

✳ ✳ ✳

"You're listening to WISE-AM, Wise All-News Radio for the Nation's Capital. I'm Bradford Morris. Traffic and weather together in just 60 seconds. But first, this message. . . . "

The inventors of radio would have smirked at what was happening inside 9807 Greentree Road, Bethesda. The whole idea was that radio hit you in the ears. You didn't need to sit and watch the receiver. Yet the six people arrayed around Larry Felder's living room were doing exactly that, with more than a little anticipation. They heard Lance Bradley, a well-known butterscotch commercial voice, launch into the script:

"The Maryland suburbs northwest of Washington sound pretty good to many people. Great schools. Lush landscapes. Thriving businesses. Excellent community spirit.

"But around the Eighth Congressional District, the gap between rich and poor is widening. Many residents go to bed hungry. Their children can't do their homework at night because the heat has been turned off. Meanwhile, too many of their neighbors say there's nothing that government can do about the problem.

"Larry Felder feels just the opposite. He is running for Congress so that everyone in the Eighth District can have a voice on Capitol Hill who will solve problems for our neediest citizens.

"You know Larry Felder from his many years as a journalist. Now that journalist is looking to put his columns and stories into action. He wants an Eighth District that is a model for the entire country.

"Larry Felder. Democrat for Congress. Felder for all the people.

After a brief blip:

"Hi, I'm Larry Felder, candidate for Congress, and I approved this message."

The room burst into applause. Billy The Intern hopped up and gave Felder an emphatic high five. A young female scheduler danced an impromptu shimmy-shimmy co-co bop, and ended it with a playful punch to Felder's right bicep. Blake Sonner tossed a pizza crust into the air and crowed like a drunken football fan after a late-in-the-game touchdown.

Felder allowed himself an uncharacteristically wide grin. Then he clapped his hands twice, for attention.

"Great, great, gang. I'm very happy with it. Blake, thank you for a great script and a great choice of narrator. I thought it sounded sincere without sounding saccharine. Everybody else?"

Nods all around.

"So is everybody on board with the decision to avoid TV and concentrate on radio?"

More nods.

"OK, great, everybody. I'm really pleased. Thank you all so much for your hard work and your excellent advice. We're looking pretty good from where I sit. Now please eat the rest of the pizza. Larry Felder doesn't run a wasteful campaign!"

Sonner had suggested a watch-the-radio party, in part because he always liked to foster team spirit around a campaign, in part to counteract a brief case of the blues, caused by a story in that morning's Rag.

Vic Printz had done a survey of media buys among congressional candidates around the Washington suburbs. Of 18 major candidates in six races, only Felder had declined to buy any TV time.

Printz had knifed him in the way that only an experienced political reporter could. He dredged up a blind quote from a "congressional campaign expert" who called Felder's strategy "prehistoric."

To avoid TV was to avoid where the voters are, this expert said. "Radio might have turned heads when Arthur Godfrey was still on the air," the expert was quoted as saying. "But I haven't noticed Arthur around much lately."

Felder's decision had not been unanimously loved by his staff. They agreed that the voters of Maryland's Eighth spent an unusual amount of time in cars, thanks to the area's legendary traffic, so radio would reach them. They agreed that TV was very expensive, and might not deliver the newer, younger and more ethnic votes they were trying to reach.

"But everyone else is doing TV, so it must work," commented Billy The Intern.

"Billy," Felder had said, "I'm not everybody else."

That pretty much closed the door to further debate.

Sonner had engaged an old media buyer friend, Harlan Spence, to analyze what kinds of radio spots would work best. Spence suggested 30 seconds in length rather than the standard 60—more memorable, more snappy. He suggested a smooth male announcer, but not someone unctuous. "Stay away from sounding as if you're selling bikini wax," he had said.

Final suggestion: Coach the candidate so he sounds fresh and young when he suddenly appears at the end of the spot. "If he sounds draggy and drudge-y, he'll reinforce the idea that he's some dust-covered old guy from the newspaper world whose ideas are dust-covered, too," the friend had said. When Felder said he had approved this message, he sounded like a combination of sunshine, Corn Flakes and July 4.

Pizza gulped, soft drinks chugged, the party was breaking up. Larry asked Blake to stay for a minute.

"I just want to show you this," he said, as he reached into his trusty, lumpy black briefcase for a sheaf of papers.

They were hot off the press from Delabar and Associates, his polling company. Larry handed the sheaf to Blake with a major Cheshire-cat smirk on his face.

Blake nodded and read, nodded and read some more. Then he looked up and said: "Awesome."

The polls showed that Felder had lengthened his lead. He now commanded a virtually insurmountable 68 percent. Bartlesby remained second at 18 percent. Five other contenders were in single digits.

"You'll forgive the cynicism, Blake, but I always subtract five percent because of home-team bias. We're the ones paying for this, after all," Felder said.

"But even if you subtract TEN percent, you're winning in a walk," said Blake.

The men shook hands. Sixteen days to go. It was all over but the shouting.

★ ★ ★

FELDER FOR CONGRESS

"Maryland's Eighth District has long been the picture-book upscale bedroom suburb of the Nation's Capital. Ever since World War Two, the problems that bedevil Washington and the rest of the region—poor schools, unemployment, racial divisions, corruption—have been hard to find among the leafy trees and ritzy cars of Bethesda, Chevy Chase and its cousins.

"But in the past decade, the Eighth has come face to face with these problems and many others. Montgomery County, now nearing a population of one million, has more than 80,000 schoolchildren who qualify for free lunches at public school. The unemployment rate in the county has risen from 4.1 percent to 7.2 percent in just a decade. The county was recently indicted in federal court for poor or non-existent environmental protection policies. And three federal agencies have shipped out to the greener pastures of Northern Virginia.

"None of these issues will be simple to fix, and no one person can fix them by himself. But in the Democratic primary for the Eighth's open Congressional seat, one candidate stands clear of the rest.

"Since announcing for the seat just five months ago, Larry Felder has captured substantial attention and even greater support. His strength has emerged across the county—from all races, all ages and all income groups. He has taken firm positions on ethical matters, and he has been very careful not to place his campaign up for sale to his largest financial supporters. If Hollywood were looking to make a film about Maryland's Eighth, Larry Felder would be the obvious choice for top billing.

"Felder's lack of electoral experience has emerged as his most critical asset. He owes no party boss a thing. His closet seems to contain zero skeletons. His motives are public and pure. He looks as if he could be a leader in Congress for years to come.

"We at The Washington Record endorse him in the Democratic primary knowing full well that Felder worked for this newspaper for a very long time. To the cynical, that will seem to be the main reason we are favoring him over his opponents. That's how the scratch-my-back world of politics works, no?

"No.

"We would have come to this decision if Larry Felder had never met a balky typewriter, a cranky editor, an immovable deadline, or anyone at The Record.

"He is that rare bird—a journalist who rose to the top of his profession and a potential public servant who can rise to the top of his new one, too. He has talent, drive, sophistication and a willingness to learn what he doesn't know.

"Lorraine Bartlesby has served the Eighth District well as a philanthropist and local volunteer. But she does not have the ideas, the platform or the personal megatonnage of Larry Felder. The other candidates in the race have shown little or no promise.

"We recommend an enthusiastic vote for Larry Felder in the Democratic primary on May 19."

Larry Felder read the editorial and thought, "Couldn't be better."

Lorraine Bartlesby read the editorial and thought, "Another nail in my coffin."

Charlise Carpentier read the editorial and thought, "Better get moving."

Kal Radin read the editorial and thought, "I need to snuggle up to this guy, as close as I can get, and soon."

Cal Cassidy read the editorial and thought, "He's never coming back."

Billy The Intern read the editorial and thought, "I can become his appointments secretary after the general election if I play my cards right."

Blake Sonner read the editorial and thought, "Well, gosh, maybe I'll try one last go-round with one last egomaniac. This guy has such big potential."

Chuck Bartlesby read the editorial and thought, "I might still be able to stop this runaway train."

★ ★ ★

Felder pitched his legs out of bed and onto the gray shag carpet with the same thought he always had:

"Why does this happen to me at midnight and not at 7 a.m.?"

Once again, he hadn't been able to sleep for more than an hour—too many plans to hatch, too many strategies to burnish. Once again, he had tried to nullify his blast-furnace energy with food.

He opened a can of apricots swimming in syrup and ate it in 45 seconds. Maybe all that sugar would settle his nerves.

Whoops! Sugar does the opposite, doesn't it? Nice going, Lawrence Felder. You just ate more sugar than half the sovereign nations on earth eat in a solid month. You might be heading for an all-nighter, you dunce.

Well, maybe some reading would do the trick. But it did the opposite.

A New York Times dispatch from Eastern Europe proved to be surprisingly compelling. So did a Philadelphia Inquirer piece about the transformation of Sylvester Stallone's image (bad to good back to bad again). Felder was homing in on a Wall Street Journal takeout about unsung causes of inflation when he noticed a pair of worn black running shoes in the corner, long ignored.

Yes. He would take a walk.

The streets and the wind were equally still. Felder dressed in a light blue windbreaker, dark blue running shorts, a T-shirt and a soft cotton baseball cap that said VOTE FELDER above the bill. He headed west on Greentree, toward the massive shopping center that had transformed the neighborhood when it opened 20 years earlier. But at midnight, the center could neither be seen nor heard. Greentree, all the houses near it and all the streets intersecting it were church mouse quiet.

Felder loped along in first gear while his mind raced in fourth.

Need to discuss guest fundraiser appearances for next week with Bill Clinton's people. . . . Can't let that meeting with the state party leaders slip any further. . . .

Must send a personal thank-you note to the officers of that women's foundation. . . . Can I afford to sleep in on Saturday now that the polls are looking so good?

A car passed him, going in the opposite direction. The radio was cranked to stratospheric levels. So were the occupants, probably.

Curious to see and hear such a car along Greentree so late at night. The burbs were always quieter than city people expect, and Bethesda along Greentree was especially silent. Crickets could be heard for blocks. So could the TV from the one house whose lights were still lit. From a block away, Felder could tell that the occupant(s) were watching a sitcom. The canned laugh track was forced, jarring and unmistakable.

Clomp, clomp, clomp—*you know, this feels pretty good. I should do this more often, especially at night, when the temperatures drop off and the humidity usually does, too.*

Clomp, clomp, clomp—*such nice cars parked along here. Is anybody ever unemployed in Zip Code 20816?*

Clomp, clomp, clomp—*Larry, old boy, this is a far better way to marshal your thoughts than staring into that computer in your study yet again.*

Clomp, clomp, clomp—*I really miss Charlie. Wasn't sure I would, but I really do. I'll have to call her once the primary is over.*

He was just crossing Ewing, almost to Fernwood, when a car rumbled to a stop right beside him. Nothing insisted that he stop walking, but he did, instinctively.

Two young men piled out, one from the front seat, one from the back. They were wearing reversed baseball caps, plaid shirts and work boots. They were heavily bearded. One was holding a crowbar. The other was holding a butcher knife.

Oh, my God, it's the car that passed me a minute ago, going in the other direction. . . . They were cruising me. . . . Damn!. . . . Should I run?. . . . No, I can talk my way out of this. . . . Whatever "this" is. . . . If they want money, they're going to be disappointed. . . .

The radio was still cranked way up there. *How dopey. Won't that attract lots of attention?* The two young men came toward him, looking straight at him. *Got to remember their descriptions, for the cops, later.* Felder backed up, onto someone's terraced lawn. *They couldn't possibly recognize me, could they?* He stumbled on a mound and fell.

"Your money," commanded the one holding the crowbar.

"I don't have any."

"Don't tell me that, man. I want your money. Now."

"Listen, I just told you, I don't have any. I'm just going for a walk late at night. I didn't bring my wallet." *Should I offer to bring money to them later?*

The one holding the knife cursed.

"I should mess you up, you know that?," said Crowbar.

"If you do that, you'll be sorrier than I'll be." *Now where did THAT little piece of bravado come from?*

"Last chance, buddy boy. Cash. We want cash," ordered Knife.

"If I had any, I'd give it to you. Honestly." He showed them the pockets of his shorts, turned inside out.

Voices carry late at night when there's nothing to muffle them. About 50 yards away, down Ewing, lights snapped on in someone's living room, followed by the porch light.

"We should kill you. You've seen us," said Crowbar.

My God, no. . . .

"Hey, Lonnie, man, we need to get out of here. Let's just teach him a little lesson," said Knife.

As Larry Felder lay there, too terrified to move, Crowbar smacked him once across the back of the head. Knife followed with a slash to his face. Then the men, their car, their woofers and their tweeters disappeared down Greentree, at what the police report would describe as "an unusually high rate of speed."

Singing. . . . My blood is singing. . . . Oooooh, did he knock my brains out?. . . . No, I can still think and I can still see. . . . Better get up. . . .

As soon as Felder tried to do so, he noticed blood dripping onto his neighbor's perfectly sculpted lawn. He stumbled and fell to his knees. He tried to stand again, but stumbled again.

The world spun. He drew a hand across the back of his neck. A handful of blood. *Oh, no. . . .*

A woman came trotting up, dressed in a magenta housecoat and furry slippers. "Don't worry, mister," she said, a touch breathless. "I'll call 911."

CHAPTER  **9.**

■ DAMNED RAG WASN'T DELIVERED
this morning. Damn, damn, damn. Here I pay all this money, and the least they could do is get it to my damned doorstep by breakfast time. Is this rocket science? They do it every other blasted day. Didn't snow overnight, for God's sake. No excuse. No wonder the ship of journalism is sinking. Damn, damn, damn.

It was a bad morning to have gone Rag-less. Charlie had not seen the story across the middle of the front page. Headline: FELDER, CONGRESSIONAL CANDIDATE, WOUNDED IN ASSAULT. While the rest of her former campaign colleagues were in shock, and were heading into Crisis Mode, Charlie dressed in her best powder-blue power suit—and in blissful ignorance--and walked 14 blocks south to the Madison Hotel for coffee with Aggie Stern.

"So what have you got for me?," Aggie began, with her usual absence of subtlety, in her usual uniform of Ann Taylor working-girl simplicity.

"We'll get there," countered Charlie, tapping the brakes. "Croissant?"

"Not here. They cost about six bucks apiece. I may look rich, but, hey, I just pound a keyboard for The Rag."

Charlie chuckled because she was expected to. Her Duke pals had counseled her via many e-mails to be very careful about how she said what she intended to say, and where she said it. Was it sane to worry about someone recording this conversation? Patsy Finkel, her lawyer friend, had answered that with a resounding yes.

"Make sure you meet in a public place like a restaurant, and make sure you sit at a table where you can see Stern's hands at all times. That way she can't conceal a recording device. Some of them are very small these days. But they work very well just the same. And remember, Char, that there's no law in the District of Columbia that requires Stern to notify you if she's recording the conversation."

Charlie had called the maitre d' an hour before her date with Stern to request Table Seven, which was as far from a wall or a banquette as one could get in the Café Beau Rivage. The maitre d' promised to hold Seven for her, and didn't ask why. Such discretion is what you buy when you order a six-dollar croissant.

"And I may look stupid, Aggie, but I promise I'm not. I'm not very full of bravado, either, or I would have suggested we meet alongside Deep Throat in a parking garage."

Now Stern laughed, because she was supposed to. The women exchanged glares—of wariness? Of disdain? Neither could be sure. Like so many high-stakes encounters in journalism, this would be a skirmish, not a romp in the park.

They both ordered orange juice and whole wheat toast with a sampler of marmalade. The toast cost only a buck less than a croissant.

"So you don't work for Felder any more?" *Wow, this woman does cut to the chase doesn't she?*

"No, we had some irreconcilable differences, so I left."

"Tough about what happened to him."

Does she mean that it was tough on him that I left? "Time will tell, Aggie. But yes, that's very likely."

"You're a tough babe, Charlie."

"Takes one to know one, Aggie."

The toast and juice arrived. Aggie twisted off the top of a miniature glass container of glowing raspberry spread and said:

"I want you to know that I don't take sides, and won't take sides, in the Felder campaign. I'm here as a reporter. But any reporter would have been excited by the voice mail you left me."

Charlie chose apricot, spread it deliberately without looking up, then replied:

"I just want a fair shake with the facts that I propose to give you, Aggie, OK?"

"Understood," said Stern.

Charlie reached into her purse—it was the oversized brown leatherette one, chosen for this purpose—and produced a red file folder. Inside was a sheet of paper, single-spaced and dense with detail. Charlie handed it over.

Stern read silently for about two minutes. She paused for regular glugs of juice and regular nips of toast. She nodded several times. She wiped her mouth with the oversized linen napkin—the waiter had carefully handed her a black one so that a white one wouldn't shed on her dark skirt—and began with a caveat:

"Charlie, I make no promises. Not how I work. But this is all very interesting. I have a whole lot of questions."

"Go."

"Nine checks, all written to the campaign on the same day. All written by the same person?"

"I'm not a handwriting expert, Aggie. But it sure looks that way. Same capital F in Felder. All the I's dotted with circles and not periods."

"Have you told anyone at AaaaaaH about this?"

"Not a soul."

"Refresh me about campaign finance laws. Is it illegal for nine guys at one company to each give the maximum allowable donation?"

"No. But if there's been an effort to conceal those donations, or to cast them as individual donations when they were actually orchestrated by the CEO or the candidate, that would be illegal."

"Illegal by them for making the gifts the way they made them, or illegal by Felder for accepting them?"

"Both."

The waiter slid up to the table and asked if everything was OK. Charlie began giggling. Stern asked what was so funny.

"I was talking to a friend the other night. She's Jewish. Loves corny Jewish jokes. Told me a good one. Four Jewish women are having lunch. After ten minutes, the waiter comes over and asks: 'Is anything OK?'"

Stern smiled—a single curl of her upper lip. "You've obviously got excellent Jewish friends," she said.

"Had this one since college. Patsy. Couldn't live without her."

Stern whipped out a well-thumbed notebook and asked if taking notes would be OK. Charlie nodded. The interrogation upshifted.

"So why are you fencing this material to me?"

Finkel had warned Charlie about reporters putting words in Charlie's mouth.

"Fencing, Aggie?" she said. "I'm not trafficking in stolen material here."

"Then what exactly are the circumstances? Where does this information come from?"

"From the campaign's files."

"You control those files even though you no longer work for Felder?"

"Yes."

"Does Felder know we're meeting today?"

"No."

"Does he know you've shown me this material?"

"No again."

"Why do you have this material if you no longer work for the campaign?"

"He never asked for it back. It was sitting in a file in my living room."

"I thought you were super-loyal to him. That's what everyone says, anyway. Why the change in attitude?"

"I just thought the public had a right to know all this, Aggie."

She smirked. "That's *my* line, usually," she said. "When some source is being ugly and reluctant."

"Do I look ugly and reluctant?"

"Not at all. But I still can't figure out what your game is. Romantic retaliation, maybe?"

"Aggie, I don't operate that way. Besides, that's none of your business."

"But you were having a thing with him, weren't you?"

"Most certainly not!" Finkel had advised high dudgeon when delivering this line. Charlie hoped that her dudgeon was high enough, and didn't sound too coached or pre-conceived.

"No hanky? No panky?"

Higher-level dudgeon: "Look, do you want to discuss what's in the material I gave you, Aggie, or do you want to make insinuations about my private life?"

"No insinuations, Charlise. I'm just asking questions here."

"Like hell. You are daring me to deny an allegation that you have no basis to make. You are floating a rumor and asking me to confirm it as fact. Do you work for The Rag or The National Enquirer?"

The blow glanced off. "Gee, golly, I've never heard that one before. Better try something a little more original, Charlise," Aggie said. Tough babe.

Charlie could feel her face redden. She was losing control of the interview.

Be sure you hold the reins very tight, Patsy Finkel had said, before reassuring Charlie that she was doing the right thing in meeting with Stern. *But now this damned reporter was going to write whatever she wanted to write, regardless of what I say. And she was going to make me out to be some hormone-addled slut. What kind of idiot talks to a reporter, anyway?*

Stern fiddled nervously with her place mat. She was doing what talented reporters always do, waiting for her quarry to fill the silence. Amazing how much information sources will spill at moments like this, without having it dragged out of them. Sources hate awkwardness. Sources hate silence.

"Can I tell you something off the record?," Charlie asked.

The waiter brought the check. Stern let it sit. The hook had been baited. Now it was land-the-fish time.

"Do I have your word on this?" Charlie appended.

"You have my word. But I am agreeing only to avoid naming you. I'm not agreeing not to run what you tell me past others, to see if they will put it on the record."

What kind of double talk is this? Do I really want to say what I'm about to say? Am I about to violate Washington Rule One: Never say or do anything that you don't want to see on the front page of The Rag the next morning?

"OK, then, Aggie," said Charlie. "Here's why I'm doing this. I believe Larry Felder has broken the law, and I believe the voters have the right to know it. But I am also doing this for personal reasons."

"And those are?"

"Personal."

Stern slapped a MasterCard on top of the padded black leatherette case that held the check. She flashed a grin at Charlie.

"Let me tell you a story, Charlie, OK?" she said.

"OK."

"Once upon a time, in this mad whirlwind of my career, I had designs on a guy and time to do something about it. He was unavailable, as they say. Way too old. Way too unaware of me. Way too married. Way too unlike what my Mom was always hoping I'd bring home."

"Yes?"

"But I'm a pretty determined gal, Charlie. I guess you could tell that, huh? So I kept dangling more and more bait in front of him. More and more frankness about my intentions. More and more skin showing above my bust. You get the picture."

"And?"

"And it was as if I was talking to a Martian. He simply wasn't in the same solar system. It never got to the point of should I take him to bed or shouldn't I? It just kept spinning around in circles. Same running up the side of the mountain by me. Same not noticing by the guy."

"So?"

"So I decided to drop a bomb on him. I decided to give up on him, but to send him a parting gift that he'd never forget."

The waiter returned with the check, the credit card and two copies of the filled-out charge slip, one headed ESTABLISHMENT, the other headed PATRON. He delicately avoided eye contact with either woman at Seven as he deposited the bad news. Beau Rivage discretion.

"And the bomb was what?"

"The bomb was something I found in his apartment one night, when I had just finished running up the side of the mountain one more time. It was a bill from a private school in Pennsylvania. Sitting out in the open on his desk. Turned out the guy had a love child, from long, long ago. He had never told me about it, and had carefully avoided telling anyone else, either. He was supporting the kid. Had been for a very long time. But he never talked about it. And here he was, this big public face of a big public organization that stood for Christianity and taking the marriage vows seriously."

"So you torched him?"

"I torched him. No fingerprints. Nothing that would lead back to me. I fed the tip to another reporter at The Rag. The guy was fired, and he slithered out of sight, and I've never talked to him again. Never regretted any of it, either."

Charlie opened her purse, exhumed a mini-hairbrush and ran it over her bangs. It was a time-honored way to buy time.

"Very interesting," she said, after a short pause. "Very, very interesting."

"Could something like that have gone on with you and Felder?" Trap sprung. Charlie walked right into it.

"You just might be onto something there, Aggie," she said. Not a yes. But certainly not a no.

They shook hands in the Madison lobby and agreed to talk again if Stern had more questions. Charlie didn't look back as they parted. If she had, she would have seen Stern grinning a little too widely after a routine interview in a hotel coffee shop on a routine weekday morning.

And if Charlie had been able to climb inside Stern's head, she would have heard a reporter giving herself a high five, licking her chops over the story to come, congratulating herself for having laid out a tale of personal romantic betrayal that was 100 percent lies, yet 100 percent effective in flushing the pheasant out of the bushes.

★ ★ ★

Lorraine Bartlesby and her entire campaign staff are horrified by the assault on Larry Felder last night. Everyone at Bartlesby headquarters hopes and prays for his speedy recovery. The Bartlesby campaign also stands ready to assist law enforcement in any way we can to bring the perpetrators of the assault to justice.

In a gesture of respect for Larry Felder, Lorraine Bartlesby will suspend her campaign for the Eighth District Democratic Congressional nomination for 48 hours. The Bartlesby campaign has cancelled all appearances and all speaking engagements during this period.

"I am looking forward to Larry's recovery and return," Bartlesby said. "The Eighth District deserves more of the same energetic campaign it has enjoyed for the last several months."

Bartlesby will discuss the future of the campaign this morning, at the Chevy Chase Holiday Inn.

FOR FURTHER INFORMATION: Bartlesby press office, 301-320-4567, or press@lorrainebartlesby.org.

The turnout was disappointing—very disappointing. Two youngsters from The Rag, neither of whom had been seen on the campaign trail before and both of whom looked as if they had recently exited diapers. Three local TV crews, including the usual blown-dry correspondents who looked lost, worried and unprepared, not necessarily in that order. One kid from WISE, who kept fiddling with some sort of electronic device (was he texting with a girl friend?).

And Martin Farnwell, age 80 if he was a day, a slight man in rumpled brown corduroys and a flannel work shirt who attended many such press conferences. Farnwell had press credentials from a long-defunct Socialist Labor Party weekly and liked to disrupt proceedings with partisan darts. He and soap were obviously having a long-running feud. But no one wanted to bar him or confront him because his sister was a doyenne of Eighth District philanthropy, and she loved to make donations to progressive politicians.

"For this kind of turnout, we paid $1,000 to rent a room at this dump?," groused Bartlesby, to her main scheduler, Millie McFall. Millie could only nod in sympathy. Newton's Third Law of Politics: When a campaign is having trouble, it continues to have trouble.

Interns passed out the press availability release to the assembled, which took all of 30 seconds. The non-throng read in silence. An intern nodded to another operative, who was waiting near the door to the Maryland Suite. He opened it. Lorraine Bartlesby walked briskly to the podium.

"Thanks to all of you for being here this afternoon," she began, as videotape shooters cranked up and started to whir. "You've all seen our press release. I believe it speaks for itself. However, I'm sure you have questions. I'll be glad to answer them."

NewsChannel 15: "Will you drop out of the campaign?"

Bartlesby: "I have never considered it, and would certainly not consider it now. Why would I do that?"

Six On Your Side: "Will Felder drop out of the campaign?"

Bartlesby: "You'd have to ask him, of course. But I assume that if he recovers, he'll be back in the chase."

Four News Galore: "Is this the break you've been hoping for, Lorraine? I mean, it's no secret that you've been far behind in the polls."

Bartlesby: "I want to win this primary fair and square. I don't want to win it because Larry Felder got assaulted by a couple of criminals. I'm sure he'd say the same if our situations were reversed."

Rag reporter: "Can you trace for us how you found out about the Felder incident and what your reactions were?"

Bartlesby: "Sure. I learned of the assault early this morning from my staff. I was totally horrified, of course. I checked with local law enforcement to see if there might be some political reason behind the assault. They assured me that there wasn't. If there had been—for example, if one of my staff members had done this, or had arranged this—I'd have fired the person right away, and I would probably have dropped out of the race."

Second Rag reporter: "Doesn't Felder's incapacitation make you the prohibitive favorite in this race now?"

Bartlesby: "I can't speculate and I won't speculate. The only thing that matters is how many people vote for me, and for other candidates, in 15 days."

Second Rag reporter, following up aggressively: "Would you urge Felder to drop out? Have you urged Felder to drop out? Will you do either of those right now?"

Bartlesby: "No, no and no. And if you're about to ask me why not, I would tell you that there's a place for politics and a place for common decency. Larry Felder is very badly injured, and he's lying in a hospital bed. I'm thinking of him as a human being right now, not as some enemy I have to crush."

WISE reporter: "If Felder recovers and returns to the campaign, what will it take for you to win? Like, he'll have the sympathy vote, won't he?"

Bartlesby: "I'm sure voters in the Eighth District are extremely sympathetic to Larry after what happened to him. But I believe they'll vote on the basis of proven leadership. I have always had more of that in my history than he has."

WISE reporter: "But, like, doesn't his injury put you at a disadvantage?"

Bartlesby: "I'm already at a disadvantage, my friend! So let's just leave it up to the voters, OK?"

Martin Farnwell: "Miss Bartlesby. . . ."

Bartlesby: "It's MISSUS Bartlesby, Martin, and it has been for more than 20 years."

Farnwell: "Whatever. I want to know whether you will now change your campaign from Plutocrats On Parade—a disgusting attempt to extort campaign contributions from the richest people in the Eighth District—to a campaign that focuses on and helps the little guy."

Bartlesby: "Martin, your question—if it's a question—is based on a false assumption. My campaign did not accept or seek contributions until two months ago. It was self-financed. I decided to change that because Mr. Felder was accepting contributions—lots of them, many of them from county business leaders. I don't want to get steamrollered in this campaign. I don't want Larry Felder to be able to out-advertise me 8-to-1. So I joined the battle for dollars. I don't love that, but I look on that as being a necessary evil. And by the way, I am not a plutocrat, and neither are any of my donors."

Farnwell (far from having been silenced): "Missus Bartlesby, when you have no room on your campaign staff for anyone without white skin, when you have not met with any groups of voters outside the richest sectors of the Eighth District, when your entire history is full of country clubs and nine irons, how in the world, Missus Bartlesby, can you say, as you do in your campaign literature, that you're a woman of the people?"

Bartlesby: "Easy. Because I am. Because all of my public efforts have always been aimed at everybody, not just at the wealthy. You can look it up, Martin."

Farnwell: "I have! I certainly have! And you are distorting the truth, Missus Bartlesby! You are ignoring the real needs of the underprivileged! You are a shame and a sham and a. . . ."

Bartlesby: "Any further questions?"

There were none.

The pencil press came forward to ask a few more follow-ups. The electronics packed up and left in a hurry. Farnwell was escorted to the parking lot by an intern who kept nodding—and kept escorting with a firm hold on the old gent's right elbow.

It wouldn't have been nice to have gang-tackled an 80-year-old man, but this intern had played high school football, he had been pre-alerted by Bartlesby's senior staff and he was ready. Luckily, Farnwell got into his turquoise Dodge Dart rather meekly and puttered off.

What a mess it would have been if a Bartlesby campaign aide had been videotaped "heavying up" on an octogenarian sort-of reporter. The story would have led the 6 o'clock news, and doubtless the 11, too. Would have made the networks as well. But a four-alarm PR disaster would not have surprised anyone aboard Good Ship Bartlesby. Newton's Third Law of Politics was proving itself by the minute.

Bartlesby was en route home, for yet another senior strategy session, when her private cell phone rang. She answered without any enthusiasm.

"Lo?"

"Yes, Chuck."

"Lo, this is awful news about Felder. But what an amazing opportunity for you!"

"Chuck, I'm not going to walk on anyone's grave to win this thing. A man is hurt and may be dying, Chuck. Where are your priorities?"

"With you, Lo. With my wife and partner. I want to come back, Lo."

"Just because I might now win this race? I don't think so, Chuck."

"Well, you think about it overnight, OK?"

"Yeah. Sure."

"Thanks, Lo. And good luck, sweetheart. Love you."

She rang off without responding, or without missing Chuck in the slightest. She turned to Bill Bigelow, the campaign consultant who had never lost a race. He was riding beside her in the back seat of Bartlesby One, one of the campaign's six leased black Ford Expeditions. He looked as if he had eaten a bad oyster for lunch.

"Bill, we can win this thing now. I know it. I can feel it," Bartlesby declared. "All we need is a little sanity from Felder. He'll drop out, won't he? I would if I were him."

"You're not him, Lorraine," Bigelow growled. "And that reporter was dead right just now about the sympathy vote. Felder might win this thing even if he dies. Don't laugh. It happened a couple of hundred times in Chicago, from what I hear."

Bartlesby stared out the window at a now-rainy afternoon along Old Georgetown Road. She slid into serenity.

Que sera sera. What will be will be. Her mother, bless her heart, had always said that her Lorraine was touched with magic. Maybe a crowbar had delivered some.

✮ ✮ ✮

"Aggie Stern."

"Aggie, it's Charlise. You know, Charlise Carpentier, who had breakfast with you this morning. . . ."

"Yeah?"

"Aggie, I feel like such a total fool! When I met with you this morning, I hadn't heard about Larry. Oh, my God! Oh . . . My . . . God."

"He's in a lot of pain, I hear."

"I'm sure he is! I'm going to head for the hospital as soon as we get off the phone. But before I go, I want to ask you, Aggie, to please, please not go ahead with the story we discussed at the Madison."

"Why not?"

"Because it wouldn't be fair to Larry! He might be dying, Aggie! Can't you just pretend that I never handed you that piece of paper?"

"Sorry, Charlise, but we don't do things that way."

"What do you mean?"

"I mean that you offered me this material freely and without any conditions. I never said I'd hold back on my reporting. I never said that I'd give you a window to change your mind about providing it to me. These are the big leagues, darling. The Rag publishes the truth, however we come by it. You offered. I bit."

"Are you serious? Are you really telling me, 'Tough luck?,' "

"That's exactly what I'm telling you. And I'm telling you one other thing, too. If you had offered that material to Larry Felder when he was still a reporter, he'd be telling you exactly the same thing that I'm telling you."

"Jesus H. Christ!"

"Even he isn't going to save you."

"You're a joke, Aggie! You're dishonest! You're vicious! You would really drag Larry through this after what just happened to him?"

"Sorry, cuteness. Them's the rules of the game."

"I am giving you one last chance. I want to cancel what I told you. I want that piece of paper back. I want you to pretend that our meeting never happened."

"In your dreams, Charlie."

Charlie banged down the receiver so hard that the casing of the phone cracked. She poured herself a grape juice, then thought better of it and replaced it with two inches of straight bourbon.

She flashed on the moment when she was in the eighth grade, and the mayor of Conshohocken had spoken at her school. He was so full of purpose and poise. That was the day the public service course had been charted. Now it had snagged her and gored her, hard.

The tears billowed down her cheeks. The sobs wouldn't stop for five minutes.

CHAPTER

10.

SUBURBAN HOSPITAL

was born in 1949, just after Bethesda was. The war was done, the economy was surging, a chicken was finding its way into every pot. Planning the suburbs seemed misguided—it was enough for newly marrieds and new arrivals to avoid the city, its smells, its ethnics and its crime. Streets of higgledy begot cross-streets of piggledy. The burbs grew like the proverbial topsy. Hospitals remained downtown.

But people still got old and sick, and teenagers still got snockered and smashed cars into trees. So Suburban Hospital was created by a coalition of town fathers and doctors, the better to care for local citizens in a boring, brick, five-story box set into a grove of locusts.

Suburban's emergency room had been winning national excellence awards for six decades. Even at 3 a.m., when the third team was on duty, the staff knew exactly what to do when Larry Felder arrived via ambulance in a bloody heap.

First, do no harm. But even sooner, stop the bleeding, check his pupils to see if he was conscious or had suffered brain damage, inspect his scalp for wounds that might not have been immediately obvious, order X-rays and an MRI. Then notify the police.

The ER resident on duty asked Felder what had happened. He said he didn't know for sure—two kids, a botched holdup. The resident checked a box on an intake form that said, CAN COMMUNICATE, NO SIGNS OF LIFE-THREATENING TRAUMA.

The detective who arrived minutes later asked the same first question. Felder gave the same answer. The officer did not recognize Felder, or his name. But the resident motioned the cop outside the over-fluorescent examining bay and explained that this was a VIP politician, and a former big-deal newspaper columnist, so please go easy on him, don't ruffle feathers. The hospital brass would report for work in just a few hours, and they'd be very displeased if Felder's case had been mishandled.

"Gotcha," said the detective, a lifer with a serious gut and a plaid sports jacket named Cornelius Schmidt. He pasted on his best unctuous bedside manner and asked Felder if he had any enemies.

"Too many," said Felder, whose hospital gown was hanging off in the front and open in the back, and whose head and neck were swaddled in bright, white gauze.

Schmidt belly laughed. Felder managed a smile, despite the ringing in the back of his skull. The resident, Manu Patel, checked another box: PATIENT ALERT AND CONVERSANT.

Schmidt asked why Felder had been out alone so late at night. Taking a walk, he explained. Schmidt asked Felder if he had gotten a look at his assailant. There were two, actually, Felder said. Both male. Both young. Both white. Sorry, can't do any better.

Schmidt asked if Felder's campaign had touched off any personal animosity. Felder said he didn't think so. Schmidt asked if Felder was known to carry large amounts of cash. Felder said he never had. Schmidt asked for a description of the assailants' car. Sorry, no clue, Felder said.

Schmidt said Felder was very lucky not to have been injured much more seriously. Felder agreed and thanked him.

But Manu Patel was not about to let his patient go on any ten-mile hikes. The X-ray results were back. They showed large amounts of bleeding at the base of his neck, and some signs of internal bleeding in his major organs.

"You will need to be admitted and watched for at least the next several days," the resident said. But Felder hadn't heard. It was 3:30 in the morning. He had nodded off on the gurney.

Manu Patel needed to contact next of kin. Basic protocol. But none was listed on Felder's intake form, and he hadn't been carrying his wallet when he was assaulted.

So he resorted to common sense. He Googled "Larry Felder campaign." The one phone number listed rang and rang, and eventually urged the caller to leave a message in the general mailbox. Patel did so. He did not explain who he was or why he was calling. He simply asked for a "senior campaign official" to call back as soon as possible.

"Can this guy really not have a wife, or a brother, or a sister?," he asked the charge nurse, Jenny O'Reilly.

"Probably an escaped convict or a Russian spy. Or maybe he hangs out with guys," growled O'Reilly, whose poisonous personality had been amply stoked by 30 years of drunks and druggies arriving at the Suburban ER.

"Maybe I should alert the PR staff about this?"

"If I were Dr. Patel, and I was looking forward to a long and lucrative career, I certainly would," snipped O'Reilly.

Patel dialed the hospital operator. She immediately produced the name and home phone number of the on-duty PR operative, Beverly Wood. Patel punched the ten digits. An unseen hand fumbled the receiver, cursed somewhat mildly and finally said, "Hello."

Patel apologized for the early hour and explained the basics of what had happened to Felder. "Call you back in ten," said the unseen Wood, who had fielded such calls many times before and well knew how to go into Red Reputation Protection Alert.

First, The Rag. She dialed the unpublished number for the city desk. No answer. Great.

Second, the president of the hospital. Ring, ring, ring, voice mail. Was he out of town? Should I try his cell phone? Yes, I'd better.

Ring, ring, ring, voice mail.

OK, how about the executive vice president? Ring, ring, ring, at last a semi-bright, "Yes?"

After sorry-to-wake-you and gee-isn't-it-a-shame, the two agreed on first steps: A press conference at Suburban, to begin at 9 a.m. A courtesy call to the chief of the medical staff. A second courtesy call to the chairman of the board. A call to hospital security, warning that the local TVs might want to set up in the parking lot for live shots starting at 5 a.m. And finally, please try to notify some high official in Felder's campaign. They are going to want to manage a lot of what happens from now on, and they should. But above all, let's stress that he's getting excellent care at Suburban.

Wood had brewed a cup of instant coffee by now—a spoonful and a half of crystals, to make it extra-potent. She fired up her computer and went to the Felder campaign page. A news clip linked from the home page reported that the new chief was a guy named Blake Sonner. She found him in seconds via some whoop-de-doo new site that gives you even an unlisted number, as long as you have the name.

Sonner had obviously been asleep, but he thanked Wood for the call and said he'd take over from here. He immediately rousted the four senior campaign staff members out of bed and scheduled an emergency meeting for 8 a.m., at Felder's home. As he shaved (quickly) and showered (slowly), he had a pit-of-the-stomach feeling that this can't-miss campaign was about to crash on the rocks.

Meanwhile, two attending physicians on Three West had welcomed Felder and had examined him. The news was both good and bad. No apparent brain damage. No life-threatening injuries. But severe blood loss, comparable to gunshots, and a likely major concussion. Also the chance of damage to important nerves that ran down the back of the neck. And they wouldn't know for several hours about internal bleeding.

Bottom line: This patient wasn't going anywhere for quite a while.

Sonner had reached the senior attending, Dr. Mark Rosenkurtz, by 5:45 a.m. His first question was whether the Felder campaign should bag itself. Dr. Rosenkurtz said he was no politician and no predictor of the future. "But I would greatly doubt that he will be in any shape to do any typical activities for quite a while," he said. "And that would go double for a strenuous political campaign."

Sonner sighed and said thanks. He needed five minutes alone with Larry, and he needed them well in advance of the inevitable live shots and the inevitable speculation.

By 6:20, he was on Three West. Felder's name was on a dry erase board behind the nurse's station. He grabbed a look at the board without breaking stride. Ignoring squeals of, "Sir, these aren't visiting hours!," he was inside Room 327-W in seconds.

Felder thanked him for coming. Sonner nodded. Felder asked if the docs were telling him everything. Sonner said they were, as far as he knew. Felder said the food in the hospital was awful, and there wasn't enough of it. Sonner smiled slightly at the timeworn joke and nodded again.

"How do you feel, Larry?"

"As if a bus hit me."

"Whatever it was, it sure hit you."

"I don't plan any replays."

Sonner ambled across the room, so carefully designed to be inoffensive, and pulled aside the curtains, so carefully designed not to be openable. Dawn was trying to break, and failing, thanks to a heavy layer of puffy gray clouds.

"Well," he said, as he turned back toward the bed, "shall we discuss the elephant in the room?"

"Which is what?"

"Which is whether you want to suspend or drop the campaign."

Felder slammed his right hand on the mattress, hard. "Is that what you WANT me to do, Sonner? Good grief! Why would I do either of those?"

"Because you've been seriously injured. Because you won't be at your best for who-knows-how-long. Because people who've been klonked in the head with a crowbar deserve to take a break."

"No chance."

"More becauses, Larry. Because you could always run again in two years, if need be. Because your funders would not dry up. Because I and the rest of the staff would come flooding back in 2008. Because you would attract lots of sympathy votes then that you wouldn't necessarily get now."

"No chance."

"Larry, please listen to reason. You're lucky to be alive. Isn't that more important than a silly old election?"

"Blake, I won't dignify that with a serious answer. One more time: I'm not dropping out or suspending anything."

A nurse came in to take Felder's blood pressure. Sonner had already elevated it. She noticed, and announced that she would discuss new medications to control this problem with the senior attending on Three West. "Fine, thank you," said Felder.

As she left, he told Sonner: "Always pays to be nice. Always on during a campaign. You never know where a vote can be won or lost. Or how many cousins she might have who are registered Democrats."

"Larry," Sonner said, a bit wearily, "we are having a press conference in an hour or so, in the auditorium of the hospital. I have got to be able to say that you're considering a pause in the campaign to protect your health. To do anything else would make you out to be reckless. You can't be worrying about the voting predilections of some nurse."

Felder, who never cursed, urged Sonner to commit an anatomically treacherous act. Sonner said he had never noticed that in his job description. Sonner tried again—wouldn't Larry authorize him to at least float the idea that the campaign was reassessing where it would go from here? With a smack to his three pillows, Felder adamantly refused.

"You are a very stubborn SOB, you know that?"

"My father always told me, stubbornness is just one form of purpose, and purpose always wins."

As a green-gowned woman brought in his breakfast, with an overly cheery, "Time for some calories!," Sonner said: "Mission understood. But I'm going to have to duck lots of rotten tomatoes."

"I know you can do it, Blake," said Felder.

Oatmeal always looks like paste, and at Suburban, it tasted like it, too. A rapidly browning banana wasn't much better. The only thing that attracted Felder's fancy was a small plastic cup of grape juice. He was able to rip off the thin aluminum covering after three tries.

Obviously, he was weak, weaker than he had ever been. But admitting that would be weakest of all.

Puerto Rico as the sun was going down.... Kat resplendent in a light blue sun dress.... A second cocktail shared beside the pool.... Larry patted her arm softly and asked what she was thinking.... "Trying to imagine you in 30 years," she replied.... "The only thing different will be my hair, or the lack of it."... A chuckle from her.... A rueful chuckle from him.... Another arm tap.... "The main thing I will promise you, Kat, is that whatever I end up doing for a living, I will mean business"....

Felder debated turning on the television, but thought better of it. He hated to rest—it was time lost forever--but he knew he needed it. His head throbbed. His neck was swaddled in so many bandages that it was hard to tell where skin began and bandages ended. The drugs were ootching him into Dreamland....

A honeymoon is only that. Then you return to your lives, and to reality.... And ours barely had a chance.... Did we use up all our luck the day the baby was born, Kat?.... Did I use up the rest when those two guys came after me? .... Should I really insist on continuing?.... Maybe Sonner has it right.... I could always write some more books, be a "media presence," take senior status as a reporter, if you will.... Being one of 435 yammering hotheads in the House, maybe that wouldn't be so terrific.... Perhaps a long break, perhaps move to somewhere warm for a year or so.... Have you ever done something just for yourself, Larry Felder?

Sonner had brought him a copy of that morning's Rag. Felder sifted through it—from back to front, as was his 30-year habit.

Sports. . . . too much rooting and jumping to conclusions, as usual. Financial. . . . would they ever define terms for the lay reader, for heaven's sake? How many people really understood the gold standard? Metro. . . . lots of good stuff about local schools and local antics, but not much about immigrants or children, as usual. First section . . . still caught between trying to be all things to all people and a headline service.

If I suspended the campaign, would I be a quitter? . . . . That's how Dick Young, bless his rotten old heart, would label me. . . . If I were ever going to be unsure of this path, I shouldn't have gone down it in the first place. . . . Hell, I was way down in the polls when I announced, and I was still dumb enough to think I could make rivers run uphill. . . . Bartlesby was the perfect candidate, until I really focused. . . . God, Charlie did a great job. . . . Charlie, damn, what would she advise me to do? . . .

A nurse appeared. She wasn't the same one who had propped up the back of his bed a few minutes before. Apparently it was against the rules at Suburban for any nurse ever to appear more than once.

She thrust a small paper cup at Felder. Two bright blue pills were in it. "Bottoms up," she said, with a leer that pegged her as a veteran of the local cocktail lounge as soon as each nursing shift was done. Larry glugged down the pills without asking what they were.

I can't quit. . . . Just can't. . . . Quitters quit, workers work, and winners win . . . . Besides, you can't go home again, can you? . . . . If I quit, what would I do, pound a keyboard at The Rag again? . . . They'd never have me back. . . . And it might be a disaster. . . . Cal might give me the cops beat. . . . Well, OK, unlikely, but I might not like being there any more . . . Might not get my calls returned. . . . No, Larry the Stoic will be stoic. . . . Stay the course, and focus on getting better. . . . Just wish Charlie were here to bounce this off, and to bless it. . . . Christ, I sound like some lovelorn kid. . . .

Felder rang for the nurse. Yet another previously unseen woman arrived. He apologized for turning her into a secretary, but could she please call a woman named Charlise Carpentier? Yes, Kar-PON-Tee-Ay. Mister Sonner will have the number. She's an old pal. Thanks so much. . . .

★ ★ ★

Aggie Stern often felt like an alien dolphin—swimming upstream, unseen, in a school of alpha males.

She felt she had long since proven her bona fides as a Rag reporter. As tough as any man. Tougher if she needed to be. Lots of honors. Lots of merit raises. Steadily better assignments. And she was still only 31.

But the masthead, and the superstructure of newsroom expectations, were resolutely all male.

If blacks always say they have to be twice as good as whites to do half as well, the same held true for Aggie and her female compatriots. When her immediate supervisor (male, dumpy, flabby) had once described her to her face as "pert," sugarplum fantasy fairies had danced in front of her eyes. The guy had just committed a cashable lawsuit of a sin.

But to have pressed the point through the legal process would have submarined her entire career. The definition of baby and bathwater.

So Aggie continued to play the good scout, wearing fresh nail polish every day, taking any assignment cheerfully, cooing dutifully over the newly arrived children of her colleagues and ignoring all the (male, dumpy, flabby) eyes that followed her rump every time she marched from her desk to the ladies' room.

"If one more guy looks at my butt that way, I might kill somebody," she confided, at the silver liquid soap dispenser, to a young political researcher named Karen Quoit.

"Don't do it until I'm there to help you load the murder weapon," said Quoit.

Part of the good scout code of conduct was to document everything, in case any Set Of Pants ever doubted her wisdom or her performance. So there would be no casual, verbal pitching of her latest bang-up "get." Aggie had been tapping away at her "Memo to Cal" since she had arrived at 8 a.m. (classic career girl thing to do—get to The Rag two hours before anyone else).

Her draft was getting too long. She had been at it for more than 15 minutes. Time to finish, Ag. Time to fish or cut bait.

She re-read it for the fifth time. . . .

"To: Cal Cassidy

"From: Aggie Stern

"Subject: Felder campaign blockbuster

"I have it from a very solid source that the Felder campaign has accepted— and may have solicited—a potentially illegal group of campaign contributions.

"My source is very close to Felder. I can't identify the source further at this time. But I have no reason to doubt the details, or the motives of the source.

"I have plenty of documentation. I'm in the process of checking it with Felder's people and others.

"I propose to write this no later than this afternoon, so we don't get beaten by anybody. I can't promise that my source hasn't shopped the same information elsewhere.

"I believe The Rag would look very ethical and principled by running this piece. Felder may have been one of ours, but if he broke the law, he should pay the piper on our front page."

Nope, that last paragraph is way over the top. What is it that Cal always preaches? "We do journalism, not vengeance?" Yep, that was it.

Stern killed her two offending sentences with one firm keystroke, then added a new last paragraph:

"I'd be happy to meet with you at any time this morning to supply full details.

"Thanks, Aggie."

She pushed SEND with a flourish.

Was it unprofessional to think of the reaction to a hot story before there had even been a story? Maybe, but such was human nature, n'est-ce pas? The Felder story had the whiff of a major goodie. Rub palms together. Silly grins. Was it PULL-it-zer or PEW-lit-zer? Let the chicken-counting begin.

Cal came to the lip of his office door about three minutes later and shouted, "Stern!" She was sitting on his mocha sofa less than 90 seconds after that.

The national editor, political editor and Metro editor were all camped shoulder to shoulder on the matching couch across the room. Stern had the passing, antic thought that the three "mastheads" looked like forlorn sardines, about to be packed into a tin.

"Aggie," Cal began, "is this memo of yours some kind of freaking joke?"

Blood rushed to her face. "No, Cal. Why would I joke about something like this?"

"Because of what happened overnight, perhaps?," said the politics editor, a certifiable worm named Justin Blanchette.

Aggie looked clueless. Cal rushed in to fill the silence.

"Felder had the hell beaten out of him at about 1 o'clock this morning, Aggie. On some street in Bethesda. While he was taking a walk. Crowbar and maybe a straight razor. Probably a robbery. Cops have no idea about motive, or whether there's any political link. He's doing fair, but only fair, at Suburban. Lots of buzz about whether he'll drop out of the campaign. So here you come, with a Felder story about money. Today, of all the God damned days! Is this some kind of sick joke?"

"Cal, I swear to you, I knew nothing about Felder. My God, how awful!"

"What's awful, my dear Agatha, is your timing," said Cal. "Maybe we'll consider your story in a few days. But for now, the news is what's left of Felder's skull, and whether he has just delivered the Eighth District to Bartlesby on a platter."

"Aggie," popped in Blanchette, "don't you listen to WISE in the morning? They've been all over this story since before dawn. You should really make it a habit to listen before you get to work." He smiled smugly and condescendingly. He was 37 trying to seem 60.

Aggie made a mental note to notify Quoit: I HAVE MY FIRST PANTS-WEARING VICTIM IN SIGHT. DO NOT MESS WITH AGGIE THE RAGGIE WHEN SHE'S ON THE WARPATH. SHE IS MORE DANGEROUS THAN A WOMAN WITH HER MONTHLIES.

But Aggie slipped into be-agreeable mode and said: "I'll have to start listening as of tomorrow, Justin."

"See that you do," said the editor. What a sicko sycophant. Thinking he can score points with Cal by being a bully and a braggart. Worse: Maybe he could. Maybe he has.

"You three stay," barked Cal. Stern got the hint. She was back at her desk in a flash.

On her computer, she cranked up the WISE web site. They were featuring live streaming audio of a press conference that had evidently begun a few minutes earlier, in the parking lot of Suburban. Stern cranked up the volume and exhumed a fresh notebook from the bottom drawer of her gunmetal gray cast iron desk.

★ ★ ★

The pout was world-class. The words came out in a soft whine. The sheets were pulled up to cover the upper chest.

"Barrykins, how can you POSSIBLY leave a woman in such an unsatisfied state?"

But Mauskopf had made the decision to abandon his latest quarry about ten minutes earlier. Half shaved, half dressed, he was about to bolt for the door and his midnight blue Lexus convertible, the one with MOUSE ONE vanity plates (MOUSE TWO rode aboard the jet black Cadillac Escalade). The call had come from Sonner. You're needed at Suburban Hospital, urgently. Felder is asking for you.

"Babykins, the good news is that tonight is another night. We'll return to the thrilling days of yesteryear."

"Barrykins, what the hell are you talking about?"

"Lone Ranger. Wore a black mask. Good guy. Caught bad guys. Before your time, Babykins."

Mauskopf wiped away the last of the shaving cream, blew her a kiss and sprinted for the carport. He estimated Suburban in less than 20 minutes, Georgetown's legendary traffic permitting. He was glad of only one thing—Ms. Latest and Greatest hadn't demanded to know if Barry Mauskopf remembered her name. He didn't.

Just as Mauskopf fired up the engine and Haydn flooded the front seat, Mauskopf's cell phone rang. The private one. Number known only to a very fortunate few.

"Hello, Mr. Mauskopf," said a resolute female voice, dispensing with the preliminaries.

"Who the hell is this?"

"Aggie Stern of The Washington Record, Mr. Mauskopf. I'm calling about Larry Felder. We need to talk."

"How did you get this number? I know nothing about the accident."

"It isn't about that, Mr. Mauskopf. It's about a story I'm working on. About campaign donations."

"Yeah?"

"Mr. Felder is your client, isn't he?"

"No comment until I hear more, Miss . . . Miss?"

"Stern. Agatha Stern."

"OK, there, Miss Agatha Stern. What can I do for you?" Mouse was already sensing a possible conquest. The voice was youngish. Wouldn't the figure be, too?

Aggie explained the bones of what Charlie had told her and given her, without identifying Charlie. Mauskopf whistled.

"You're serious?," he asked.

"Serious as a heart attack."

"Well, Miss Agatha Stern, this is the wrong time on the wrong day. I'm en route to confer with Mr. Felder right now. Can we talk this afternoon?"

"That would be just great, Mr. Mauskopf. I'll call you then."

"Please do," said The Mouse, as he cut across Reservoir to Foxhall.

Nice voice this dumpling had. Wasn't a nice voice a harbinger of niceness in other body parts? The Mouse, too, was counting his chickens.

CHAPTER 11.

"LARRY! OH, MY GOD, Larry! I'm so sorry! Are you OK?"

Why does one always run out of hands when one is lying in a hospital bed? Felder asked Charlie to hold on for a second. He placed all five sections of The Rag on his skimpy, kidney-shaped bedside table. Three promptly fell to the floor. He re-propped his three pillows in a nice, neat stack, the better to sit upright against them. They promptly slid to the other side of the bed, in an untidy heap. He tried to pull the phone closer, but the cradle promptly slipped off the bedside table and dangled like a man on a gallows.

"Charlie, I'm sorry to make you hold on, but I'm making a mess here."

"Oh, Larry, please don't worry about the small stuff. I'm so upset! Are you really, really OK? Are they treating you OK?"

"They're giving me so many drugs, I wouldn't know it if they weren't."

"Well, Larry, I'm sure that's for the best. You need rest! This is your mother speaking!"

"You were always a lot more fun than my mother ever was, Charlie."

"I'm going to take that as a compliment."

"You should."

Pregnant pause. Charlie filled it first.

"Larry, I realize that I have no standing to ask this, but I have to ask it. Are you going to bag the campaign?"

"Charlie, I have been asked a lot of lame questions in my life. And I have asked a lot of lame questions in my life. But I can assure you, Charlie...."

"Just what I thought you'd say, Larry. Bully for you. Keep on trucking."

"No choice, Charlie. No alternative. I haven't come this far to let a couple of strung-out cokeheads steal my future from me."

"Is that who they were, Larry?"

"Actually, I have no idea. But that's what the cops are guessing. Couple of guys who were out of money and out of drugs at the same moment. That can be a witches' brew."

Another pause. "Larry, I have to ask you something."

"A preamble! Don't get all bashful and cautious on me all of a sudden, Charlie, or I'll think this isn't really Charlie on my phone."

"Larry, do you want me to come back to the campaign? I'll do it if you want me to. In a split second, Larry. I joined up with you because I believed in you, and I still do, despite all the.... all the ... all the other stuff."

Longer pause. "I don't think that would be a good idea, Charlie."

"You really don't?"

"No, I really don't. I suppose that's not what you wanted me to say. Maybe not what you expected me to say. But that's what I'm saying. You closed that door, Charlie. It stays closed."

"Larry, I could really help you in the rest of the primary. I really could."

"Charlie, it would be a disaster. You put your cards on the table. You want to make me your boy friend. Or whatever the right phrase is these days. Sorry, but I'm all business, Charlie. There are plenty of other guys out there, Charlie. Go find yourself one."

"Larry, it isn't that simple! Yes, I certainly want you to be my guy. I said so. But that never meant that I wouldn't or couldn't manage your campaign well at the same time. I can do both, Larry!"

"Charlie, you're dreaming. You're delusional. When I said no to your guy-girl idea, you became a woman scorned. How can a woman scorned also be a woman employed and a woman trusted?"

"Larry, you are sometimes so hopelessly 1950s that I want to scream! Are you saying that I can't control my raging hormones long enough to arrange press briefings and set up conference calls with the House Democratic Campaign Committee? My lust isn't so overwhelming that I froth at the mouth, Larry!"

"Charlie, I don't want to hurt your feelings. I really, truly don't. But I am going to repeat what I said to you at that restaurant a couple of weeks ago. I am married. I intend to stay married. I take that seriously. You should, too."

"Larry, my offer stands. Check that. Both offers stand. I want to see you win this primary, win the general and go on to a long career in the House. And I want a life with you, Larry. Yes, you're married, but it's obviously a shell and a sham. That's all it is. That's all it can be. We could be so great together. Don't you want a woman who will give you everything she's got?"

"You are being offensive, Charlie. Kat would give me everything she's got if only she could."

"I'm sorry, Larry. Not my best choice of words. Let's try these instead: I love you."

"Good Lord, Charlie!"

"He has nothing to do with it. I love you. There, I said it again."

"Charlie, I am lying in a hospital bed with my head doing loop-de-loops around the room thanks to the pain drugs. This is not the best time for me to wrap my brain around what you mean by saying that."

"Then wrap your brain around this, Larry. All you ever have to do is call me back and say I'm rehired. Don't worry about my salary. I'll take what you were paying me before. We can take the I-love-you stuff as it comes. Maybe it goes nowhere. But at least you know where I stand."

It never occurred to Larry Felder that Charlie had already started to destroy him, out of pique. It never occurred to him that her loyalty had ended when her employment had. He took her, and this phone call, at face value. He saw her at this moment as he always had—as a useful functionary, a loyal poodle, who happened to be female. When she quit his campaign, the "useful" piece quit, too.

"Charlie, I don't want you to get your hopes up. My campaign will go on. I assure you that it will, even though some of these doctors don't see how I can manage that. But you're not part of the team, Charlie."

She had half-expected this. She hung up softly. Was it rage she was feeling? No, more like resignation. And resolve.

She dialed Stern at The Rag. Got kicked to voice mail. The message she left was brief and crisp:

"Aggie, Charlise Carpentier. Are we a go? Do you need more from me? When is the story going to hit? Please let me know where our project stands. You have my number."

★ ★ ★

One cold winter's night, long ago, some of the guys at The Rag had decided to educate the occasionally too-stern Miss Aggie Stern. The setting was the swoopy, futuristic bar of the Madison Hotel. Three men, one Aggie. Bourbon was the pour of choice. Vic Printz was holding forth.

"Aggie Stern, you are young enough to be my daughter, so let me give you some fatherly advice," he had said. Stern had folded her hands in front of herself, a bit too daughterly, a bit too demurely. Vic's advice was 8-to-1 to be obvious and forgettable, as usual.

"Men don't think with their heads, Aggie, and they aren't governed by their hearts. They are propelled by their gonads."

"That doesn't end when college frat parties do, Vic?," Aggie had asked.

"Not a chance, Aggie," Printz had said. He took a pull on his Old Grand Dad. "And at The Rag, in the upper echelons of management, it only gets worse." The two other guys said yup, they'd drink to that.

Now, about eight years later, here was Aggie, pushing all her chips into the middle of the table, perhaps endangering her career, sitting in Cal Cassidy's office and begging him to reconsider. Would he please use his brain and his heart instead of that other equipment? Would he please publish her Felder story right away?

Cal could upshift into Rant Mode without much prodding. He was already pushing the red line, even though Aggie hadn't uttered more than a couple of sentences.

"Aggie, it might seem to you that we at The Rag simply let fly with any good story whenever it's ready to print," he said, with the occasional windmill of his arms to punctuate.

"But we have to keep many things in mind. Fairness to the subject. Fairness to the reader. Not just how things are, but how they might seem."

"So are you telling me to go fly a kite, Cal?"

"No! No such thing! The day I don't get my private parts in an uproar about a great news story is the day I'll take up shuffleboard, Aggie! No, no, a thousand times no!"

"So are you telling me that you'll publish the story, Cal?"

"No again. And the reason isn't because I've suddenly gone soft in the head, or soft in another critical part of my anatomy. The reason is that if we publish this now, it will look as if we're piling on Felder. The guy has so much misfortune landing on him right now. We shouldn't add to it. We'll be lambasted for being ugly and uncaring. And maybe for rooting for Bartlesby in our news columns."

"And if we don't publish the story," Aggie said, "it will eventually leak that we could have, and we'll be lambasted for pulling punches to protect a guy who used to work at The Rag."

Cal got up and wandered the room, tracing concentric circles. Aggie noticed for the first time that his thin, pewter carpet was worn in a neat loop right in front of the couch on which she sat. Obviously Cal had circled many quarries in his time as the big cheese.

The rant continued.

"Perhaps some day, Aggie, you will have a position of responsibility around here. Perhaps some day, you will have to weigh the short-term effects of a quick hit against the long-term value of The Rag's reputation. Perhaps you will come to understand why I'm not saying no, but am saying: Not now."

"I do understand, Cal," she said, trying to simmer down, trying to seem reasonable. "But it seems to me that we do more to endanger our reputation by holding my story than we would by printing it. I mean, aren't you the guy who let fly against Bob Dole when it might have looked as if you were piling on?"

The Dole episode had led to much gnashing of many teeth, and to many irate yanks of many ads. Four days before his doomed presidential race in 1996 against Bill Clinton, Dole had fallen off a stage at a campaign event. To the casual TV viewer, it was just a stumble and a tumble. But the next day, Vic Printz landed a large, flapping fish of a story: Dole had probably stumbled because he was having an ischemic episode, Printz learned, from Dole's former physician. That might be taken to mean that Dole was medically unfit to be president.

Cal had literally bounced through the newsroom, declaring that his private parts were as hard as they had ever been now that he had read Printz's story. It ran the next day across the top of page one.

Reaction took typical forms.

Republicans accused The Rag of wishing so hard for a Democratic victory that it had dragged the garbage pail and come up with the Dole story.

Democrats went holier-than-thou and said that a statesman and patriot like Dole didn't deserve this. Besides, they said, Clinton was going to win anyway— all the polls said so. They thus wanted it both ways, as they so often did.

Meanwhile, press haters declared the end of the world to be at hand. Only truly malicious rats would publish such drivel, and publish it at a time when it would do maximum damage to the Dole candidacy. Why was the American press allowed to be free via the First Amendment when freedom produced such vicious, groundless attacks?

And the Kumbaya-crooning letter writers were right there with their handwringing. Couldn't The Rag concentrate on issues and not personalities?

Couldn't we hear about Dole's wonderful grandchildren and peerless war record instead of his blood pressure? Can't we all just get along?

Cal had dismissed every objection. He was happy to flesh out the caricature of the great, bold editor. Stand in the schoolhouse door against the bullies and the special interests. Run over his grandmother to get a good story into print. Do his thing without fear or favor. Print that baby! And win the battle of the post mortems as they were fought over bourbon at the Madison Hotel bar.

Cal buttoned his dark blue cardigan in mid-wander. "Getting chilly in here," he observed. *Does he mean I'm cold and heartless?*, Aggie caught herself wondering. But Cal immediately jerked himself back to the issue at hand.

"Aggie, that's a cheap shot," he said. "The Dole story had to do with who was going to be the leader of the free world. Your Felder story has to do with a would-be freshman Congressman who's going to represent cookie-cutter shopping centers along Rockville Pike."

"I'm going to assume that's a joke, Cal."

"It is. Sort of. But you have to keep all this in proportion. Would we go bananas over any other congressional aspirant's finances if he were just Joe Candidate?"

"That isn't the point, Cal, and you know it! Felder is about to represent the largest segment of readers The Rag has! He isn't Joe Candidate. He's a guy who might very well be a major leader in the House one day."

"We'll cross that bridge when we come to it, Aggie. For now, I'm not even sure he'll stay in the campaign beyond sunset."

Cal clapped his hands. An idea had just struck him.

"Let me propose a deal to you, Aggie. If Felder is still an active candidate 24 hours from now, we'll take another look at running the story. If not, it sits on ice, and might sit there forever. Deal?"

Aggie got up and shook the big boss's hand. "It'll have to do," she said.

"If it wouldn't get me sued, I'd give you a big hug right about now," said Cal. Aggie glared at him as she turned and stalked out.

Cal didn't do mulling well, or much. He was what he liked to call a "nuclear reactor." He liked to respond from his gut, and he often went nuclear. At an office birthday roast years earlier, he had been presented with a mock diploma. It awarded Cal Cassidy a PhD in Impatience and Skin-Deepness. The diploma now graced his south office wall.

But the Stern visit had caused him to hit the pause button.

He sipped from a two-liter bottle of Evian. He pushed aside a stack of performance reviews that he hadn't yet signed. He wished that he could fire up a Marlboro Light—but those bastard docs had made him quit 15 years ago.

And then the light bulb went on.

He picked up the phone, dialed Suburban Hospital and asked for the patient room locator.

★ ★ ★

"Hey, Chuck. Kal Radin. How's it going?"

"Real fine, Kal. Good to hear from you, old buddy. What can I do for you?"

"Just need a little advice. I know you're good for plenty of that!"

"Only my first client could say something like that and remain a client!"

It was the serve-and-volley of old friends. In 1974, Bethesda-Chevy Chase High School had been a hotbed of anti-war protests and long-haired druggies. But 33 short-haired young men still came out for varsity football. Kal Radin and Chuck Bartlesby had been two of them.

The team finished 1-8 that year. Radin and Bartlesby rode the bench, even though they were seniors. Neither played a second until the final game of the year, when B-CC trailed Northwood, 33-0, and the coach decided to take pity on his scrubs.

Radin made a tackle in the final minute. Bartlesby made none. Radin had been lording it over Bartlesby ever since.

"How does it feel," he now asked, "to be talking to a man who made 1,000 per cent more tackles in his high school football career than you did?"

"Marvelous," retorted Bartlesby. And they chortled as they had 32 years earlier, when everything had seemed possible, with the possible exception of playing college football.

"Chuck," said Radin, shifting gears, "I need to discuss something confidential with you. Do I have your vow of silence?"

"What is this, some Mafia hit about to happen?"

"I'm not that classy. No, pal, I need to discuss something about income taxes."

Bartlesby had never done these, for Kal or anyone else. He was strictly a fee-for-service financial advisor. But he would certainly lend an ear. Being a financial advisor was a little like being a parish priest. One heard many confessions.

"Shoot," said Bartlesby, as he picked up a felt-tipped pen to take notes.

There would be no need for that. Kal Radin wanted to know if donations made to a political candidate were deductible on federal and state taxes.

"Not deductible," proclaimed Bartlesby. "Sorry. Your donation was the act of a concerned citizen, but not the act of a tax dodger."

"You put it so nicely," said Radin, with a soft chuckle. "Remind me to double your fee."

"That won't be hard," said Bartlesby. "Two times nothing is still nothing." The two men laughed a little too richly, a little too long.

Radin coughed and said he needed to add one thing, in strictest confidence. The campaign donation in question was made to Larry Felder. He wouldn't be donating to Lorraine Bartlesby.

"Kal," said Chuck, after half a beat, "it's a free country. I can't stop you from giving to the candidate you want to support. Lorraine would have appreciated a check from you, but, hey, let's be honest, she's heading for the same fate as our B-CC Barons in 1974."

Kal was suddenly grave. "Chuck, I know you're not a tax expert, but I just want to be sure I haven't made the gods angry somehow. If I suggested to my senior management staff that they also make contributions to Felder, is that going to put my rear end in the soup?"

"I'd say the same thing to them, Kal. They are free to make contributions to whoever they want. But I will also say this. All the senior staff at one prominent company making gifts to the same candidate . . . it might not pass the smell test."

"So what should I do, bud?"

"I'd suggest asking Felder to return all those donations. He doesn't need your money, anyway. He's within just a few days of the primary. He's on final approach to a big, big victory. He can win without another cent. Hell, he isn't even buying any TV time or any billboards. Of course, for Lorraine Bartlesby's husband to make these comments might sound as if he's trying to steer support away from Felder and towards her. Just so we're clear, that isn't my intention."

"Gotcha, Chuck," said Radin. "Thanks a bunch."

"Hold on, hold on! Are you saying you DID suggest to your senior staff that they make contributions to Felder?"

"Yes, I did."

"And did they?"

"Yes, they did."

"And were the amounts large?"

"Depends on what you mean by large. I gave the federal limit. A thousand bucks. I suggested that each of them do the same. I assume they did. Damn well better have, if they know what's good for them."

"And did they cough up the money, or did you?"

"I did."

Bartlesby chained and then unchained a pair of paper clips. Was this divine providence, arriving into his left ear? Was this the break that his almost-former wife needed? Was this a gift-wrapped way for him to return to her good graces?

"Kal, I will not tell a soul about this. I'm glad you let me know. But I would advise you to undo these gifts, very soon. This could be very embarrassing to a certain soft drink company and to a certain CEO."

"Not to mention a certain guy named Felder."

"Yes, indeed."

The two men rang off as they always did—with an off-key mutual rendition of the final eight bars of the B-CC Barons fight song (.... *and we shall fight, till Baron might, spells vic-tor-eeeeeeeee*). They promised to meet for coffee or beers very soon.

And as soon as they hung up, both were on the horn again. Radin was calling Felder campaign headquarters and asking for Felder himself. Bartlesby was calling his difficult, distant Lorraine.

★ ★ ★

Nearing midnight.... Gotta sleep but can't do it.... Can't help the drifting, the cogitating, the worrying....

Once a newsie, always a newsie, I guess.... Will I ever stop trying to answer the question, why?.... Only if I'm trying to answer the question, how?....

Back to why:.... Why are the digits on every machine in a hospital room red?.... I can understand the blood pressure thing-a-ma-doo.... But why the clock?.... And why the TV clicker read-out?.... Maybe in my next life, it'll all be clear....

I need to make a decision.... Soon.... If I'm going to drop out, I need to do it without stewing any further.... No one will believe it, but I want to be fair to Bartlesby.... She can be a total rhymes-with-witch, but she has treated me honorably....

Or do I hang in there?.... This is a childhood dream, isn't it, Larry Felder?.... Long way from the Grand Concourse, bay-bee.... Is it really like you to quit five feet short of the finish line?.... You have faced down tough before .... You could say you've faced it down every day for the last umpty-ump years .... You didn't have to do that, but you did. . . . Winning this primary would be something like a victory lap. . . .

Set a deadline, Larry. . . . Three days max?. . . . Three days max. . . . Shake on it . . . . Writing it on my little note pad beside my bed. . . . Done. . . .

A firm shake of his right shoulder.

Must have drifted off. . . . Must be time for more Percocet. . . . Oh, joy, oh rapture.

But this wasn't the overnight nurse with the thighs as wide as Detroit. This was a slightly battered 60-ish man in a slightly battered green windbreaker.

"How you doing, Larry, you old bastard?" whispered Calloway Cassidy III. "Shhhh. Keep it down, you dumb piece of lint. That nurse out there is going to have us both for breakfast if she catches me in here."

CHAPTER

"BA-BA-BA, BA-BARBARA ANN

"Ba-ba-ba, Ba-Barbara Ann
"You got me rocking' and rollin'
"Rockin' and a-reelin'
"Barbara Ann."

It was bad enough whenever Barry Mauskopf sang in the shower. When he sang in public, it was enough to make children cower and rats desert sinking ships.

The famed advocate could not come close to carrying a tune. But that didn't keep him from trotting out the Beach Boys' mega-hit of 1965 as he rounded the bend of Three West and blasted—unannounced, uninvited and undeterred--into Larry Felder's room.

"Mouse, you've just made me smile for the first time in the last 24 hours," Felder quipped, as he offered his right hand.

"Just for you, old man," retorted Mouse. "Remember Murray the K and his Swingin' Soiree?" Then came another bit of show biz that Mauskopf had never quite mastered, and never quite would: A send-up of the radio patter made famous by the legendary New York DJ, Murray Kaufman, when Felder and Mouse were barely teenagers.

"Hey, baby, we're sending this one out to Barry and Larry and all them fine folks up on the Grand Concourse, you hear me? Let's get down with the Beach Boys and Ba-ba-ba, Ba-Barbara Ann!"

"Now you've made me LAUGH for the first time in the last 24 hours," said Felder.

"You getting any in here, Larry?"

"Mouse, even if I had a chance to do that, which I haven't, my body wouldn't let me."

"Wouldn't stand in MY way, my man."

"I hope you're going to leave your male parts to medical science, Mouse. The world needs them."

"The women of the world are already GETTING them, my man."

"You have a one-track mind."

"The women don't love me 'cuz of my mind, Larry, let me break it to you."

"I truly appreciate your clearing that up."

Mouse peeled off his jacket and tossed it onto a nearby chair. Like a prize fighter discarding his robe, it was Mouse's signature move. Time to get down to business.

"OK, what we're about to say here is covered by attorney-client privilege. Which means I don't leak and won't leak. But I need to hear the TOTAL truth, Larry. Because your hindquarters might be in a sling, and it's my job to undo that."

"What are talking about, Mouse? My only problem at the moment is this." He tapped the back of his neck.

"Wish that were so, old man. It's not. First question: Do you know somebody named Aggie Stern?"

"Of course. Aggie the Raggie. A young political reporter at The Rag who's on her way up."

"If it were up to me, she'd be on her way DOWN. But be that as it may...."

"Mouse!"

"Hey, man, the life force is in me. What can I say?"

"I've got the idea."

"Anyway, Larry, this Aggie called me and said she's getting ready to unload a ton-of-bricks story on you. About finance violations in the Felder campaign."

"What?"

"You heard me. Seems that she has learned about a whole bunch of money given to you by one major donor and all the senior staff at his company. That might be illegal if the CEO insisted that they all contribute at the same time, and in the same amounts. It might be VERY illegal if the money was actually his, but he tried to conceal it by passing it off as donations by others."

"My God! Is she going to write this?"

"She wants to, obviously. I got her to agree that she won't do it unless she talks to you. But I was a little sneaky there, Larry. Won't be any such conversation. As your lawyer, I don't want you to talk to her, and I don't want you to comment in any way. Let me handle it. Don't take any calls from her. Your Mouse is in the house."

"Mouse, did she say who fed her this information?"

"No. I kept asking. She kept refusing."

"Charlie.... had to be Charlie... It's all starting to make sense now." Felder slammed the mattress with the flat of his left hand.

"What are you saying, you babbling brook?"

"Mouse, my former campaign manager, Charlise Carpentier, I think you met her once or twice...."

"Once. I gave her about a 9.5. I would VERY much have wanted to meet her twice."

"Jesus, Mouse!"

"OK, OK, I'll simmer down."

"Anyway, Charlie and I had a major disagreement about a week ago and she left the campaign. I have a hunch she decided to talk to Stern so she could nail me out of spite."

"Tell me more."

"Well, Mouse, she wanted to be my girl friend. She offered, very pointedly, and I declined. Not only would that have been a huge conflict of interest, since she was the key person in my campaign, but I'm not like you, man. I am still married. I can't just toss off a few female conquests here and there as if I were eating a cupcake or two."

"Maybe some day you'll learn."

"No way. Anyway, I have a strong hunch that Charlie is Stern's source."

"What does she know about your campaign's finances?"

"Everything. She ran them. In fact.... oh, my God!.... I think she still has all the records. I never got around to asking her to return them."

"Not good, Larry. Not good."

"Did Stern say she had actually seen records?"

"She didn't say. Wouldn't say. Wrapped herself in the First Amendment and got all huffy when I demanded to know the answer to that question. 'I never burn sources, Mr. Mauskopf,' she said. All high and mighty."

"Mouse, if Charlie leaked documents to Stern, couldn't she be prosecuted?"

"No, because these aren't public documents. They're Felder documents. We're not talking about state secrets here, Larry. And nobody stole anything, as far as I can tell."

"Am I in trouble, Mouse?"

The advocate ran his hands up and down his starched sleeves, which ended in monogrammed cuffs. "Depends on the donations that got Stern so hot and bothered," he said. "Think hard. Which donor could she be talking about?"

"No idea."

"Think harder."

"I haven't attracted all that many big gifts. Haven't needed them. We've depended mostly on free media. You know, it's a good story when the former columnist goes rogue and decides to be a candidate."

"Think harder."

"Mouse, it might be Stewart Costinian, the real estate developer. He gave me a grand, the max. But I don't think he bundled anybody else. He would have said so if he had, braggart that he is. It might be Harry Higbie. Used to be a serious, bookish, downtown think-tank guy. Then he married into the Holiday Inn family. Second marriage for both. Big bucks. Now he's a country squire type, living the high life. He took a shine to me. Also gave me a grand. But again, he wouldn't have log-rolled other donations."

"Keep thinking."

"The only other guy it might have been is Kal Radin. The AaaaaaH drinks guy. But I wouldn't know about other donations under his control without looking at the records."

"Can you get this Charlie to return them to you?"

"Under the circumstances, I doubt it."

"OK, let me get cracking on that. I think I can get a judge to order her to turn over all the records, now that she is no longer on the payroll. Kind of like a divorce decree. Neither party should be able to hold onto documents that might incriminate or inconvenience the other. But that's going to take time, Larry, and Stern could publish at any moment."

Felder slammed his hand on the mattress again. This time, he managed to dislodge his IV drip. Glucose solution and pain medication dribbled down his arm and began to douse the sheets.

Mauskopf shouted for help. Two nurses came on the double. As they reattached Larry and retaped the clear plastic tube to his left forearm, he began to sermonize about the issues at hand. Mauskopf shooshed him with a punch to the other bicep.

The nurses told him to be more careful and left, their sneakers squeaking on the tan linoleum. Mauskopf nodded. Felder could now resume.

"This is really tough, Mouse. The newspaper guy in me says we shouldn't do anything to stand in Stern's way. Journalism seeks truth. Chips need to fall where they may, and all that. But I'm not about to get ridden out of this campaign by a newspaper story or Charlie's hurt feelings. Not after all this work, and not when I can see the tape stretched across the finish line. Let's fight, Mouse. Let's fight hard."

"That's my Larry," said Mouse.

They made a plan. Mauskopf would pursue legal action against Charlie. Meanwhile, Felder would try to sweet-talk her into revealing the name of the key donor and relinquishing the campaign records. And both men would pray, hard, that they weren't overtaken by a front-page story in The Rag.

Felder knew he should be telling Mouse about the visit overnight from Cal. He should be passing along what Cal had passed along—that Stern was ready to publish as soon as she had a quote from Felder, that Stern was champing at the bit, that Cal was holding her off but couldn't justifiably hold her off forever, that Cal had agreed to hold the story until Felder made a go-or-no-go decision about his campaign, that Larry had promised Cal first crack at his decision. But Felder withheld it all. Sometimes, he figured, lawyers know too much for their own good.

"Time for all good mice to be down on K Street, earning serious money," said Mauskopf.

"Be safe, Barry."

"All I got to say, Larry, is (hum of a note somewhere near middle C).... *Went to a dance/Looking for romance/Saw Barbara Ann/So I thought I'd take a chance....*"

"Two things. Get out of here. And don't quit your day job."

"I'll call this afternoon." Hugs. Waves. Big questions hanging in the air.

★ ★ ★

Why had he ever agreed to return his key to the front door? That was like relinquishing all hope. But Lorraine had insisted on it.

"Point of no return, Chuck," she had said, with her right palm upraised and outstretched.

"And if I want to return?" he had asked.

"You won't," she had said, with that irritating certainty that she had always used as a weapon. She had pocketed the key. He had listened as it clanked against her others.

Ring, ring, ring. God, the battery in that doorbell must be about shot. And the hedges could use a few minutes of clipping. Getting brown around the upper edges. But that's all Lorraine's problem now, isn't it? Graystone Manor Drive is hers and hers alone. The way she wanted it.

The door swung open. Lorraine nodded a greeting. She was dressed in her Junior League best—a black pants suit with a tight-waisted jacket, a white underblouse, shiny black pumps, an obviously new ivory kangaroo purse. Clearly she was making a grudging minute for Chuck before heading out to a campaign stop. She motioned him inside with a flick of her chin.

"Good morning, Lo."

"Good morning, Chuck."

He sat on the lemon canvas-covered sofa without being invited. "Well, now that we've gotten that out of the way. . . . ," he said, with a forced grin.

"Chuck, I'm a very busy woman. You asked to see me. What about?" Her right foot tapped the hardwood floor. A classic impatient Lorraine tic. She had never suffered fools, even when the Bartlesbys were both 23 and couldn't stand to be out of each other's sight (or arms) for more than 25 minutes.

"OK, OK, I get it, Lorraine. Final days of the campaign and all that." She glared. "And it might be about to be a victorious campaign," he added, with a cat-just-caught-a-canary gleam.

"Would you mind telling me what the hell you're talking about, Chuck?"

"I'd be delighted. I have it on good authority that Larry Felder might have accepted illegal campaign donations."

"What?"

"Yep. Larry the saint. Larry his holiness. Larry the paragon of principle."

"How do you know this?"

"I can't tell you just yet. But trust me, it comes from a very good source, with the Good Housekeeping seal ink still drying on the page."

"One of your clients?"

"Lo, I told you, I can't say. Please don't go barking up that tree. Just trust me. I'd never be telling you this if it were a whim or a guess."

"Trust you the way I trusted you to run our retirement accounts? Trust you the way I trusted you as head of the investment committee at the family foundation?"

"Lo, markets go up and markets go down. I wasn't the only guy to take a flying leap at tech stocks. To blame me for the downs is like blaming the manager of a baseball team when the clean-up hitter strikes out."

"You never did anything BUT strike out."

"Unfair, Lo. But it's all water under the bridge, isn't it? Anyway, I'm here because I want to help you win this primary, not because I want to re-litigate a bunch of stock positions that I shouldn't have taken."

"Chuck, unless you tell me the source of this information, it does me no good. It's just gossip."

"Lo, here's all of what I know. My source knows about gifts made to Felder. First-hand knowledge. This isn't something he overheard on the L-2 bus, Lo. He asked for my advice about whether the gifts are tax deductible. They aren't, of course. And in the process of the discussion, he told me that not only had this person he knows made a gift to Felder, but all the ranking executives at his company had, too. Probably he shouldn't have told me all this. He knows who my soon-to-be former wife is, after all. But I'm not going to bite the hand that feeds me such terrific information."

Lorraine glared at him, but allowed her brow to soften about 25 percent. "When luck falls out of the sky, catch it," her older sister had always told her. Was this the stroke of luck her campaign had needed for weeks, and hadn't gotten?

Sensing her interest, Chuck went on:

"Lo, here's what I suggest you do. Don't get near this information yourself. Let me leak it to The Rag. Not to just anyone there. I'll figure out the right person. Let that journalist connect the dots. No fingerprints left by you or anyone in your entourage. The story will blow Felder right out of the water!"

"Chuck, haven't you heard about what happened to Felder two nights ago?"

"Yes, of course I've heard, Lo. Terrible. Absolutely terrible. But I can't believe he's going to drop out of the campaign at this late date. Not with the lead he has in the polls. So please give me permission to do the leaking. Opportunity is knocking, Lo."

"I can't feel good about this, Chuck. What if I let you do the leaking and you crow about it to all your buddies around the bar at the country club?"

"I give you my word that I wouldn't do any such thing, Lorraine."

"The way you gave me your word you wouldn't tell Brent that my sister wanted to divorce him? The way you told Bo that his soccer coach didn't think he was good enough to start as a junior?"

"Those were different."

"But you aren't any different, Chuck. You're like a mangy old sheep dog, always brushing against my leg and angling for approval. You probably think I'm going to walk over to you, pet you and say you're welcome back into my life."

"I can hope."

"No, you can't, Chuck! Jesus H. Christ! I told you months ago that we were done, and I meant it!"

"OK, OK, please don't blow a gasket, Lorraine. I'm here to help you, not to get you all upset."

"You've been getting me all upset for years, Chuck."

"Well, I can't change that now. But I can light a fire under your campaign. Say yes, Lo. Please say yes to me."

Much against her better judgment, she nodded. He beamed. She asked him to keep her posted. He promised that he would.

Back out in the driveway, amid the dogwoods and the flying pollen of a Washington spring, Chuck fired up his hand-held device and went directly to The Rag's web site. He entered "Larry Felder, candidate" in the search field. Three of the first five articles that came up had "Agatha Stern, Washington Record Staff Writer," across the top. He dialed 202-223-5000 and asked to speak to her right away.

★ ★ ★

Aggie Stern had made a pact with herself years ago. As a serious female professional journalist, she would never curse during the swift completion of her appointed rounds.

If a source was being reluctant, she wouldn't resort to F-bombs. If an editor was acting more like a meat cutter, she wouldn't rip that fool with unholy verbiage. If a male colleague offered her career advice, but was really more interested in a private showing of her private body parts, she wouldn't tell him where to go the way a sailor might.

Her mother had worn out the famous phrase: "You catch more flies with honey." Not that Aggie was some latter-day Julie Andrews. She could be forceful, definite, pointed and persistent. But why be more scabrous than men? It wouldn't get her anywhere. She was big with the please and the thank you. She was iron will wrapped in velvet and lace.

But now, the phone operator at Suburban Hospital was telling Stern for a third time that Mr. Larry Felder was not accepting any phone calls. Stern was explaining for the third time that this was very, VERY important, that she was going to press with her story at any moment, that her editor had insisted that she speak to Mr. Felder, that she needed to speak to Mr. Felder right away. The operator—iron will wrapped in velvet and lace—stood her ground.

So Stern pulled rank. She demanded to speak to the public relations director. That got her precisely nowhere. "The senior medical staff has ordered this," said Beverly Wood.

Stern demanded to speak to the president of the hospital. She was duly transferred. He came on the line, all oil and honey. "We simply can't let you speak to him, Ms. Stern," explained Martin Garcia-Lopez. "It would violate our first job: Help the patient get well."

Stern reached deep into her satchel and came forth with the oldest self-serving trick in the reporter's tool box: I am about to publish, I am going to mention Suburban in a major way and it wouldn't look good for Suburban not to be quoted in my report. Unspoken—but heavily implied—was the threat of a directly negative portrayal of the hospital in Stern's story. Of course, no Rag editor would ever let a reporter's pique or threat seep into a straight news account. But what hospital presidents didn't know wouldn't hurt them.

No dice. Garcia-Lopez wouldn't budge. More oil, more honey, but the man knew where his limits lay.

"I wouldn't let you speak to ANY patient who had requested no phone calls, Ms. Stern," he said. "This isn't just because Larry Felder is Larry Felder."

Stern thanked him (for what?) and hung up. Stymied? For the moment. But maybe Cal—who had demanded a quote from Felder before he would publish her story—could be sweet-talked into changing his decree on appeal. She was heading for his office when. . . .

Ring, ring.

"Agatha Stern."

"Ms. Stern, you don't know me, but my name is Chuck Bartlesby. How are you this fine morning?"

Fifteen minutes later, Stern had yet another notebook full of scribbles, a dose of extra resolve and a case of major excitement. She headed for Cal's office at a semi-trot. Cool. Game-changing. Surely this call from Bartlesby was the extra depth charge that would blow up Cal's caution.

★ ★ ★

It wasn't the greatest place to hold a pity party, but it would have to do.

Charlie had gotten there first, in her el cheapo red rent-a-car, after an excruciating seven-hour drive through traffic so clotted that it could make you scream. The agent had said the place was extra-nice and extra-quiet—no frat parties down the road, no screaming kids next door. "We're still a couple of weeks short of Memorial Day, so you've picked a perfect time," she had said. "You will love Duck. Duck will love you."

The small North Carolina resort was right up the beach from where the Wright Brothers had launched their famous (if brief) flight. Charlie had admitted to Patsy Finkel that she had been seeking too much solace in too many bottles of Captain Morgan rum. Patsy, ever the well-intended interventionist, had proposed a weekend rental in Duck, just the two of them. Patsy would be arriving later that evening, as soon as she had escaped yet another pointless (but billable) meeting with yet another nervous-nellie client.

Charlie had resolved not to pop the fresh bottle of Captain until Patsy arrived. But that vow expired about when sunlight did. Three fingers over three ice cubes. A stout swallow. Mmmm. Nice.

Patsy called. The bridge traffic near Virginia Beach was a total bear. Might be two more hours. Might be three. Charlie had better get dinner on her own.

Her sandals slapping, her jacket lapels flapping, Charlie chose the Tropical Hut, a mock-Hawaiian place a few hundred yards away, with a deck overlooking the ocean. Why any restaurant would want to evoke the Pacific when it sat right beside the Atlantic was more than Charlie could figure. But apparently, Abe Lincoln had never been in the food business. Evidently, you could fool half the hungries all of the time.

Charlie had just ordered chowder, fried catfish, hush puppies and iced tea—and had just broken off eye contact with the 55-ish guy eating alone at the next table—when her cell phone rang. She did not recognize the number.

"Charlie, it's Larry."

Briefly, she considered hanging up. Would Judas take a call from Jesus? She could always say the signal was spotty there on the Outer Banks, or that she had already spoken her piece to Larry, so why speak further?

But hope sprang eternal. If you want to land a fish, you sometimes have to cast your line more times than you'd like. That went double if you were after a Felder fish.

She said "Hi, Larry," half cautiously, half eagerly. It was the precise mix of moods she was feeling.

He leapt right in, guns blazing.

"Charlie, did you torch me to Aggie Stern?"

"I spoke to her, Larry. Torch you? No, I don't think I torched you."

"You don't THINK? Don't you know?"

"Larry, you know better than anyone that when you speak to a reporter, the result is out of your hands. Even the most honest reporters will bend and twist what you tell them. So I have no idea what Aggie Stern will do with what I told her. Has she published yet?"

"Not as far as I can tell. But it can't be very long until she does. OK, Charlie. What did you tell her?"

"That you might have a problem with campaign donations."

"And did you give her any documents from our files?"

"Make that YOUR files, Larry. Maybe you've forgotten that I'm not on the payroll any more."

Felder blew right past this stop sign. "Charlie, why in the world did you do this?"

Weakly: "Because I believe in truth, Larry." And then, weaker: "Because it's better for this to come out now than after you're sitting in the House, Larry."

"Charlie, you were trying to submarine my campaign! And God damn it, you might have succeeded! Oh, my God. What a disaster!"

Charlie's eye fell on the menu. It was festooned with sketches of pineapples and pictures of stud muffin surfers in cargo pants. Both the pineapples and the surfers were smiling. Nothing could have been more out of keeping with the tenor of the Larry-Charlie phone call.

"Larry," offered Charlie, softly, "I'm sorry."

"You can't possibly mean that, Charlie! Is a murderer sorry?"

"I didn't murder anybody, Larry."

"I wish I believed that, Charlie." A brief, awkward silence. Then: "Charlie, I never want to see you or speak to you again. Never. Clear?"

She hung up without responding. A waiter appeared. He said his name was Alex, he'd be her server tonight and would she like to hear about the special cocktails and desserts this evening? She nodded.

Maybe too much deep-fried seafood would help her past her treachery. That and a couple of Captain Morgan nightcaps.

CHAPTER

13.

■ THE DOCS WERE PLEASED.

Patient Felder was turning the corner.

He had been allowed to start walking up and down the corridor, and he had tackled that opportunity with gusto. The attendings had allowed his senior campaign staff to visit—ten minutes max, please. Blake Sonner and crew had crisply managed all the publicity and all the speculation. Both had been voluminous.

Felder and the saga of his nearly-crushed skull had grown far beyond the jagged, gerrymandered boundaries of the Eighth District. USA Today had placed him on the front page, complete with a thumbs-up photo from his hospital bed—and a sidebar collection of "Dear Larry" get-well cards from readers. The New York Times had devoted three paragraphs to the assault and Felder's medical prospects—and the next ten to the political fallout, both in the Eighth and nationally. The CBS Evening News had brought in an artist and a mystic. The artist sketched what the faces of the two assailants might look like. The mystic declared that both were hiding in plain sight—"my intuition says Gaithersburg."

In the presence of his staff, his nurses, the guys who delivered sprawling thinking-of-you floral arrangements, Felder was all smiles and all systems go. But the phone call with Charlie had begun to spiral him into the dumps. His good humor and sense of purpose were circling the drain.

When he had made the fateful decision to chase a seat in Congress, Felder had felt similarly crummy at first. This was cuckoo bananas. What was he thinking? To abandon a dream career for a lark, a whim, a likely failure? Why not play it safe and secure? Why not ride ten more years until his pension kicked in? He could be the go-to, gravitas-spouting graybeard of Talk Show America for the rest of his life.

Because no one ever got anywhere by taking the path of least resistance, Felder had told himself, during yet another soul-searching shave.

Because exceptional is as exceptional does.

Because it's just too damned easy to sit behind a keyboard and aim rockets.

Placing yourself before actual voters—as crazy and as kinky as they could be—was the ultimate test, and the ultimate reward.

But now, facing a challenge and surmounting it, and becoming a national leader, were not going to be sufficient rewards. There were worse things than losing a Congressional election. Being portrayed as a slime was one of them.

As a journalist, Felder had never wavered in his devotion to ethics, even when it was very inconvenient and even when it meant waiting three extra hours at his desk for one last phone call to be returned. You had to live with yourself, Cal Cassidy had always preached. Do not cut corners. Do not get down in the muck and expect to be able to rinse it off.

So an idea was forming. Drop out. Or rather, drop out for 2006 and keep the door very slightly open in case he ever wanted to drop back in.

It could all be done with total, disarming honesty. Not via the easy path—my neck hurts a lot, and I don't want to represent the people of the Eighth District without being able to give the job my all. No, he would acknowledge that he had been sloppy with campaign donations, and he would acknowledge that he couldn't bear to continue his campaign under such a cloud. Very neat. Very Boy Scout.

But how to make the decision? And when? And how to reveal it? And what would become of him next?

It would all depend on what Cal said.

On the back of a slightly sodden paper towel, Felder scribbled a list of pros and cons.

Pros: If I drop out on my terms and my timetable, I can appear to be the white knight. I can head off any legal proceedings. I can own up to a real failing. I can sleep at night.

Cons: Just one—a lifelong dream would die a-borning.

Was it ethical to seek the famed editor's advice before making this hard left turn? Felder decided that it would be. Any ethical mushroom cloud would form on Cal's end of the phone, not Felder's. Besides, Felder was prepared to offer Cal a major scoop. That would surely sweeten the deal in a big way. And Cal The Legend had always liked playing the role of Felder's big brother, anyway.

No, Larry, don't pick up that phone just yet.... Let it simmer for a while....No wine before its time, and no epic phone calls, either.... On the other hand, Aggie Stern might be ready to drop a cluster bomb in tomorrow's paper....And, knowing what's up with that new web site editor at The Rag, she might torpedo my candidacy even earlier.... Like ten minutes from now, for instance....To be overcautious is to discover tire tracks running up the front of your torso....Should I call Mouse first?....Nah, no need....Time to man up, Larry....

Millie the secretary was all gush when he announced who was calling Mr. Cassidy. "I've been so worried about you, Larry!," she told Felder. "Hang on, I'll put you through to the old son of a bitch right away."

Remarkably, uncharacteristically, Cal did more listening than talking over the next five minutes. Even more remarkably, he agreed to every morsel of Felder's proposal.

He commented that Aggie Stern might have to be re-nicknamed Aggie The Fraggie, because she might be coming after him with a fragmentation device when he broke the word to her. "But I've been through worse, Larry," Cal said. "Three divorces. Three mothers-in-law. Three alimony checks every God damned month." He told Felder that he'd call him back within the hour.

The candidate eased back against his pillows. His neck really was feeling better. The medical look-ahead was all pretty sunny. No long work days, the docs had decreed, and no craning his neck from side to side for the foreseeable future. But there had been no broken bones and no brain damage, and the concern about internal injuries had dissipated. Felder was going to be 99 percent very soon.

But where would he go, and what would he do for the long haul, after the solution that he and Cal cooked up had played out? Larry Felder had never been without a path or a plan. Now, uncomfortably, he was without either.

✷ ✷ ✷

The Eighth was bubbling.

The county Democratic club's voice mailbox was so full that it couldn't accept any more messages. Bartlesby campaign headquarters had laid on three extra volunteers to handle walk-ins, most of whom were urging her to step aside out of compassion for Felder. Felder One was regularly approached at red lights by earnest pedestrians of all political stripes, who urged Felder to drop out and worry first about his health—and by the way, why wasn't the Felder campaign using electric cars, to set an example?

The Montgomery Clarion, the county's largest weekly, did not take a position about the campaign on its editorial pages. It went for the usual on-the-one-hand-on-the-other-hand.

If Larry Felder wants to stay in despite his awful injuries, well, by golly, he should stay in. If Lorraine Bartlesby wants to redouble her efforts on the chance that Felder will drop out, well, by golly, it's a free country. As for those also-ran candidates (there remained five of them), well, by golly, their candidacies are exactly what makes America great. It added up to a pile of such deep circumspection that no one could tell where the Clarion stood—the Clarion included.

Outside Suburban Hospital, TV news trucks still congregated around the clock, satellite dishes sprouting from their rooftops like some mad strain of mushroom. The Felder story still led every 5, 6 and 11 o'clock local news show, even though the story hadn't moved or changed for at least three days. Of course, that didn't stop news directors from rushing their $2 million mobile studios to the scene of the non-news, so that they could show their audiences, live and in color, just how on top of the non-story their stations were. As Cal Cassidy loved to say, "TV can always be counted on to kill every story it touches."

Meanwhile, at the county office building in Rockville, the staff was noticing a phenomenon they hadn't seen since 1992, when a neo-Nazi ran for county executive on a platform of Hitler curriculum in the public schools, and the good burghers of the Eighth massed to defeat him. There were lines. People wanted to register to vote. The biggest beneficiary was the Taco Trolley, a food truck that usually did quite well at lunchtime on the streets of Wheaton. It did twice as well outside the Office of Election Services.

Blake Sonner had insisted on regular press conferences, even when developments had basically dried up. "Feed the beast," he said, repeatedly. The media were very grateful to be fed.

By Day Five, interest in the Larry Felder story had actually started flagging, but no newspaper or TV station was gutsy enough to move on until the rest of the herd had done so. Sonner, a wily veteran, realized this early. The beast therefore never lacked for regular updates about Felder's blood pressure (stable) or his latest jaunt down the hallway of Three West (he was wearing his blue pajamas, the ones with the aqua trim that his wife once gave him for their anniversary, and he hugged one veteran nurse, who squealed).

Letters to the editor in The Rag were split—but letters to the editor are always split. One repeating tack: Violence is always awful, and Felder's assailants must be arrested as soon as possible. Another: Felder is now the overwhelming sentimental favorite, but let's decide this seat on the basis of issues, not emotions. A third: regardless of who stays in or drops out, the Eighth is traditionally the home of good government, and that must endure long after Felder's wounds have healed.

There was even the obligatory nut case/conspiracy letter: Felder had orchestrated the assaults because his private polling indicated a precipitous drop in his support. The writer knew so because unidentified voices from a parallel solar system were telling him so. Followed by the obligatory replies and ripostes the next day: Why did The Rag publish such swill? What was the letter writer's evidence? And it's a good thing that Montgomery County offers free mental health services, because here's one guy who can certainly use some.

Meanwhile, some kids who needed more to do took a ride through Germantown on the fifth night Felder lay on Three West. Armed with a spray paint gun, they "edited" four of his campaign lawn signs. Instead of a simple FELDER FOR CONGRESS, on a red, white and blue background, the four signs now bore free-form black crowbars.

Asked to comment at one of his press briefings, Blake Sonner said: "We were all kids once." Asked to comment at a briefing of her own, Lorraine Bartlesby said there was no place for such stupidity in the nation's most educated county. Asked to comment at his regular weekly press conference, the police chief said with a straight face that he had ordered the force to be on red alert for teenagers with spray paint guns. He was swiftly taken down a peg by an editorial on WISE, offered up by the station manager, who pointed out that vandalism was not exactly the greatest threat to western civilization.

Felder read about all of it in "Felder Three West," his staff's sarcastic nickname for the effective campaign headquarters. He laid down that morning's Rag with a sigh.

"I think everyone needs a couple of weeks off," he commented, to Billy the Intern, who had been sneaking him jelly beans and Reese's Pieces on a regular basis.

Felder's breakfast was arriving, as always, right on the stroke of 7:30 a.m. Billy was happy to accept the offer of Felder's whole wheat toast. "Supplements my massive campaign income," Billy said—every single morning. "With my blessings," Felder said—every single morning. "I am happy to feed cardboard to my energetic young campaign staff."

Giggles. Grins. Clearly, Felder was very much on the mend.

Just as clearly, the hospital staff knew the same. On this morning—the dawn of Day Six—a Hallmark card had wormed its way under Felder's plate of rubbery eggs and wilted fruit salad. Larry cracked it open. The card had been signed by "All the guys and girls on Three West." Someone had written: "If you're half as good a Congressman as you've been a patient, the Eighth District will rule the world." Below that and all around it were many, many signatures—Bess and Bill and Stacy and Ruth.

Felder rang his call button. Thighs The Width of Detroit appeared. "I just want you to know, I'll miss all you guys," said the patient. Thighs hugged him. "We never want patients to stay around here, but you've been very special, Mr. Felder. You've been great," Thighs said. Billy memorialized the moment with his cell phone camera.

The phone rang. Sonner. "Just been reading the National Journal," the campaign operative reported. "They've got a survey piece about 2008 on the front. They name Larry Felder as a dark horse for the 2008 presidential nomination."

"Maybe if those kids had broken all of my ribs as well as my head, I'd be leading in fundraising already," Felder joked. He reminded Sonner not to drink any greater-ambitions Kool-Aid. First things first. The primary was in just ten days.

Billy had overheard, and couldn't resist. "Larry," he half-whispered, "would you EVER consider it? I mean, in your wildest dreams?"

"Billy, I'm much more worried about what I'll say when the cops arrest my two friends with the crowbar," Larry replied.

"This guy really does have his feet on the ground," Billy thought, to himself, not for the first time.

A day earlier, Felder had agreed to open his bedside phone to calls. He had soon done a 180. The first five people who got through were, in order, a palm reader who saw great things in his future, a woman he didn't know who proposed marriage, a PR man who thought he could nab a syndicated talk show for Felder for a very small retainer, a woman who had been in his high school class (he didn't remember her, but he claimed that he did) and a neighbor who asked if Felder wanted his lawn mowed by a truckload of itinerant Salvadorans.

"None of this used to happen when I typed for a living," he told Billy that day, with a rueful shake of the head. Billy nodded. Sometimes the boss just needed to vent about the career path he had chosen, and the one he had left behind.

The deal he had struck with the hospital operator was: If they say it's really important, and you think it is, patch them through. Otherwise no.

At exactly 7:42 a.m., the phone rang, five times, in rapid succession. Felder picked up.

"Listen, you malingering bastard," said a voice that he knew very well. "Aggie Stern is sitting here in my office. She's all hot and bothered for us to print her story because she's got some new corroboration. Good stuff. Major-league stuff. She knows nothing about the deal you and I cooked, Larry. So I'm going to be all transparent, the way all the kids want me to be. I'm going to put Aggie on the speaker as soon as Millie gets in here and sets it up. Millie! Now! Thanks, cookie.

"OK, Aggie and Larry, here's what I've decided to do. If either of you doesn't like it, tough beans."

★ ★ ★

Kal Radin retracted the 20-by-20 space-age screen with a push of a button. With a dull whir, it began to fold up into the cream-colored ceiling. Behind it, on the south wall, hung a 10-by-10 oil portrait of Radin's father. El Founder. He was posing uncomfortably. He obviously would rather have been hitting a four-wood or analyzing sales figures. The old bird seldom cared about anything else.

Neither did his oldest son. Kal Radin insisted not only on regular Friday morning meetings of the senior staff, but his own cranky ground rules during them. No gum chewing. No checking hand-held devices. No asides. No interrupting.

And no short-sleeved sports shirts.

Radin had always considered them a little too Muscle Beach show-off-ish for his taste—and his taste was what ruled this roost. So nine men (the senior staff contained no women) were attired in their best pinpoint oxford long-sleeved dress blues. The last thing they wanted to hear was yet another Radin expostulation about the ambiguity and the sloppiness of business casual.

The one concession in the conference room to creature comfort, and variations in style: A mammoth display of all nine AaaaaaH product lines on a teak sideboard. The senior staff could choose any flavor, in any sized bottle, at any time. Ice buckets and glasses had been laid out in perfect rectangular formations. Help yourself. As many refills as you like.

As the screen thunked into its slot in the ceiling, the CEO thanked the assembled for the April results. "Best spring month we've ever had, as the figures just showed us," he crowed. "And thanks to global warming, we can expect a hotter than usual summer. So look out below for the July and August results."

The guys applauded. Radin beamed.

"Got some more thanks to pass out," he said. "To all of you. Thank you for making those gifts to the Larry Felder campaign. The guy's obviously on his way to a big victory, despite that business with the two kids who beat him up. We badly need to be on his radar as far as import duties are concerned. Your gifts will definitely make that possible. To give to his campaign was smart. It was timely. And it was necessary."

The guys applauded some more. Yet it was an emperor's-new-clothes moment.

None of the senior staff had the nerve to point out that the dough had been Radin's, although the signatures on the checks had been theirs. But, hey, the boss is the boss, and after those April numbers, we can all look forward to fat bonuses and sales seminars in Aruba. Not to mention more corporate success via a boss who obviously will have this Felder character in the palm of his hand.

★ ★ ★

"I can't believe I came back to this place. Last night, the food was working overtime to get to mediocre."

"Well," said Patsy Finkel, to her oldest and dearest friend, as their Tropical Hut pancakes arrived, "at least you're not washing away your breakfast with Captain Morgan."

Charlie had spent most of the previous evening doing precisely that to her sorrows. Half the bottle of rum she had brought with her was gone. Her temples felt as if the good captain were practicing the pole vault inside them.

But Patsy wasn't judging. She was only listening. And Charlie had a lot for her to hear.

Since Duke, the two women had made a rule and kept to it: Always honest. Always a shoulder, either to lean on, or cry on, or both. Always a friend of last resort.

Patsy had been receiving lovelorn e-mails from Charlie for many months now. It was time to trot out an extra-heavy dose of "always honest."

"Charlie," she began, "I'm very worried about you."

"I'm very worried about me, too."

"Do you need to uproot your life? Just move to, I don't know, San Francisco and start over?"

"That would only push the obvious problems aside, Pats. My head and my memories would accompany me to San Francisco, Pats."

"OK, then how about chasing a guy who isn't named Larry Felder?"

"It isn't the guy-ness that I'm missing, Pats. If I just wanted that, I could go for a taste of him." She nodded in the direction of a table across the room. The 55-year-old from the previous night was there, again. By himself, again. He had been staring at Charlie, again, ever since the two women had walked in.

"So it's Larry or bust?"

"Always was."

"And you decided that the way to this man's heart was to destroy his campaign?"

"Well, he'll certainly notice."

"What are you, Char, some six-year-old who doesn't like being told to clean up her room so she throws her socks all over the place? There is no chance, zero, that Larry Felder will suddenly hurl himself into reverse and come rollicking to your bedside. Surely you can see that."

"Don't WANT to see that."

"But, sweetheart, it's my job to prevent pain from creeping into my Charlie's life. How else can I do that except to point out the obvious?"

"It isn't obvious."

"Charlie, just what do you see in this guy?"

"Sincerity. Stands for all the right things. Solid as a rock personally. Alert to me. Sensitive to me. Cares about the world. OK, maybe the brown socks aren't my favorite, but guys NEVER get it about the small fashionista stuff, do they?" The women chuckled and took turns with the maple syrup.

Patsy said she had been thinking about something that Charlie had said last night, somewhere between Blast One and Blast Two of Captain.

"You said that you're half-assuming that Felder will drop out of the race. And if he does, that he will have time to rediscover Charlise Carpentier."

"That's what I said."

"Just why do you think that has a snowball's chance of happening?"

"Because Larry Felder has never come to a dead stop in his entire life, Pats. He blew right into the newspaper business after college, and right through it. He hasn't ever stopped to take a breath. He hasn't needed to. But now, if he drops out of the campaign, he's going to get all moon-y and mope-y about oh gosh, oh gee, what should I do next? The answer to that might very well be me."

"Tell me what you're visualizing."

"Being the other woman. Not demanding a choice between me and his wife. Being accommodating to Kat. Accommodating to his obvious sense of responsibility to Kat. Just having whatever percentage of him I can have that isn't sewn tightly to her or to whatever his next career is."

"Honey, you know what you're describing? You're describing pure misery. You're describing something from an advice column in Redbook. You're describing waiting by the phone like some lovelorn teenager, hoping that he'll call and ask you to the prom, and hating the fact that he has all the control over the relationship and you have none. This isn't why we're women of the modern era, Charlie."

"Well, didn't you do a lot of waiting by the phone when Mark was in law school in Chicago?"

"That was different. We had made a commitment to each other. It was like a business trip for him to be out there. Besides, he didn't have a wife and I didn't have a husband. The route was clear."

"Pats, let me straighten something out. It isn't the sex part. Really, it isn't. Obviously, Larry would be mediocre at best in the rack. But my libido is hard-wired to my psyche, Pats. I want him because I admire him and I respect him. Is that too tough to understand?"

"What's tough is accepting the back seat that that makes you take."

Alex, who will be your server today, came by to ask if everything was OK. The women asked for a little more coffee. "Sure thing," he said, and set off in search of some.

"Now, with that rear end, our Alex could redirect traffic," said Patsy. Charlie nodded, but she hadn't noticed. Her libido and her psyche were hard-wired seven hours to the north.

"Just promise me this," said Patsy, as Alex brought the check with a cheery, "Pay me when you're ready. No rush." (That always meant, "Pay me right now so we can have the table.")

"Just promise me that you will not twist in the wind forever about Felder. Promise me that you will resolve this, up or down, within ten days."

"I can't swear, but I'll damn sure try."

"That's my Char."

"And you're my Pats."

As they got up to leave, Mr. 55 Years Old came over to their table. He was holding his breath slightly so his paunch wouldn't be quite so obvious.

"Ladies," he said, "I've noticed you having breakfast and I've noticed that there are no gentlemen with you. Would you like to join me for a beachside drink?" He smiled the way he must have for grudging family photos long ago—a little too wide, a little too toothy.

"Sorry," said Patsy, "but we don't date men."

She grasped Charlie's right hand. Mr. 55 skittered away as if he had seen a rabid rat. The two women roared with laughter for the rest of the day, as they made the balance of the Captain disappear.

CHAPTER

THE TWO ARTICLES WERE,
in newspaper parlance, twinned. That meant that they ran side by side, each under its own headline.

A larger, terse, bold headline sat above both articles, which had been placed above the fold on page one. The main headline read:

INJURED FELDER DROPS OUT.

The article to the right was by Agatha Stern, Washington Record Staff Writer. It reported that Larry Felder had decided to "abandon" his race for the open Eighth District congressional seat in light of "the recent late-night assault on him on a quiet Bethesda street" and because of "allegations that his campaign accepted—and may have solicited—illegal campaign contributions."

Stern's story named Charlise Carpentier and a "person close to the Lorraine Bartlesby campaign" as sources for the allegations. Stern reported that the United States Attorney for the Southern District of Maryland was investigating.

Felder was quoted as saying that he planned to return every cent of his unspent campaign donations, and was consulting counsel as to whether he should return donations that had been spent. Felder "wholeheartedly" urged his supporters to back Bartlesby, for months his principal opponent. He apologized "for the disappointment this will cause among my supporters, whom I have clearly let down." Unnamed "political observers" were quoted as crystal-balling a huge Bartlesby victory in the upcoming Democratic primary.

The article to the left bore a familiar Rag byline. "By Larry Felder," said the single strand of 11-point type. Right below it was an editor's note, in italics:

"Larry Felder spent more than 30 years as a reporter and columnist for The Washington Record. With this essay, he rejoins The Record as a regular staff contributor."

Felder had long been a legend in "the biz" for not milking dramatic moments, for letting them speak in print without adornment. He was true to form in that morning's Rag:

"I took my eye off the road. I deserve the crash that has followed.

"I take full responsibility for the odor of scandal that has attached itself to my now-abandoned Congressional campaign. I was excited to campaign among my neighbors, and I was excited at the possibility that I would represent them. I believed I could be a force for good as the Eighth District and the country confront difficult and important issues.

"But no one is exempt from the law, or from bad judgment. I have dropped out because of both.

"I am enormously lucky to have the chance to return to The Record as a senior political correspondent. My thanks go to the editors and the owner, without whom I could never have had my previous career. Because of their faith in me, I look forward to my next.

"I strongly urge all my former supporters to align themselves with Lorraine Bartlesby's campaign. She will be outstanding as the Eighth District's next member of Congress.

"Many readers and potential voters will have further questions about my campaign, my behavior and my decision. I will be happy to answer any and all, personally. My direct phone number is 202-223-5151. I will pick up the phone myself. I never hid behind a wall when I was a candidate, and I won't hide behind one now.

"There is a certain irony—no, a boatload of irony—when a former political correspondent commits the kind of fiscal carelessness that he so often wrote about. But irony would not have been enough to make me drop out of this contest. Public service is what the name implies, and no one is worthy of serving the public if he cannot run a forthright, honest campaign.

"If there are legal consequences to my failure to observe campaign finance laws, I am prepared to meet them.

"In the meantime, I thank all my well-wishers for the cards, calls and e-mails that have flooded into Suburban Hospital over the last ten days. My recovery was much easier and much faster because of your kindness and support.

"I had nothing to do with the preparation of the article that appears beside this one in today's Record. I did not see it before it was published, and I was not consulted about any details by any editor. Agatha Stern is an outstanding journalist, and Calloway Cassidy is an editor-in-chief without peer. They worked closely together to prepare Stern's report, and would never have asked—or allowed—me to affect it ahead of time in any way.

"In my experience, The Record is one of the few large media organs where taint never touches the product. That has always been true, and it is true today, even though I worked for The Record for decades before deciding to run for Congress and even though it might seem logical that The Record would seek to protect me. Cynics may assume that this happened, and will go on happening. But those who work for The Record know the truth.

"In the days ahead, I—and all of you—will learn whether I and my campaign broke any laws. If I did so, I did so unwittingly. I never promised favors in return for campaign contributions, and I never provided any during the campaign. I never looked for ways to skirt the law. I never would.

"I am sincerely sorry that a former senior member of my staff seems to have been the person who reported suspected campaign irregularities to the media. I am not responsible for her decision to do so. However, I am glad that she did so if it clears the air and allows me to begin clearing my name.

"In the months ahead, I will not cover the Eighth District race, or any political story that might touch it in any way. My new assignment at The Record will be to cover national political trends and the early stages of the 2008 presidential campaign.

"Once again, I apologize as sincerely as I know how, to all the voters and residents of the Eighth District. You deserve better. You will now get it."

Mauskopf was on the phone to Felder before the sun had finished rising.

"Bravo, baby doll," he began.

"I'm going to be depending on you to be the Mouse that roared," said Felder.

"I'm on top of it. So far, the news is all good," the renowned lawyer reported. "Doesn't look as if the U.S. Attorney is going to seek an indictment in the current grand jury term. That doesn't mean he can't, or won't, or won't in some other term. But my nose tells me he doesn't think there's much fire here. Some smoke, yes, but no crime that will imperil the future of the republic. I predict that Felder skates."

"Mouse, what about the financial records? Can you get them back?"

"Trying, baby doll. Trying hard. I've filed a proposed order with a federal judge. He won't schedule a hearing until your good buddy Charlie gets lawyered up. She hasn't yet. Once she does, we're good to go."

"Mouse, I'm worried about what the public will think. They might decide that my essay is self-serving."

"Hey, man, it is! Of course it is! But you didn't brag, and you didn't strut. You were offered a platform, and you took advantage of it. Isn't that what the First Amendment is all about?"

"Have I told you lately, Mr. Mauskopf, that even though you're a slimy rat bastard, and you treat women like Cream of Wheat, and you give the Grand Concourse a bad name, I love you?"

"Nice to hear it when a client respects the help."

"Keep me posted."

"Always."

"Later."

"Ciao."

Felder opened the French doors and strolled out onto his patio. It was suffering from massive neglect. Leaves, dust and mounds of yellow pollen had blown into the corners beside the low retaining wall. Moss was forming near one drain. Somehow, a Styrofoam coffee cup from Dunkin Donuts had blown three miles from the nearest outlet and had found its way onto the rows of terrazzo tiles.

"Kat," said Felder, to the woman who had once lived here but never would again, "I think it's all going to work."

★ ★ ★

Winston Churchill was alive and well on Graystone Manor Drive. Across the front door of Lorraine Bartlesby's home, a campaign operative with a strong sense of history had strung a makeshift bedsheet banner. It bore Churchill's famous wartime exhortation: "Never, Ever, Ever Give Up."

The candidate wanted to speak to the staff before they fanned out across the Eighth for the duties of the day. No smashed coffee cups this time. The Bartlesby campaign had just been handed a gift that most campaigns can only dream about.

"Everybody, I just want you to know that overconfidence is the enemy of success," said Lorraine. "We still have a primary to win and a general to win. We could still stub our toe."

A grin spread slowly across her carefully made-up face.

— 170 —

"But I have to say that I like our chances a WHOLE lot better than I liked them yesterday."

War whoops. Hugs. High fives. It felt like a college fraternity mixer, and for good reason. Most of the staff was 25 or younger. They had signed on to the Bartlesby campaign for the experience, to stuff greater ballast into their resumes. Now it looked as if they had backed a sure-thing first-time winner. Many were already imagining business cards that read, "Director of Legislative Affairs" or "Staff Director, Committee on Ways and Means."

"People! People!," called Bartlesby, shooshing the uproar with two hands. "I still have neighbors! And around here, the neighbors will sue you if they don't like you."

Guffaws. Giggles. Knowing smirks.

"So let's be sure we do our jobs thoroughly and well over the next few days, please. On to Primary Day! Questions, anyone?"

A driver-gofer named Charlie Corriveau had one: How do we respond to questions about Larry Felder's decision?

"We refer anything that has to do with breaking the law to Felder. And we very carefully say that our campaign is about the voters and the citizens of the Eighth, not about what another candidate may have done or said."

Mick McGuire, a press aide, wanted to know if Bartlesby had re-examined her own fundraising, and had checked to see that she hadn't made the same mistakes as Felder.

"Great question, Mick, and I'm delighted that I can set your fears to rest. Bill Bigelow and I hired an accounting firm today. It will go over every donation we've received with a fine tooth comb.

"I have no reason to be worried about any of our gifts, by the way—mostly because we've gotten so few of them!" The room rocked with laughter. Even Lorraine, a notorious Gloomy Gus, had a wide grin plastered across her mouth. In politics, nothing ever succeeded like success.

"Now let's get going, gang. Coffee is ready. Free! Please take a cup with you as you go, if you want. Have a doughnut, too. Just be sure to drive safely. This is your mother speaking!" The staff loaded up on both kinds of provisions and headed for the cars.

Jim Phillips, the communications czar who was suddenly fielding a million requests from the press, stayed behind. He wanted Lorraine to agree to a pop this coming Sunday morning on "This Is Washington," and an "availability" that afternoon for the national press. She nodded yes to both.

"We're going to get some lifestyle interest now, too," said Phillips. "Guaranteed to be some back-of-the-book scribes who will want to write about you as a woman, your personal life. How would you like to handle that?"

Gloomy Gus returned.

"Jim, I have to be honest with you. Chuck and I are having some trouble right about now. The last thing I want is for that to appear all over the county, or all over the country. Might cost me a lot of momentum. Please discourage this kind of thing."

Phillips nodded. In previous jobs, he had kept the press pack away from the dalliances of sitting Congressmen, and away from a candidate who regularly honed campaign strategy by communing with the devil. A garden-variety marital rift would be baby stuff by comparison.

Bigelow also wanted a minute with Lorraine.

Would she be willing to take a phone call in an hour from the House Democratic Congressional Campaign Committee staff director? Absolutely.

Sane Nuclear, a left-leaning lobby, had e-mailed a demand. Would Bartlesby pledge to vote against nuclear power plants if elected?

She frowned. "Don't want to tie my hands before I've taken the oath, right, Bill?," she said. Bigelow said, "Check," and made notes on a clipboard.

And would she be willing to talk to The Rag about her campaign, and where it would go from here?

"Who from The Rag?"

"Not sure. Might be Aggie Stern."

"Hasn't she collected enough scalps for one week? God, these reporters! Unquenchable thirsts. Well, what do you think, Bill?"

"I don't see how you can say no."

"Then I'll say yes."

"What kind of a story are they planning?"

"My guess would be something like, Bartlesby suddenly wakes up as the favorite, and what that means as far as changes in her platform are concerned."

"OK, Bill, OK. If I said no, that would raise more hackles and questions than if I say yes. I just wish Felder could cover me!"

More guffaws. More giggles. In just one morning, Larry had slipped from dominant opponent to no-threat laugh line.

★ ★ ★

Larry Felder deliberately did not show up at The Rag until late morning. He wanted the day to belong to Aggie Stern. He also wanted to avoid the gossipy front-runningness of his colleagues.

Whenever a story led the paper, it developed a vapor trail of notoriety. The busybodies around the newsroom—and what other kind of animal inhabited a newsroom?—always wanted to know what else there was to know, especially if the "extra" might be juicy.

Secret sexual intrigue never failed to get tongues flapping, and led to many casual visits to the desk of the reporter covering the story. Political speculation wasn't far behind. If a Rag story didn't quite say that someone was running for president, maybe the reporter would confirm it in a quickie one-on-one chat. As for high-octane exclusives–a tell-all about a movie star, or a groundbreaker about the chances of war in Eastern Europe—the path to a reporter's desk was well-worn, as long as the reporter was seen as a Cassidy favorite and as long as his stories got consistently excellent play.

But this was a different Larry Felder on this Monday morning. Eight months earlier, he would have been open to chats, yarns, gripes, bad jokes, and he would have expected all four. After the premature death of his campaign, however, he felt like damaged goods—as if Cassidy had extended him a life raft that he didn't quite deserve.

He had cashed in his "one of the Rag-a-muffins" status when he had decided to run for Congress. Now he would be pounding a keyboard again. But would he be welcomed back? Accepted? Respected? If Felder had been a betting man, he would have wagered "No" to all three questions.

Vic Printz was the first person he encountered, in the main lobby. The elevator ride to the sixth floor took 15 seconds. Printz made full use of the time.

"Never would have suspected it, Larry," he said, gravely. "Not from you. Not from such a total altar boy. But welcome back." Felder stared at the red emergency button on the control panel and said nothing.

Lindsay Baron was waiting in the elevator lobby when the doors opened. "I hope you'll forgive me, Larry," said the longtime Felder assistant, "but I asked the security guard to call me and alert me when you were coming up." She wrapped him in a serious hug, pushing her breasts against the glasses and pens in his shirt pocket.

"I cannot TELL you how happy I am to have you back," she added. With Linz, you never knew if she was angling for romance or merely displaying enthusiasm. But she and Larry had agreed long before not to turn their relationship into something steamy.

"Thanks, Linz," Felder said. "Thanks so much."

"Wouldn't be looking for an assistant, would you?"

"Too soon to say, Linz," said Felder, "Let me float that one past Cal. I'd be delighted if it worked out." They exchanged a fist bump. Linz had taught him how to execute these only a year earlier. A sure sign of how young she was, and how young Larry Felder wasn't.

Felder ambled into the newsroom, onto the showroom floor. It had been subdivided, prettied up and labeled about a decade earlier. Baby blue signs hung from the ceiling—METRO here, FINANCIAL there. But there was no concealing the essential disorganization. Corridors were often blocked by yellowing heaps of newspaper. Coats that would have been hung in closets at law firms had been slung wildly across file cabinets here. Even loose change was left in open sight—pennies and nickels tossed into saucers, forgotten leftovers from that last late-night cup of coffee that had gotten a reporter past one more crushing deadline.

Millie was on the phone. With an index finger, she gestured to him to wait. Behind her, Cal's office was dark. He was a notorious late-arriver. Rag wags speculated that he had a ravenous mistress, or at least a secret drug habit.

The truth was more typical of a 60-year-old man. His prostate gland had developed a mind of its own, and he was up at least three times each night to empty his bladder. That blew his sleep patterns to smithereens. He regularly arrived at 10 because he had regularly been wide awake at 4.

"Thank you, sir. Thank you very much," Millie was saying, as she rolled her eyes. What a diplomat! She heard every day from irritated subscribers, irate sources and imploring PR people. And yet her eyes still danced with life.

Down went the receiver. Out went her arms.

"Larry, babe-u-lah, I missed you!," she screeched. And here came Felder's second hug in less than a minute, complete with more pushed breasts, more squished glasses and pens.

"I missed you, too, Millie. More than I can say."

"So say it already! This girl can always use a little praise. Especially with that old creep as her boss." She yanked a thumb toward the dark office.

"You deserve combat pay, Millie," said Felder. "Without you, this place would have gone down the tubes long ago."

"Tell it to HIM!," she bellowed. "Tell the son of a bitch that I need a raise!" Felder promised that he'd do that.

"Hey, Millie," said Felder, grinding the gears and trying to shift them, "did Cal assign me a place to sit?"

"He did, Larry. You may not believe it, but he put you right next to Aggie. Right out there, in the middle of the politics pod." She pointed to her right, into the center of the vast room.

"Cal never loses his sense of humor, does he?"

"Son of a bitch never had a sense of humor to lose, Lar."

"OK, let me get moved in. Good to see you, Millie. Good to be back."

"I was so worried, Larry!"

"No need. I'm almost completely healed. And I promise that I won't be taking any late-night walks again any time soon."

She blew him a kiss. He blew one back. He made his way to the politics pod. Stern was at her desk, speaking with great animation and intensity into her phone about the Eighth District. She was dressed as if for a job interview. Felder guessed that she had been booked for mid-morning cut-ins on the local TV news channels.

She asked whoever she was interviewing to please hold on.

"Aggie." A nod from Felder.

"Larry." A return nod from Stern.

"Good to see you."

"Thank you. Good to see you, too."

Nobody was budging an inch.

"Aggie, is this the right move?," asked Felder. "To have me right next to you out here? Somebody who doesn't like The Rag is going to hear about it and get the wrong idea. Might look as if your story and my return were all cooked up long ahead of time."

"That kind of thing is way above my pay grade, Larry. Better ask Cal. He's the one who put you here. It's all the same to me." She resumed her phone call. Obviously, she was interviewing someone—a Republican, perhaps?—who wasn't cooperating with her follow piece about the campaign in the Eighth.

At that moment, the king arrived, and surveyed his court.

"Is everybody HAPPY?" bellowed Cal Cassidy. "Are all the children playing together nicely in the sandbox?"

Felder shook Cassidy's hand. Cassidy cuffed him affectionately in the right bicep.

"I didn't think it would look right to give you a private office right away," offered Cassidy. "So you're back out here, in the pigpen."

"I can work anywhere," said Felder.

"You and Stern going to kiss and make up?"

"We were never feuding, Cal."

"Not what she says."

"Not my problem, Cal."

He nodded and interrupted Stern's phone call without apology.

"Aggie, you and this dude had better get over it. Now," he ordered.

"Sure thing, Cal," said Stern. She shot daggers at Felder. He held her gaze blandly.

"I'm not going to have some kind of pissing match out here among all the pigs," Cal Cassidy said, sharply. "You can both piss in private."

"I usually do, Cal," said Aggie.

"Same here," said Felder.

Cassidy rumbled away. Stern whirled in her chair, pointedly turned her back to Felder and began to study some notes. Felder sat down at his new desk and began to organize his pencils and his paper clips. Not for the first time, not for the last, he was glad to be back and sorry to be back, in approximately equal proportions.

★ ★ ★

A bike ride when the thermometer reads 61 always clears the pores and the nostrils. Charlie was hoping that this one would also clear the soul.

She and Patsy Finkel had just spent an hour on the phone, going over the twinned pieces in The Rag line by line. Then Charlie called her old pal, Amanda Prosser, in Arizona. They went at it for another hour.

Both friends had been cooingly empathetic and repeatedly encouraging. You have nothing to be ashamed of, Charlie. . . . The problem was caused by Larry, not Charlie. . . . If he was careless with campaign donations, he deserves what happened to him. . . . He'll slip right back into his status at The Rag, and he probably never should have left. . . .

But all of that was beside the point, as all three women well knew.

If Charlie had remained as Felder's campaign chief—if she had never let her feelings get in front of her duties—she would be on her way to a major career boost right about now. And didn't daily closeness at work often lead to nightly closeness in someone's bedroom? Charlie wanted reassurance that she hadn't stupidly committed romantic and professional suicide.

Neither of her friends was quite ready to let her slip off the hook.

"Of course you complicated things tremendously when you spoke to that reporter," said Amanda. "But these things with guys take flight if they're meant to take flight, and they don't if they aren't. What you need, Charlie, is a quick fling with someone whose abs are very strong and who gives great hugs. That will restore your sense of feminine worth."

"The book just closed," said Patsy. "Larry Felder is no longer available, if he ever was. I cannot let you beat yourself up over this, Charlie, or let you keep on mooning over him like a 15-year-old. Do you want me to introduce you to some of the younger associates here at the firm? Some of them are actually pretty promising."

Now Charlie was pushing herself and her scarlet British 20-speed along the Capital Crescent Trail, a reclaimed rail line that pierced the woods of Northwest Washington. Her mother had Fed Ex'd her a hope-you'll-feel-better chocolate cake. That, plus chamomile tea and the two Felder stories on the front of The Rag, had been breakfast. Monday morning traffic on the trail was light, and super-dedicated. Only joggers who weighed 140 pounds and bikers who seemed to be Olympians were out and about.

The hill north of Arizona Avenue was especially nasty—four miles of a ten-percent grade. But Charlie was handling it—huffing-huffing-huffing while her mind kept pounding-pounding-pounding.

Should I call him? . . . . Would he talk to me? . . . Should I just leave it all alone for three months and try again then? . . . Will he ever forgive me? . . . . Maybe I should arrange an accidental 'bump' that isn't really an accident. . . . Yes, I'd be stalking him. . . . But I'm not the first woman whose man needs a little persuading. . . .

Up the long asphalt path she pedaled. Wrens cooed. Hedges rustled in the light southerly breeze. She imagined a possible resolution.

If I tell him that it isn't about sex, but just about closeness and click. . . . If I tell him that we can go clean slate, fresh start, no recriminations from either of us. . . . If I promise to stay completely out of his new life at The Rag. . . . If I make sure never to encourage him to try again in 2008. . . . If I accept his marriage and his desire to stay married . . . Doesn't all this give me a fighting chance?

Only if Felder agreed to see her and talk to her. Which he very directly and unmistakably had said he'd never do again.

As she pedaled past the discreet brown wooden sign announcing that she was leaving the District of Columbia and entering Montgomery County, Maryland, Charlie began to face the unmistakable music. Wasn't going to happen. She had no shot.

CHAPTER

LORRAINE BARTLESBY SURGED
to an impressive victory in the Eighth District Democratic primary. She captured 68 percent of the vote. Her five competitors split the rest. It was one of the largest margins of victory in the state's history.

For her victory party, Bartlesby decided to go small. She had attracted a few heat-seeking missiles during the last days of the campaign from various political web sites—Lorraine spends money like water, Lorraine will spend whatever it takes to win, Lorraine doesn't understand how it looks to be so rich when so many of her constituents are so poor. So, to celebrate her smashing win, she booked into a rather ordinary public library lobby in the rather ordinary town of Silver Spring. A minority-owned catering firm supplied the (rather meager) food. Another minority-owned firm provided the (rather lackluster) drinks--beer, wine and soda only.

Bo Bartlesby, age 16, and his sister Amanda, age 17, were right beside their mother as confetti flew, videotape rolled and cameras clicked. Chuck Bartlesby was right behind the three of them.

He smiled hugely, and kept waving to greats and near-greats among the assembled dozens. He hadn't planned to show up. Why should he? He had been sidetracked, dumped, discarded. But Lorraine had implored him to do it, "for the sake of the kids and for my sake, too, Chuck." Reassuring himself that no one could tell how frayed the Bartlesby marriage was as long as he kept smiling, Chuck was playing the part of Proud Spouse very nicely.

Lorraine's speech was clipped and brief. "This is only the beginning," she said, as a high school band kept attempting—and mangling—"Happy Days Are Here Again." "I am proud to have the backing of so many of my friends and neighbors. Let's roll on to victory in November!"

Larry Felder had called her about an hour earlier, once the results were firm. "I'm delighted for you, Lorraine. You'll have this seat for as long as you want it."

"Thank you, Larry," she had replied. "Thank you very much." Icicles were hanging from her voice. Felder couldn't help but notice.

Aggie Stern had booked a solo interview with Bartlesby for the next day. Stern had been very explicit about the kind of piece she was planning to write. "I want to get at a Lorraine Bartlesby that the public doesn't know," Stern had said, to Lorraine's press chief. "I want to peel the Bartlesby onion." Stern did not say she was writing her piece for The Rag's much-loved (but also much-feared) Lifestyles section. But that implication was obvious.

As the library began to thin out, and the Bartlesby kids disappeared in Amanda's new Toyota Rav 4 (a gift from their father—the market was doing a lot better lately), Lorraine finished up her TV interviews and had a brief sit-down with a correspondent from Der Spiegel. She was marching toward the parking lot, and her own Chrysler, when Chuck caught up to her.

"Lo, can we talk?"

"Not here." Her pace picked up steam.

"When, then? And where?"

"Not soon, Chuck. And probably not anywhere."

"Lorraine, this isn't fair. You're treating me like some worn-out shoe. I'm a big part of your life, Lorraine."

She drew him into an alcove, where there were 300 children's books and a small helping of privacy.

"Chuck, listen to me. We are done. I am done. This is irrevocable."

"Please give me another chance."

"To do what? To prove that you're more interested in golfing with your pals than you are in me and the kids?"

"That really isn't fair, Lorraine."

"But it's accurate, Chuck."

She made briskly for the back door. Chuck began to fall behind. He lengthened his stride so he could continue to plead while right beside her.

"Lo, you never even thanked me for the leak I gave Aggie Stern. I made this evening of yours happen, Lo! Don't I get some credit for that?"

"None, Chuck. Obviously, Stern had most of the story already. You just gave her the final button to push. Don't exaggerate, Chuck. God, I hate it when you do that!"

They were beside Lorraine's Chrysler now. With a clicker, she opened the door. Chuck stepped between her and the handle.

"Lorraine, let me ask you a question. What would it take for you to have me back?"

Lorraine wormed around him, opened the door and slid behind the wheel.

"It would take a miracle, Chuck. A freakin' miracle." She started the car, stepped on the gas a little too hard and roared out onto Georgia Avenue.

★ ★ ★

Larry Felder decided to go AWOL from The Rag on primary night. He didn't think his presence could help. He checked this decision in advance with Lindsay. She gave it a thumbs-up and him a fist bump.

Felder had worked election nights since he was a pup. They were always somewhat the same, yet always temperature-raising.

Not only was this the perfect night to see democracy at work, right there in the political Petri dish, but the challenge for newsies was both obvious and stirring. There would be more readers of your work the next morning than usual, maybe more than ever. So get it right. Do it extra-fast (because deadlines were usually moved up). Make extra-sure you didn't tilt toward or away from any candidate. Treat it like the seventh game of the World Series: Tell who won, who lost and why. Put your best foot forward.

Day's work done, it was time for Felder to vanish. As he loaded up his briefcase and slipped on his sports jacket a little after 5 p.m., Aggie Stern was just arriving for work.

She had been unremittingly hostile to Felder throughout the nearly two weeks that they had been deskmates. Why? Was she jealous of Felder? Disdainful of him? And why couldn't he find a way to bury that particular hatchet? He had never borne grudges or incubated jealousies. Aggie Stern hadn't dashed his congressional hopes. His own carelessness had. That and the stealth piece of leak-ball played by one Charlise Carpentier. He and Aggie had never had any history before he left the paper, either good or bad. Why the freeze-ball now?

He decided to ask her.

"I have no beef with you, Larry," she replied, evenly, as she unpacked her briefcase, put down her plastic carryout cup of Frappuccino and began firing up her laptop. "I'm not looking to acquire one, either. I just want to go my way, and let you go yours."

"Aggie, I'm not going to get in the way of your career. I never have. Let's be civil to one another, OK?"

"Sure, Larry," she said. "Sure. OK."

But she turned away abruptly and began to strap herself into the general notes computer drive, so she could prepare to write the national lead-all for Senate races. Obviously, Larry's attempted thaw job would need more time.

"I can't imagine why," replied Lindsay, when he sought her out to ask her take on the situation. "I happen to think she's a very major ego case, and not nearly as talented as she thinks she is. But that doesn't speak to your question, does it?"

Vic Printz wasn't much more help.

"Larry," he said, his portentousness growing as if he were about to address Parliament, "Aggie Stern was tremendously wounded when Cal held her scoop for so long. She will always believe that you big-footed her with Cal, based on your long history with him. You can tell her that never happened till you're blue in the face. You can tell her that she's an early favorite for a Pulitzer. You can tell her whatever you want. But the woman is going to believe what she's going to believe."

Cal didn't choose to play, either.

"Felder," he said, as he slammed a fistful of papers onto the disaster that was his desktop, "I have a half-billion dollar budget that I have to prepare for that nincompoop upstairs, I have two reporters who are in love with each other's spouses, I have two editors who are threatening to sue me for age discrimination, I was up peeing at least four times last night, and you want to bother me with THIS? Are you an infant? Go work it out with her before I kick your ass."

He tried.

"Aggie, Cal has asked me to try to make our relationship better. Will you join me in that effort?" A bit pompous, a bit Printz-ly, but there it was.

Stern had the look of a woman who wanted to say one thing, but decided to say another. She considered. She started to blurt something. But then she said:

"I'll write you an e-mail."

She did, between editions, that night. Larry read it when he arrived the next morning. It was a corker.

"LARRY: I am ticked at you not because of anything having to do with my career, my story or your campaign. I am ticked at you because of your treatment of Charlise Carpentier.

"After she told me about the campaign finance records, she told me all about the hot mess that's Larry and Charlie. We bonded in a way that men simply can't understand. We talked for hours. She cried for most of that time.

"Here was a woman who was totally open with you, and totally available to you. And you treated her like dirt. You barely listened to her. You wouldn't give her an even break. And you wouldn't be honest with her—or with yourself-- about why you were saying no dice.

"Larry, this is 2006. A man with a wife on life support for 14 years doesn't say no to a talented, dedicated, pretty young woman. It wouldn't be a slur on your wife. It wouldn't reveal some drastic character flaw in you. It would just be natural. It might even be kind of fun. Sex between consenting adults is UNDERSTOOD these days, Larry.

"Charlie has not given up on the possibility of a relationship with you, and I don't think she ever will. She sees in you what so many people do—Larry Felder the rock, Larry Felder the real man when so many other males are just overgrown kids.

"I know you were never under any court order to give her the time of day. All's fair in love and war. I understand that.

"But I've been kicked around by so many men in my time that I couldn't help but identify with the tortures that Charlie is going through. If I've been cold to you, that's why.

"AGGIE."

Felder read the e-mail three times. He told the message center that he'd be back in 15 minutes. He had some errands to run.

But he didn't have any. He wanted to take a walk and let his brain comb what he had just learned. The last time he took a walk, his life had turned on its head. This time, maybe it ought to do so again, in a different way.

Out onto 11th Street and north toward Massachusetts:

No, I can't call her. . . . She'd misunderstand, think she was back in the hunt . . . . I'm nowhere near ready to lead her on like that. . . . And really, why should I even care about whether she cried to Aggie? . . . This woman just mashed your future, Larry! . . . She thought more about herself than she did about you. . . . That's not much of an endorsement of her character, is it? . . .

Yet Felder had been wrestling for days with the notion that this epic change in his career should perhaps lead to others. He didn't believe in signs from above. Each decision was distinct from all others, and needed to be. To believe otherwise was to believe in mystical mush.

But everything in his life had been outward-facing for so long--his journalism, his campaign, his speeches. Where and what was the Inner Larry? Did he owe himself a respite from the grind, a few gumdrops of pleasure and frivolity? Could he even enjoy them if they were right in front of him? Had he become such an accomplishment machine that that was all there was?

He let the idea tickle him—Charlie in his bed, Charlie declaring her adoration, Charlie pulling him (probably with difficulty) into the worlds of biking and hiking and light-heartedness. But he quickly refiled the notion in his out box. Larry the Boy Scout just could not do this. No, no, no. Wrong, wrong, wrong. If Kat were dead, no problem. But Kat was his North Star.

Left on Massachusetts and west toward Scott Circle:

I can't really trust her, can I? . . . The damn woman already ran a sword right through me, and I'm seriously thinking of giving her another chance? . . . And then she went and blabbed to Aggie. . . . Not good. . . . Besides, I'm more than 20 years older. . . . I'll never marry her and have children with her. . . . She might tell me she doesn't want children, but the woods are thick with women who tell that to older men, and then turn up with fat bellies all of a sudden. . . . And yet, when you come to a fork in the road in life, Larry, you can't go straight ahead. . . .

Larry did a rewind on life at The Rag since he had returned. It wasn't anywhere near the same as it had been.

He was being tolerated, but not embraced. His stories had gotten good position, and no editor had tried to nickel him about writing long. But those were just the fumes of his reputation at work. If the excitement of journalistic discovery was going or gone, if he was no longer propelled by the motor that had made him pick up the phone and place one more call for more than 30 years, maybe he should be gone, too.

But not soon. Not yet. He had always been patient, and he would be again. Early in their dating lives, Kat had once suggested eloping. He had looked at her as if she had ingested loco weed. Larry Felder was never, never impulsive.

Left on 16th Street, and south, directly at the White House:

If I'm going to get involved with a woman who isn't Kat, why Charlie? . . . Mouse once told me that, with my reputation, I could have any woman I wanted . . . . Shouldn't I investigate how true that is? . . . That's what Larry Felder would do with a news tip. . . . Same with women, I'd think. . . . And yet, Charlie was always so easy to be around. . . . So alert, so smart, so efficient. . . . Could that be the basis of a relationship? . . . Then again, what if we hopped into bed and discovered that we were Pluto and Jupiter? . . .

He dodged a bus and crossed into Lafayette Square. The White House was right in front of him. Summer tourists by the dozen were snapping photos. The yellow tulips on the north lawn were in full flower.

You know, I don't care if I ever could have gotten to live here. . . . I doubt I ever had a serious shot, anyway. . . . The first Jewish president won't be some mopey guy with a cracked-open skull. . . . He'll be a visionary and a great stump speaker. . . . I'm neither. . . . So what am I, then? . . . A guy with tons of sources and lots of experience at a newspaper. . . . But could I do more? . . . Could I do it elsewhere? . . . Could I really live life differently at my advanced age?

A week later, he pushed a sealed note under Charlie's Dupont Circle apartment door. It read:

"Let's talk. Larry."

★ ★ ★

Kal Radin seemed to have dodged the first burst of anti-aircraft fire. Aggie Stern's story in The Rag did not name him, or his company. Nor did it name his lieutenants, or hint at who they were. He didn't care if Felder returned the donations. He cared about whether he was in the legal soup, even if he had not been out-ed in the newspaper.

Like his investment adviser, his personal lawyer was a boyhood friend. Carl Matthews had played left field when Kal had played third base for the Bethesda Boomerangs of the Little League. That meant that Matthews regularly retrieved ground balls that had gone through Radin's legs.

Radin had called on Matthews for many reasons across many years—on behalf of employees who had been busted while driving drunk, on behalf of the children of employees who had been caught dealing drugs. But this latest one had Radin himself squarely in the crosshairs.

Matthews' office was in a snazzy new office building right beside a snazzy new Turkish restaurant in downtown Bethesda. There had been nothing snazzy about Bethesda in the old days. It had been a collection of forlorn branch banks, ratty diners and the occasional hardware store. Now French cafes offered valet parking along with escargots, and people came all the way from downtown to sample Middle Eastern fusion fare.

"Let me tell you a good joke, Kal," said Matthews, as he welcomed his old friend into his private office.

"I could use a good joke," Radin said.

"Question: What happens any time a regime falls anywhere in the world? Answer: A new ethnic restaurant opens in Bethesda."

Matthews whooped at his own joke. Radin smiled knowingly.

"Well, it isn't the same Bethesda, Carl. And it isn't the same Kal Radin. Let's get going, OK?"

Matthews was already poised over his yellow legal pad, his ball point uncapped. Radin began at the beginning. AaaaaaH needed help with import duties. Larry Felder was obviously en route to victory. What harm could there be in making a campaign gift, with the implicit assumption that AaaaaaH would get something later in return?

"Well, now you know the answer to that question, Kal," said Matthews.

Radin resumed. "I decided that if one check was good, nine more would be better. I didn't check the campaign finance laws, and I still haven't. But the story in The Rag was pretty damning, wasn't it? Made me out to be some kind of Bonnie and Clyde."

Matthews leaped in to correct the record. "You haven't been accused of anything, and you haven't been named. Nor have you had any contact with Felder since the day you sent him those checks, right? So it's possible that sleeping dogs are still sleeping," Matthews said.

"And if they're awake?"

"I am not all that worried, Kal. You have never given to a candidate before, right?" Radin nodded. "So you are not some habitual influence-peddler or influence-seeker. You're a businessman who made a legal gift and wanted a favor in return. That's totally red, white and blue."

Radin arose and began pacing nervously. "Yeah, Carl," he said, "but I wouldn't be sitting here if I were the Virgin Mary. I did something shady. You know it and I know it. The question is what to do next."

"I recommend two things," Matthews said. "One, let me do some discreet investigating to find out if Felder has spent the money you gave him. If he has, we'll just let sleeping dogs stay asleep. If he hasn't, we face different and bigger problems. If Felder tries to return that money to you—and he said in The Rag that he would—then you are going to be identifiable, which you aren't at the moment. If and when that happens, I'd recommend that you let me begin plea bargaining with the U.S. Attorney. They always look favorably on people who approach them early, rather than waiting for the FBI to kick down their doors."

"What about the guys who work for me?"

"Was the money they gave theirs or yours?"

"Mine."

"That makes it a serious offense, but I'd give you the same answer. If your name leaks as the donor, their names and place of employment will leak in another two seconds. Then it's back to the U.S. Attorney. I'd tell him that you were a first-time donor, that you didn't exceed the legal donation limit, that none of your employees did either, that you fronted the money because you weren't sure it was fair to ask your senior staff to make donations to a candidate they might not favor. I'll paint you as naïve, but not actively criminal. That happens to be the truth, Kal, by the way."

"And how do we handle the damage to AaaaaaH's reputation?"

"By casting this as a piece of personal political aggressiveness on the part of Kal Radin, but not as a new corporate strategy. Hell, man, people love your drinks. They aren't going to stop loving your drinks because the CEO made a rookie mistake."

Radin shook his old pal's hand. "Still using baseball metaphors, I see," he said.

"The game's never over until the final out," said Matthews.

"Thanks for the reassurance and the help," said Radin. He waved to Matthews' secretary on his way out. As he veered onto the express lanes of Interstate 270, he felt better than he had in days.

★ ★ ★

"Thank you for the cake, Mama."

"Oh, Charlise, it was my pleasure! I made it with new cocoa icing this time. Did you like it?"

"I loved it, Mama. Thank you."

"You're very welcome. I hope you shared it with your friends."

"I didn't, Mama. I haven't been going out with friends much lately. I ate the whole thing."

"Not all at once, I hope!"

"Well, pretty close. It took me three sittings. But don't worry, Mama. I've been biking a lot, so I've been burning off lots of calories."

"Charlise (coughing slightly), may I change the subject?"

"Of course."

"Are you really all right? I mean, your name has been in the newspapers and all over TV and all. Your Daddy always said that a lady should only be in the newspapers twice—when she marries and when she dies."

"Well, I haven't done either of those yet, Mama."

"Yes, I know. But I can't help but worry. Here I am, all by myself up here in Pennsylvania, and your name is all over the television, and I can't HELP you."

"You don't need to help me, Mama. I'm doing fine. I just need to let all the storm clouds blow over."

"Charlise, if that doesn't happen, and if you find yourself really, really sad, please let me know. I'd be happy to pay for a psychiatrist."

"Mama, no psychiatrist can fix what's wrong with me."

"Don't be so sure. When Martha's son was going through all that trouble...."

"Mama, Martha's son was caught in a smuggling case. All I did was talk to a newspaper reporter."

"But you said it made you so SAD."

"When I told her about my feelings for Larry, that did make me sad. But those feelings always make me sad."

"Charlise, my offer stands. And by the way, I hope you aren't drinking the way you were the last time you visited."

"Mother! I'm a grown-up!"

"Sometimes, Charlise, I wonder about that. I love you. Good night."

CHAPTER

CHUCK BARTLESBY DIDN'T quite know how to introduce himself to strangers these days. Was he the trailing spouse of an about-to-be member of Congress? Was he the former spouse? Was he the sort-of spouse? Was he the on-the-way-back-into-her-good-graces spouse?

So Chuck took the path of least resistance. He shook hands with one and all and said, "Hi, I'm Chuck Bartlesby. My wife, Lorraine, is the Democratic candidate for Congress." That formulation seemed to dodge every possible misunderstanding.

But Lorraine had vehemently slammed the door on a possible reconciliation. Chuck had no way to veto or overturn that decision. What he did have was a regular get-together of barflies. They gathered on weekday evenings at the Burning Tree Country Club.

Whiskey flowed freely. So did confessions. So did accusations.

On the Tuesday after the Democratic primary, the Burning Tree Bar Boys were camped around a rough-hewn oak table, right under a wide-screen television. They were each nursing scotches. They were also nursing wounds.

The biggest beefs had to do with the stock market. It had dipped again in the last week—sharply. Although the men around the table were all business-people and financiers, and should have been above panicking over one week's bad results, they were biting their nails—and biting off Chuck Bartlesby's head.

"Dammit, Chuck, you told me to get into techs, and I did, and I lost my shirt," said Carter Porter, he of the J. Press pinstripe suit and the yellow plaid pocket square.

"And you told me to load up on airline stocks, just before all those bastards in the Middle East began charging triple for oil," groused Bill Martinson, he of the blue Brooks Brothers blazer and the horn-rimmed glasses.

"And what a bath I've taken on bank stocks," said Frank Fosworth, whose family real estate firm had built most of Chevy Chase and much of Rockville. "You told me that consolidation was done. But it was only just beginning."

The three men, Bartlesby brokerage clients all, leaned forward for an explanation. Bartlesby had offered many of them in the recent past. He reminded the men that they were dealing here with incremental dips, not fatal ones. "None of you guys is about to miss any meals," he noted.

But they weren't satisfied, and they weren't happy. Another round was ordered. The grumping now extended to politics.

Other than Chuck, the men around the table were all virulent, lifelong Republicans. They didn't understand how a guy with such impeccable breeding like Bartlesby could go to bed every night with—they held their noses when they said it—a card-carrying liberal.

Chuck was almost through his second scotch, so the wraps could come off. He told the guys that as a matter of fact, he and Lorraine were on the outs. The serious outs.

"My God, you poor man," said Fosworth. "And here we've been complaining about our brokerage results. You're about to get socked for alimony the size of Wyoming."

Not necessarily, Chuck reassured the gang. I'm hoping to get back with her. I'm hoping that we can reconcile. I'm hoping that my wife will fall in love with me all over again.

Porter was always very direct. "Somebody else?" he demanded.

No, I don't believe so, Chuck said. It's just the accumulation of many years, many slights, many sins.

"But didn't you deliver the primary to her on a platter by going to The Rag?," Martinson wanted to know.

Lorraine won't come back to me because I helped her win the primary campaign, he told Bill. She will come back to me because she believes in me all over again.

"Maybe I can get Marlene to help," Martinson said. He and Chuck locked eyes. They both knew exactly what he had in mind. Marlene Martinson and Lorraine had been girlhood chums. What this needed, maybe, was a girl-to-girl intervention.

"I'm on it," Martinson said. "Tonight. Least I can do for a guy who cost me half a million dollars this week alone." In honor of that bon mot, the group ordered a third round.

If his tongue had been loosened before, it was now four-sheets-to-the-wind loose. Chuck was now capable of saying just about anything. He took a deep draw on Dewar's Number Three and revealed to the guys that he had gotten the best of Aggie Stern and The Rag. As the price for corroborating her story about Felder's financial activities, he had demanded that she paint Lorraine favorably in her Lifestyles feature of two days ago.

Indeed, Stern had nearly canonized Lorraine Bartlesby. She found Lorraine to be an "inspiring speaker" with a "focused outlook" and an "unlimited political future." She never mentioned the fact that the candidate had a tornado of a temper, that she regularly chewed up and spit out staff, that she was pretty much absent as a mother and that she had used her family foundation connections to arrange get-out-the-vote phone trees.

The result was what newsies call a "puff job." Puff as in creampuff. Whispers had been the order of the day around The Rag when Stern's piece appeared. Was she hoping to go to work for Bartlesby? Had she left her talons at home by mistake? Was she so annoyed by Larry Felder that she had over-boosted Bartlesby?

"Chuck," said Porter, whose drawl always became thicker as his third scotch went down, "you mean to tell me that The Rag made some unsavory trade—your information about Felder in exchange for favorable publicity about Lorraine?"

"That's uh-zactly what I mean to tell you, Carter," said Chuck, whose third scotch was already down the hatch, and would soon be joined by a fourth.

The men parted about 20 minutes later amid plans to play nine holes together that Saturday. The baseball game on the wide-screen TV had ended long before. The bar was thinning out. Thanks to that thinning, a man at an adjoining table named Hunter Holleran had heard every word the four pals had said.

Holleran and Cal Cassidy had been fraternity brothers at Dartmouth four decades earlier. They had never been close, either then or since. But Holleran, who ran a huge department at the Department of Education, knew a bombshell when he heard it. We executives have to stick together, no?

From the lobby, he called Cassidy from a pay phone (yes, the venerable club still had one). He asked Cassidy to call him back as soon as he could. Very important.

★ ★ ★

Charlie offered tea because that was all she could think to offer at first. She quickly filed an addendum.

"Uh, you wouldn't want some rum, would you?," she asked. Felder said tea would be just fine.

She had been sitting lotus-style in the middle of the living room before he arrived, in jeans, and now she reassumed that position. Felder sat on the skimpy couch. He wore brown slacks and a short-sleeved brown dress shirt, his usual deeply geeky uniform. Awkwardness hung in the air.

"So, you wanted to talk?," she said.

"Yes. Yes, I do, Charlie. But let's set some ground rules first. No recriminations. No rehashing the past. That won't get either of us anywhere. I want to talk about the future."

Charlie got up to pour his tea—into a clay cup that she had bought the previous summer at a roadside crafts fair in West Virginia, for a buck-fifty.

"Yes, Larry, that's fine," she said. "I'm all about the future."

Felder had obviously planned his peroration carefully. He began with conditions.

"Charlie, I'm here because I want to be here. I'm here of my own free will. But I do not want you to make any assumptions about my motives or my feelings beyond what I'm about to tell you, OK?"

She said OK.

"I'm here because I want to discuss a possible future together. But I want to be crystal clear, Charlie. It would be a limited future. I'm not going to cash out my career. I'm not at all interested in marriage. I have zero wish to be a father again. I'm not offering to merge our bank accounts. I'm here simply because I've been a little lonely lately, Charlie. A little lonely and a lot alone."

"I can well understand, Larry, what with everything you've been through." Was she hearing this correctly?... Was he crossing the Rubicon?...

Felder got up and began to pace—toward the bay windows, then back, toward the windows, then back. The late spring evening was turning a little cool. Charlie excused herself to fetch a cardigan sweater. She slipped it on and returned to the middle of the floor.

"Cold?"

"Not really, Larry. Just eager to hear the rest of what you have to say. Maybe that eagerness is making me chilly." I'm tingling. . . . Stop tingling, Charlie, you silly fool. . . . But I can't help it . . .

"Well, OK, please hear me out," Felder said. "I'm proposing a period of experimentation, Charlie. I heard you loud and clear a few weeks ago when you said that you wanted a relationship with me. What I'm saying is that I think we can tiptoe into that. Tiptoe, got that?"

She nodded. Oh, my God! . . . Oh, my God! . . .

"I am not offering to move in with you. I am not offering you my heart. I am offering to begin a sexual relationship with you. It may go somewhere. It may go nowhere. But we'll never know until we try, right?"

Charlie wanted to choose her words carefully. Patsy and Amanda flashed through her mind. They would urge caution at this pivotal moment, mixed with boldness—and they wouldn't worry about the contradiction. Don't go too fast, Charlie. . . . Don't lunge at him. . . . He's more scared than you are. . . . Let him set the pace. . . . Reel him in. . . .

She played for time by rising and pouring herself a Captain Morgan. Three fingers over three cubes. Than she sat next to him on the couch and put her right hand on his left forearm.

"Larry, you're not offering me what every girl dreams about—a house in the suburbs, over-average kids and languid summers in Maine. I understand that. I understand your fears. I really, really do. It's amazing that you have any positive energy left in you at all after what those two kids did to you."

Felder nodded. He placed one of his hands on hers and kept it there—a heap of hands on his hairy forearm.

"But Larry, I am not your typical girl. I am not looking for all or nothing. I am not demanding that you divorce Kat, or that you spend every waking second with me. I'm not exactly saying that I'll take what I can get, Larry. But you know what? I'll take what I can get."

He removed his hand from atop the pile and began to knead his forehead with it.

"There are many, many worries here, Charlie," he said. "I could be legally vulnerable if you handle this in the wrong way. You could ruin my reputation, even more than you have already ruined it. We might be incompatible. We might fight. You might run. I might run."

She shooshed him by placing two fingers across his mouth.

"Larry," she said, "I've been a risk-taker all my life. You're a risk worth taking." Oh, my God! . . . Oh, my God!

He kneaded across his eyebrows and down onto his cheeks. "Charlie, I never like to credit people who say that everything happens for a reason. You know, this forced cheerfulness that you hear? A piano falls out of a third-floor window and kills an entire family, and the parish priest says, 'Oh, well, everything happens for a reason.'"

Charlie nodded. Was this damned guy about to talk himself out of getting going with me? . . .

"But, Charlie, I'm feeling adrift and uncertain. I've never really felt that way before, not even 14 years ago, when Kat had the baby, and the bottom fell out of my life. This time, I'm feeling some force outside my control. It's saying to me that now that I've made a huge about-face in my career, I should make others. That maybe, at 55, I should toss the whole damn show up in the air and reinvent myself."

Charlie smiled at him, to encourage him to continue. He is so cautious and so rigorous. . . . He is walking all around the car and kicking all the tires before he buys it. . . .

"So that brings me here tonight. That brings me here to humble myself a little. That sense of the moment, that this is the time to unplug and replug, says to me that maybe, despite all your disloyalty to me, that maybe everything happens for a reason. And maybe it's time for us to happen, for a reason."

"What would that reason be, Larry?"

"I already mostly told you. I want to chart a new course. I want to have a partner who can take my intensity and my caring and handle it—like it, even. I have all this energy, Charlie, and all I've ever done is devote it to a computer keyboard or a political campaign. What if I devoted some of it to a young woman who obviously thinks the world of me?"

Charlie got up, smoothed her jeans, cinched the sash on her sweater and took a deeper-than-she-should-have sip of Captain.

"Larry," she said, "this isn't the most romantic proposal I've ever gotten. You're saying to me: Charlie will settle for ten percent of Felder and like it, dammit! I mean, have you brought an affidavit for me to sign?"

Felder chuckled. "I know I sound like some anxious, two-bit teenager, Charlie. But anxious describes me very well."

She sat beside him and pulled his chin toward her. They kissed, but not epically. For maybe a second and a half.

"Charlie," said Larry Felder. "I'm very out of practice."

"I haven't exactly been dating up a storm myself," said Charlie.

She reached for his belt. He reached for hers.

★ ★ ★

"Aggie," said Cassidy, "we've got a little problem here." The old man got up and started pacing.

"No, Aggie," he self-corrected. "We've got a big problem here."

Millie had not told Aggie why Cal wanted to see her. But she made it very clear that right now meant right now. "He's pissed, girl," Millie warned.

Aggie assumed that it had to do with her tiffs with Felder. She blew through the ladies' room for a check of her clothes and hair. With a nod to Millie, she was past the secretary's desk and into Cal's inner sanctum in less than a minute.

"What's the big problem, Cal?"

"You're the big problem, Aggie."

She twitched uncomfortably. Could this be about a story she had written? No one on the desk had raised any red flags. Usually, when a storm cloud forms over a news story, it forms early. There had been no such atmospherics over her Bartlesby pieces.

Cal was warming up.

"Aggie, you've had a nice run here over, what is it, eight years or so?" You could cut his sanctimoniousness with a knife.

"Eight and a half."

"Eight and a half. I stand corrected. But Aggie, there always comes a time when a person could have done better, and hasn't." Now he was chiding.

"What do you mean?"

Cal fumbled around his earthquake of a desktop for a yellow pad. He found it after 20 seconds of scrambling. He read from it.

"You ever heard of Hunter Holleran?"

"Sorry, no."

"He's an old Dartmouth pal of mine. Called me last night. Said he had been sitting in a country club bar near Chuck Bartlesby. He heard Bartlesby bragging to his drinking buddies that he had made a deal with you."

"What kind of a deal, Cal?"

"Holleran says that Bartlesby traded you the corroboration in the Felder campaign finance story for the promise that you'd go light on Lorraine in all future pieces about her. Is any of that true?"

Aggie wriggled, a classic fish on the line. She could go for the big lie. She had never done that before, but obviously she was in big trouble. Cal could never prove anything against her, could he? He didn't have tapes, did he? And how reliable was an overheard bar room conversation, anyway?

But Aggie Stern chose the convoluted explanation route.

"Cal, what I told Chuck Bartlesby was that I was an ethical reporter, and I couldn't make a deal like that. But he insisted that he wouldn't give me his bombshell information without that promise. I really, really wanted the Felder story to see the light of day, and soon. You remember that you sat on it for a long time, right? So yes, Cal, I told Bartlesby that I would give Lorraine very careful coverage. I may have said favorable coverage. I don't remember, to tell you the truth. But my motives were simple: To get you to publish my story."

"Aggie, you know that we don't make deals with sources?"

"Yes, Cal, I know."

"And you know that we don't make promises to sources about future coverage?"

"Yes, Cal."

"And you know that, really, the only thing we have each morning is our reputation. No matter what else is going on—whether it's some cranky old editor sitting on a story—nothing, and I mean NOTHING, can be allowed to threaten that reputation." Now he was thundering.

"I understand, Cal."

"But you made a deal that threatened our reputation, didn't you, Aggie?"

"Yes, Cal, I guess I did."

He took a breath and reloaded for more.

"Aggie, let's talk for a minute about the profile of Lorraine that you wrote for Lifestyles the other day."

"OK."

"Aggie, as you surely know, we always go for balance in profiles like this. I'm especially buggy that we do that when we're writing about Democrats. I'm so up-to-here sick of the calls I get from Republicans and all their knucklehead sympathizers, about how we protect and promote Democrats in The Rag. We do no such thing! I'll be damned if we ever do!"

Aggie nodded.

"Aggie, I didn't see your piece before it ran, but if I had, I would have sent it back for a rewrite. It was whipped cream, Aggie. It didn't ask or answer a single tough question. It didn't place Lorraine in any kind of context. It deified her beyond all reason to do that. For God's sake, she's only a candidate from the Maryland suburbs at the moment, Aggie! Because of the pact you made with Chuck, you made her out to be the Speaker of the frickin' House! Or maybe God Almighty!"

Aggie's dander was up. "I did no such thing, Cal! I would never scratch Lorraine Bartlesby's back! I'm a serious reporter, Cal!"

He pressed the intercom button on his phone.

"Not any more, you're not," he said.

A woman from human resources came briskly into the office. She was carrying a large plastic bag. She told Aggie that her employment had been terminated as of that moment. Aggie would be allowed to load the contents of her desk into the plastic bag. She would then be escorted to the front door. While she had been meeting with Mr. Cassidy, her computer access had been terminated. Her final paycheck would be mailed to her. It would include a payoff for all of her accrued, unused vacation.

Stern began to cry—fat, self-pitying tears. Cal said to her:

"Don't try that woman's tears crap on me, Aggie. I've been around way too long."

Felder was sitting at his desk as Aggie and the HR woman approached. He didn't realize at first what was happening. All he noticed—how could he not have noticed?—was that Stern was wailing and sobbing, and slowly cramming a whole bunch of stuff into a large plastic bag.

"Aggie," he blurted, "are you all right?"

"Yeah, Larry," she replied, between sniffles. "I'm just terrific. Have a nice life."

★ ★ ★

Barry Mauskopf had not called ahead for a reservation. Barry Mauskopf never called ahead for a reservation. All he had to do was show up and the crew at the greeters' podium would scramble a good table for him. Yes, Mr. Mauskopf. Happy to be of service, Mr. Mauskopf. Right this way, Mr. Mauskopf. Enjoy your lunch, Mr. Mauskopf.

Larry Felder was waiting for him, right at Table Two, on Celebrity Row, at Mauricio's, Washington's legendary steak, bourbon and politics luncheon spot.

"So you're early for a change, eh?," said the often accusatory Mauskopf.

"I'm not early. You're late," said Felder, who had learned, over a lifetime of mousedrops, to parry.

Mauskopf sat with a sharp thump. He had been gaining weight regularly over the last few years. But he assured Larry regularly that it wasn't cramping his romantic style.

"In fact, Larry, I have just learned that in certain primitive civilizations, women went especially ga-ga for guys with big cans. Gave them something to hang onto when the rocking and the rolling started in earnest."

"Whatever you say, Mouse," Felder replied, smoothly. The Mouse must be slipping. It had just taken him 14 seconds to begin bragging about his sexual talents. That was eight more than usual.

Waiters brought menus and wine lists. The men ordered ahi tuna steaks, salads and iced tea. Mauskopf shut off his cell phone with a flourish. He leaned in closer.

"So, you wanted to see me, boychick?"

Felder pushed his greens around the edges of his plate. He wasn't sure that Mouse would understand what he was about to say. He wasn't sure that he understood it himself.

"Mouse," he said, "I'm leaving The Rag."

Mauskopf speared a tomato wedge, shoved it down the hatch and widened his eyes.

"Are you serious, Felder,?" he blurted. "You did that just a few months ago, to run for Congress. Are you running again?"

"Maybe so, Mouse. Running from the past, you might say."

Mauskopf leaned over and stage-whispered to his friend that they should talk about baseball for the next 35 minutes. They couldn't discuss serious things in here. The walls had ears. The waiters had very good ones, too.

The tuna was inhaled quickly. The bill was covered by Mauskopf with a wave (he ran a tab). The two friends made for nearby Farragut Square. Homeless guys were camped all over the benches, but so were fresh-faced accountants and eager summer interns, munching sandwiches and enjoying the sun. Mauskopf gestured for Larry to sit beside him on the lawn. He motioned for Larry to explain himself further.

"The Rag just ain't got that old ring-a-ding-ding, Mouse," he said. "I'm being patronized. The middle-level editors don't want to mess with me because they know I'm Cal's fair-haired boy. But that isn't the same as respect."

Mauskopf asked if his brief Congressional campaign was chilling the air.

"I don't think so, but maybe. You know how newsies are. Once you wear a different colored jersey, you're no longer on the team, you know what I mean?" Mouse nodded that he did.

"So, old man, I am thinking of getting a book contract—maybe for two books, maybe three—and heading off into the sunset. Leaving this old river city behind."

Mouse said he'd be available to negotiate the deals, of course. Felder said he wouldn't go to anyone else.

Then Felder said there was one other thing he had neglected to mention.

It wears a skirt.

Mauskopf got up and began to dance a jig. The homeless guys briefly looked at him and decided that this dude in the $800 suit must be crazy. Maybe he was.

"Larry, I haven't heard better news since this latest dish I've landed told me the other night that my manhood does it for her like no other manhood she has ever had."

"Mouse," said Felder, "I'm not going to name names. But my lady told me pretty much the same thing the other night."

"Mazel tov!," blurted Mouse. "Double mazel tov! You have rejoined the human race!"

"I never left it," said Felder. "I had just forgotten that some parts of it are still there. But give me a little while, Mouse. I'm just getting started."

CHAPTER 17.

SINCE LATE AUGUST, 2006, the couple had lived in a small, somewhat ramshackle house beside the sea in Del Mar, California. Million-dollar condos had long ago displaced most of the postwar two-bedrooms, but not all of them. Felder and Charlie had found one that was still in pretty good shape—and looked as if it might withstand a big-league typhoon. They had rented it on the spot, for a year. Recently, a year had become four.

Felder awoke every morning at 7 sharp (he had set the alarm on his watch). He teed up a pot of coffee and a Shostakovich prelude, in that order. Then he sat down at his computer, in shorts and a t-shirt that read IT'S FIVE O'CLOCK SOMEWHERE, and began to write.

Charlie joined him in the realm of consciousness about an hour later. Most days, she had her own start-your-engines ritual. Brush teeth. Retrieve Los Angeles Times from doorstep. Check headlines. Peck Larry on top of his increasingly bald head, once, but only lightly, so as not to disturb his concentration. Then either pick up a piece of junk fiction (the Del Mar public library had lots) or start in on a consulting project.

She needn't have done any consulting, because the couple had more money than they needed. Larry had barely delved into the $5 million insurance settlement of several years ago. Plus, Mouse had gotten Larry a three-book deal with Random House, with an option for a fourth.

The books were about American politics since the 1960s. One was an analysis, one was a history, one was a personal memoir. The total advance was three quarters of a million dollars.

Mouse had cut his fee in half, in honor of "this lady of yours and her massively, actionably, unconscionably lascivious behavior."

Larry didn't correct him. That would have been inaccurate.

Long ago, the couple had worked out their "dailiness." Whenever Larry was typing up a storm, he wasn't to be bothered or interrupted. Whenever Charlie felt the urge to hit an art gallery, she would hit it. And when Larry retired for the evening, after a 12-hour day of muttering, drafting, rewriting and arguing by phone with editors, he was seldom in a mood to be studly.

But at 5 a.m., as the breezes were picking up over the Pacific, Charlie would reach for him. She had long since proved herself a bit of a tigress. Meanwhile, Larry Felder was on the verge of his 60th birthday. His sexual stamina and performance were beginning to flag because of age. But most early mornings, he was tiger enough.

Charlie often rode her bike—the same 20-speed she had brought from Dupont Circle—along the oceanside path. Ten miles north sometimes, all the way up to Carlsbad, or 10 miles south, to the Navy base at San Diego. She volunteered from time to time at a homeless shelter in the next town. The consulting work had followed her from Washington—a gig with a PR firm to craft strategy for legislation that was soon coming before the House Government Affairs Committee. The number four Democrat on that committee was a woman from Maryland named Lorraine Bartlesby.

Larry and Charlie never discussed politics. Who needed an open can of worms, or a cracked rear-view mirror? They sold their television set and most of their books. Larry gave four of his suits to Goodwill (he kept two). Charlie bought most of their food at the fish store in town and the farmer's market that convened three days a week in a nearby church parking lot. She often made too much dinner, so that there would be leftovers. Larry praised her frugality. She beamed.

Amanda came from Arizona to visit. Larry was polite-out-of-the-book. But he didn't open his soul. When the two college pals went for a walk, Amanda expressed her concern. Why was Charlie so committed to a two-dimensional guy, when she operated so fully in three?

"Mandy," said Charlie, "my only concern is how many more years we can have. This is what I want, Mandy."

In 2009, the couple had their first extended argument. Charlie wanted to throw a dinner party. She had met some interesting artists at the gallery, and she thought that Larry might enjoy them, too.

He said he wasn't looking to acquire friends, thank you. He had all he needed—Mouse by phone, some old-time Rag-a-muffins by email and lately Marnie Moskowitz, who had found him on Facebook and wanted, benignly, to stay in touch. No more running for senior class president, Charlie. No more making nice with strangers.

Charlie accused Larry of being set in his ways. Larry pointed out that this was what she had signed on for—he had never misled her into thinking that he and she would be aboard a social merry-go-round.

Charlie said he never smiled. Larry said his smiles were all inward.

Charlie said she needed a little more flash and splash in their lives. Larry said, well, dammit, go find yourself a playboy, then.

Charlie said he was being peevish and childish. What you see is what you get, Charlie, he replied.

She calmed down, with the help of Captain Morgan. They had never raised their voices to one another again. Even when Larry said he was getting worried about her drinking, she didn't bristle or get defensive. She simply dropped the Captain, for the sake of world peace.

Charlie's mother called often. Charlie never invited her to visit, and her mother didn't press the point.

Their conversations followed the same well-worn paths: What the girls at church were saying, what she wanted for Christmas, what she had seen on "60 Minutes" last Sunday, how much she missed Charlie's father.

Then, from Charlie: The weather out here has been fabulous, the swordfish steaks are especially tasty this month, I've lost six pounds, I'm booking lots more consulting work.

Her mother never asked how Larry was. She never asked to meet him, or asked about his wife. She knew better than to tear off half-formed scabs. All she wanted to know was whether her Charlise was happy.

"Yes, I am, Mama," she would say. "Happier than I've ever been."

Every two weeks, her mother would Fed Ex a chocolate cake. Usually, it would have cocoa icing. Charlie would eat it, across three breakfasts. Then she would call her mother and thank her, as the sun set and the gulls bayed.

$$\bigstar\ \bigstar\ \bigstar$$

"Bon soir, monsieur."

"Ça va?"

"Comme ci, comme ça."

It had been raining the proverbial cats and dogs when Felder parked in the last available space outside the Devonshire's front door. 'Twas the night before Christmas. Charlie had not returned to Washington with him. She was with her Mama in Pennsylvania. Here in Montgomery County, Maryland, not a creature was stirring, not even a mouse.

Maybe the rotund nurse from Grenada was going to be off today, Larry figured. But no, she and her movie magazine were both at their usual battle stations. Felder wrote his customary monthly check. She thanked him.

"Monsieur, you haven't been visiting as much as you once did," the nurse commented.

"Yes, I know," Felder said. "Only once a month. I live far away now. Our house in Bethesda, I rent it to this nice couple from New Jersey. They moved here for jobs in aerospace. They pay the rent, right on time."

The nurse nodded and scribbled out a receipt for Felder's check.

"How's she doing, ma'am?"

"Oh, about the same as ever, monsieur."

"No change?"

"There's never no change, monsieur."

Felder pocketed the receipt and headed down the hall. A left, a right, and into Room 208.

"Hi, baby."

She slept fitfully. The room had a residual aroma of fake pine-scent cleanser. He was very used to it.

"So, Kat, I was telling you the last time I visited about the books I'm writing. Yes, plural. I'm trying something different with these three. I'm alternating between them, just to see if it keeps my mind and my writing fresher. I think it may have, but the editors haven't weighed in yet."

He took off his windbreaker, clomped over to the sink and wiped away the raindrops with a paper towel. "Sorry to have stopped some storms on my way in here," he said. "Or maybe they just find me more often than they find other people. With my luck, it wouldn't surprise me."

He rested his cheek against Kat's. She felt cold and clammy—always a startle-producer, even after all these years. His mind flitted to Charlie, and her warmth. Often, he would simply rest his stubble against Charlie's cheek and sigh. He had to admit that he wasn't tempted to do much of that with his semi-comatose wife.

"So, Kat, let me tell you some more about California. I finally registered to vote, Kat. Had to do it. This idiot is running for the school board out our way. He wants to make English the official language of the schools. He doesn't seem to understand that kids who grew up with Spanish need help acclimating to English. You can't just declare that everyone will speak and read and write the language you want. False patriotism! So I am going to vote against him in the spring. He deserves to lose."

Kat snored. Her blood pressure numbers vacillated every four seconds from 110, up to 112, back to 109. An endless loop.

"Kat, I'm not really sorry that I didn't get to Congress. Not sorry at all. It was a daydream, and daydreams seldom come true, Kat. I haven't been following Bartlesby much, but she keeps getting re-elected. I guess that speaks for itself.

"I did see one newspaper piece about her, in the San Diego paper. She had some splashy ceremony with her husband, in Ocean City. Remarried him. I don't know why. Something in the story about a girlhood pal talking some sense into her. Kind of surprising, really. He was always kind of a schmo, I thought. Maybe she thought she needed a full nuclear family in case she wants to run for the Senate in 2012. Maybe she was lonely. Or alone. Like someone else I know.

"Kat, I've arranged for you to have a special dinner for New Year's. Candied yams. Your favorite. I always have you in the front of my mind, Kat.

"But now I have to go. I'll be back very soon. You can count on me."

Kat stirred. She turned reflexively, half to her left, away from Larry. He had not said a word about Charlie during his four-minute visit. He never had.

Years ago, the ethical trapeze of philandery had seemed hazardous. Was Larry Felder still married? Was he a garden-variety cad? Both? Neither exactly? Was he playing both ends against the middle and getting away with it somehow? Justifying it somehow? Can you be faithful in your mind and your soul, but not in your reproductive organs?

But now, time had sanded down the ambiguities and much of the guilt. He had achieved a measure of peace. Peace with duty. Always with duty.

He waved farewell to the nurse from Grenada. She wished him Godspeed. He dodged the drops, fired up the rented Chevy Cobalt and headed back to the cheapie motel near National Airport where he would spend the night.

Three days from now, he will meet Charlie at San Diego International. He will have laid on some Diet Coke and some walnuts, both favorites of hers. They will sip, chomp and listen to Shostakovich, all the way home.

ACKNOWLEDGMENTS

NONE OF THE WORDS you've just read would have been written if I hadn't been hired by The Washington Post when I was a 22-year-old sapling. Ben Bradlee saw something in me that I wasn't sure I saw. Thank you to the most inspiring editor there ever was.

Thank you, too, to the hundreds of quirky, brilliant, dedicated and astoundingly talented colleagues I had over my 36 years at the newspaper. They were my teachers, whether they knew it or not. But I knew it—and many of them appear in *LARRY FELDER, CANDIDATE,* in one way or another.

Thanks to whichever lucky star brought me to Montgomery County, Maryland, and vice versa. Yes, some county residents like to clonk their neighbors over the head on summer evenings. But so many of my neighbors are among the best people I know. Hats off to them, and to the Eighth District.

A big tip of the cap to the friends and colleagues who read, critiqued and helped produce this book, especially John Branston, Alice Lawson, Debra Naylor, Emily Niekrasz and Mitch Gerber. You folks can play on Team Levey any time.

One more special salute—to a college English professor of long ago named James Miller. Jim first waltzed me down the path of literary analysis. He said it would make me a better writer, no matter which form of writing I chose. He was right about my journalism. I hope he would say the same about my fiction.

A bow in the direction of our children—Emily Levey and Alexander Levey. Both raised in Montgomery County, both deeply thoughtful, both committed to making this stricken globe a better place (although neither has plans to run for Congress).

And then there's their mother--my partner, my sweetie, the final set of eyes on just about every sentence I fashion. Jane F. Levey has kept me headed into the wind in every way for more than 40 years. Please keep it up, beautiful.